ABORIGINAL MUSIC

ABORIGINAL
MUSIC *Cross-cultural Experiences from South Australia*
EDUCATION FOR LIVING

CATHERINE J. ELLIS

University of Queensland Press

ST LUCIA • LONDON • NEW YORK

First published 1985 by University of Queensland Press
Box 42, St Lucia, Queensland, Australia

Typeset by University of Queensland Press
Printed in Australia by The Dominion Press–Hedges & Bell

Distributed in the USA and Canada by University of Queensland Press,
5 South Union Street, Lawrence, Mass. 01843 USA

Cataloguing in Publication Data

National Library of Australia

Ellis, Catherine J. (Catherine Joan), 1935–
   Aboriginal music, education for living.

   Bibliography.
   Includes index.
   [1]. Pitjantjatjara (Australian people) — Music.
   [2]. Aborigines, Australian — Music. I. Title.

781'.71'94

Library of Congress

Ellis, Catherine, J.
   Aboriginal music, education for living.

Bibliography: p.
   Includes index.
   1. Australian Aborigines — Australia — South Australia
— Music — History and criticism. 2. Pitjantjatjara
(Australian tribe) — Music — History and criticism.
3. Folk music — Australia — South Australia — History and
criticism. 4. Music — Instruction and study — Australia —
South Australia. I. Title.
ML3770.E44   1984   781.7'29915   83-10630
ISBN 0-7022-1992-4

Contents

Variety of musical styles, their uses, and views about the value of
music; The nature of musical communication; Music as a
channel of communication; Music therapy: a special-purpose
communication; Music education

Performers' insights into the nature of music; Different systems of
thought; Bateson's theory of learning; Music, myth and spiritual
experience

The three main musical styles in South Australia; Disintegration of
traditional forms; Ways in which Aboriginal music is used;
Understanding the song text; Pitjantjatjara terminology; The story
of Miniri/Langka

Perceptual background; Larger-scale interlocking of structures —
music and meaning; Smaller-scale interlocking of structures — the
elements of music; Positioning of the song text; Rhythm and text;
Duration; Beating accompaniment; Rhythmic patterns and
rhythmic segments; Melody and duration; Melodic structure and
text; Melodic identification across tribal boundaries; Conclusion

Figures and Table

Preface

This book is about a number of different cultural and inter-cultural problems, each viewed primarily from the perspective of the music performed by the group involved. It shows how the Pitjantjatjara view of their world is reflected in their music. The system these central Australian Aboriginal people have developed to deal with the expected and the unexpected in life is symbolized in their musical expressions. The book is also about problems of communication where children grow up within a cultural framework different from that of their parents. And finally, it is about the experiences that people face when they must think and act in a culture different from that in which their first informal, unreflective perceptions of the world are made.

It seems to me that before any individual sets out to examine the views, ways of thinking and life-styles of other people, he should first examine his own views, ways of thinking and life-style. While this process may be precipitated in the first place only through contact with differing concepts, many unconscious errors of judgment can be made unless introspection is deliberately developed. In cross-cultural situations it is possible for people to develop one mode of behaviour to please those around them in the professional situation, and to live by completely contrary standards.

This in itself is not unusual (though surely unhealthy), but when the unconscious values of the life experience are conveyed in the professional sphere many contradictory situations arise. These can be avoided by each individual being prepared to discuss his own view of life as a valid and authentic expression of his own cultural heritage, and by his being prepared to listen intelligently and sympathetically to the views of those with whom he works. Without such personal dialogue many contorted views can be propagated in cross-cultural interaction.

I have therefore attempted in this book to make clear my own position, and to distinguish this from both the theoretical writings of other scholars, and from my observations of Aboriginal situations. As well I have presented Aboriginal views of Aboriginal and Western concepts and situations, and these, too, I have clearly identified.

When a book is about people and the experiences they pass through in an endeavour to communicate with one another across cultural barriers, it is possible to present the material in a detached statistical or theoretical mould. Yet statistics, and even theory developed from direct experience, have little to do with the act of making music. All the interactions represented in this book have taken place one way or another through the emotive agent of music making. I have attempted to achieve a balance between intuitive and analytic material by allowing the personal experiences of the music makers to be stated as a counterfoil to analysis where this helps to extend the meaning.

The opposing demands of objective examination and subjective expression of the feelings of people present many problems. Pirsig, in his book *Zen and the Art of Motorcycle Maintenance* (1976), identifies two basically different ways of perceiving the world (already suggested in the title of his book), calling one "classical" and the other "romantic". In part, my book deals with the effects of this difference which is so tellingly described by Pirsig and which often remains unconscious and therefore undetected in our daily thinking. However, the writing of it has provided me with ample opportunity to experience the split between these basic systems of thought. I am deeply indebted to the professional people from many different disciplines who have patiently read the manuscript and advised me on ways of making the material more widely understandable. Without exception they have encouraged me to continue and the eventual emergence of the book is due to this assistance.

The advice which came back from these readers made clear that the book itself represented both systems of thought: the predominantly "classical" in chapters 1–4, and the predominantly "romantic" in the second part of the introduction and in chapters 5–8. It was not my intention to make such a division but, rather, to allow the material to develop in the most natural way. However, those readers who found the classical sections exciting and informative were embarrassed by the more romantic material, while the romantic readers were often unable to read the analytical material.

This problem was most extreme in relation to chapter 4 and no amount of rewriting or separation seemed to improve the situation for romantic thinkers. For this reason, the book was ultimately written so that the reader could omit this chapter without gross injustice to the argument as a whole. Again I was reminded of Pirsig: in his fruitless attempts to define "quality" he made the important discovery that both classical and romantic thinkers knew what was meant, yet "quality" could neither be analyzed nor defined; and he concluded that the problem lay in the nature of the analysis itself, the rational process, rather than in "quality". So too, the problem of chapter 4, which lies in the analytical process and in readers' willingness to follow it through, rather than in the quality of Aboriginal music.

There are certainly some facets of thinking which are not suited to exclusively abstract methods of presentation. The experiences I have written about cover the time of my formal education in Australia and subsequently when I carried out my research. My closest companions throughout this soul-searching work have been my husband and my children. We have all had to share the hurt that multicultural work involves, and while we as adults understood the choice we had made in order to work on a basis of mutuality with members of other cultures, this was harder for our children.

They had to face their first experience of antiwhite action directed against them when they were aged four, thirteen and fifteen. Not only this, but because we live in an area where many newly migrated families have settled, their peer groups at school consisted mostly of children of European birth. At one time there were only three Australian children in our son's class of thirty. He could therefore find small solace for his perplexing cross-cultural anxieties among his own friends, and none from his educational experience.

As parents we understood the cultural confusion our children had to face; as educators in a multicultural situation we knew this was infinitesimal in relation to the disorientation that Aboriginal children and those from other minority groups deal with every day of their lives. I have written this book with these many teachers and students facing cross-cultural dilemmas in mind.

Acknowledgments

Financial assistance for all the early field research, discussed mainly in chapter 3, came from the Australian Institute of Aboriginal Studies, and from the University of Adelaide. As the work progressively involved the active participation of Aboriginal people themselves, the Aboriginal Arts Board of the Australia Council generously provided major grants. For funding of the actual research and writing of this book I am again indebted to this Board as well as to the Arts Development Division of the Premier's Department, South Australia, and to the Myer Foundation, Melbourne. Through the interest and support of these bodies it has been possible to employ two part-time assistants and a typist, who have made a major contribution to the work as a whole.

Mary Brunton, from her years of working in the Centre for Aboriginal Studies in Music, has helped extensively with the development of the explanation of the theoretical frames of reference. Guy Tunstill worked particularly with the analytical and diagrammatic representations of chapter 4 and its appendix, and with chapter 5. Margaret Bruce and Louise Fox patiently and skilfully dealt with all typing and layout problems. Malcolm Fox, Lecturer in Music Education, Elder Conservatorium of Music, the University of Adelaide, kindly advised on matters concerning music education in South Australia. I also thank Marjorie Payne who produced all the diagrams; Josie Townsend for the original drawings of *Nyi:nyi, Langka* and *Miniri*; and Vladimir Adamek for the music engraving.

Among the many Aboriginal people — both individuals and groups — who have generously helped with time and material, I wish especially to acknowledge the following: the Pitjantjatjara Council for permission to use *Inma Langka* in the form in which it appears in this work; Hilton Walsh for permission to quote the text of his song which appears on page 144; Cherie Watkins for permission to quote "Prison's Nothing Special" (page 146); and Cherie Watkins and Cyril Coaby for permission to quote "The Carrington Hotel" (page 147).

Finally, there were thirteen readers from three different states in Australia who coped with the manuscript at various stages of its preparation. Some of them made available large amounts of time to discuss with me the various theoretical problems and how these could best be explained to suit the needs of the many different disciplines on which this work impinges. For their generous assistance in this manner I gratefully acknowledge the help of Ruth Buxton, then Principal Education Officer in Music, Education Department of South Australia; Robert Cannon, Director, Advisory Centre for University Education, University of Adelaide; John Colmer, Professor of English, University of Adelaide; David Galliver, Elder Professor of Music, University of Adelaide; Dr E.A. Iceton, Lecturer (Community Development), Department of Continuing Education, University of New England, Armidale; Ian Knowles, Tutor in Ethnomusicology, University of Adelaide; Clemens Leske, Director of the Elder Conservatorium of Music, University of Adelaide; Rev. G.S. Martin, Superintendent of the Port Adelaide Central Mission Inc.; Dr Richard Moyle, Research Fellow in Ethnomusicology, Australian Institute of Aboriginal Studies, Canberra; Peter Sheldrake, then Reader and Director, Education Research Unit, Flinders University of South Australia; David Swale, Senior Lecturer, Elder Conservatorium of Music, University of Adelaide; Meriel Wilmot, then Executive Secretary, Myer Foundation, Melbourne; Professor Emeritus Sir Roy D. Wright, Chancellor, University of Melbourne and Consultant, Howard Florey Institute of Experimental Physiology and Medicine, University of Melbourne, Victoria.

Acknowledgement is also due to Macmillan Publishers Ltd for figure 4.2, prepared for *The New Grove Dictionary of Music and Musicians*, ed. Stanley Sadie (London, 1980).

Introduction:
Education Through Music

One day during my secondary schooling, in the 1940s, an incident occurred which I have since frequently recalled. Our class was asked to undertake an elimination debate where the three speakers selected represented people adrift in mid-ocean. Since only two were to survive, it was each speaker's aim to convince the class that his profession was indispensable and he, therefore, worth a coveted place on the raft. We each chose our profession. There was a lawyer, a minister of religion and myself, a musician. The final decision as to which speaker went overboard lay with the class, teenagers from families whose main common interest was their children's education. The class expressed its unanimous decision through vote and word: the musician was to perish.

My friends were all very cross with me. "We wanted to vote for you but we couldn't. Why didn't you say you were a teacher, or a nurse, or a doctor? A musician is no use for anything." And I sat miserably confused, since I felt that the misunderstanding centred on matters of fundamental importance, yet I had no way of knowing what these were.

It was not for many years that I learned something that related directly to that experience. I was told by an Aboriginal man that the most knowledgeable person in a tribal community was the person "knowing many songs". This individual encompassed, within his knowledge of music, the wisdom of his people. Here, I felt, was an understanding of music unknown to my classmates, but sensed by me when I decided to become a musician.

Within the field of music education, which focuses primarily on the technical aspects of music, polarities of attitude are found such as I have defined through my story about my own classroom experience and the much later comment by my tribal friend. My reason for discussing education through music, therefore, is to highlight the possibility that human beings can rise above such polarity. Through experiencing music, people can attain a perspective which allows validly opposite opinions to coexist without damage to either. In the process of the education of the total person which occurs through the use of music, the student may learn relatively little about music (although this is not necessarily so). But he inevitably gains a great deal of experience in reconciling and rising above contradictions both within himself and in his relations with others. This occurs as a group process when people centre their attention on the common goal of making music together.

There are many aspects of Aboriginal/white interaction in Australia which represent opposites. It is not productive to think they can be overcome by proposing a midpoint on the continuum of cultural attitudes. Indeed, any point along the continuum causes imbalance, whether it be a black policy of Black Power, or a white policy of assimilation which absorbs all cultural identity in a cultural melting pot. Rather, it is necessary to make a shift in thinking which places the continuum with its opposites in a larger, all-embracing frame of reference.

As this is an unusual concept for people to grasp, some analogies may help. For instance, the idea of east and west being two extremes on the horizon when one faces north or south is no longer valid when one moves into space and sees the east/west continuum on a sphere. Or, in music, the highest and lowest C on the piano may be used to illustrate the opposites in pitch of high and low; yet when viewed from the standpoint of Western harmony, these two lose any sense of distance in the concept of the expanded unison.

In each of these cases a diagram could be drawn showing the opposites at the extremes of a line representing a continuous gradual change. The new vantage point not only enables a

triangle to emerge, but also enables the ends of the base line
to be joined in a circle to form the base of a cone. At that
moment, the opposites exist side by side in a new dimension.

If we now return to the two views about music expressed
at the outset it is possible to place them on a continuum
which concerns music as communication. The Western attitude as represented by my classmates suggests that music is
not a useful channel of communication. The tribal attitude,
on the other hand, sees music as a useful and perhaps even
the *most* useful channel of communication. A cone shape can
symbolize the nonverbal experience of music both as artform
and as message. This way of looking at it can reconcile the
apparent opposition and enable one to see the two polarities
as merely aspects of a larger concept. (See Figure I.1).

I am postulating that through music we can each shift to a
different vantage point in which cultural opposites are

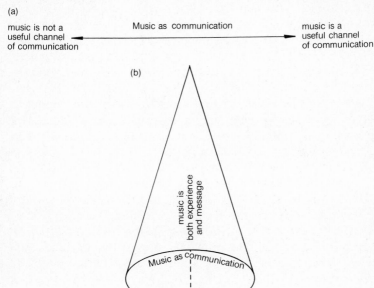

Figure I:1
(a) The continuum "Music as Communication".
(b) The cone "Music is Both Experience and Message".

merged in a larger whole. In order to expound this, I have had to show how real these differences of attitude are and how damaging the conflicts are that arise from them. My own experience as a first generation Australian has helped me to understand the nature of these conflicts in the first place. And I have had to explain how music, when thought about and experienced at deeper levels, can offer this merging process. The merging seems to occur, however, only when the structural aspects of the music are taken into account alongside the functional, emotional and aesthetic ones.

With this background of awareness one can then examine specific instances of misunderstanding or conflict. Sometimes members of one culture move to a higher level of thought and unification while members of the other remain uncomprehendingly at the lower level, unaware of the possibilities of transcending their present limited experience. For example, it often happens that the Aboriginal tribal elders attempt, from a far-seeing standpoint, to educate the white people at a level that calls for no compromise on either part; but because many white people involved remain at a lower level which disparages tribal education, they fail to hear what the tribal teachers have to say. It has also happened that fine Western and non-Western musicians from a similar, high-level standpoint have reached across to tribal people, only to be greeted with misunderstanding and misrepresentation of their deep musical and personal insights.

Within the Centre for Aboriginal Studies in Music in The University of Adelaide it has been our great good fortune to have experienced situations where, in the words of the tribal people, *nganana tjunguringanyi* - "we are all becoming one". This has been achieved through mutual growth, not cultural compromise. From the previous opposition of black and white we have achieved, not a murky grey, but a new blend of colours.

This book deals with how it is possible to facilitate such a positive shift of emphasis. It is a book for all people who are concerned with living and learning in a multicultural world and arises out of the academic discipline of ethnomusicology. I have gained a great deal from the published works of outstanding ethnomusicologists such as Blacking, Hood, Merriam and Nettl. These studies show that music is important in all known societies throughout the world, for many different reasons. Only Western society seems to ignore this fact. Music forms part of communication and plays a significant role in the social behaviour of members of all other societies. While music may structurally be very different in each particular culture, the purposes for which it is performed are remarkably similar, as are the views of the musicians, the communicators, about the depth and peculiarity of this communication.

Communication through music stimulates lively interaction and one of the reasons for this is that it conveys concepts which are not, or cannot be, verbalized. I do not need to know anything at all about tribal music to be caught up in the oneness of a tribal performance, to feel the delight, excitement, joy and deep reverence it engenders. Without a doubt, I know better why it had this effect on me as soon as I study the subject matter more, but my feelings towards the performers are hardly altered by such a study. My direct experience of the music provides all the essential emotional information I require.

While I have dealt primarily with Aboriginal music as it has been performed in South Australia over the past twenty years, this book first touches on these nonverbal apects of music in general — on the deeper values of communication and education through music — because they are directly relevant to all that is said in the remainder of the work. The book is therefore much more than a purely technical study of Aboriginal music. It is the study of tribal music as it occurs now, not as it occurred in times before contact with white people. It is a study of traditional musical techniques and how they are used in a contemporary situation. It is a study of the impact of Aboriginal music both on white people, and on Aboriginal people who have lost their own tribal traditions and live in a world where they are acceptable in neither the white nor the tribal education system. It is about Aboriginal music not only in the purist's sense, but also as it is used by Aboriginal people in education today, for white people as well as for themselves. As such it is not written exclusively for specialist students of Aboriginal music although it contains much that is relevant for them.

The book is also a study of the use of music in cross-cultural education. Many people argue that the tribal Aboriginal person should be left, with his tribal traditions unchanged, to live in isolated areas without the damaging impact of Westernization. This is simply not possible. Aboriginal people are politically and legally part of today's community no matter where they live. Some have a background built on thousands of years of tribal learning. Others have added recent learning from the many minority groups living alongside one another in outback mining towns. Still others have had a predominantly Western, middle class education which they have chosen either to absorb or to discard. Whatever the circumstances, the learning is part of communication within today's society.

White Australians also have many shadings in their cultural background. Some are third or fourth generation descendants of early European immigrants to this country. Others, like myself, have had to grapple with the experience of being first generation Australians, experiencing the rejection of our parents' culture by some Australians, as well as its enthusiastic reception by others with the same ancestry. Other more recent arrivals were born in their own countries. All these groups intermingle in contemporary Australian education.

My own experience when I first went to school has some similarities to that of Aboriginal people of today who choose to study within the Western system. There is now little financial restriction on Aboriginal education, yet finance answers very few educational questions. The similarity of my own position to theirs lies first within my experience as a child seeking an education which did not negate the knowledge of my parents; secondly as a young adult entering the university among the first group of recipients of commonwealth scholarships (which allowed the infiltration into upper levels of Australian education of many people who had no previous background of higher education in their home enviroment); and thirdly as an individual proud of my cultural heritage in a society where that heritage was not always appreciated.

I spent my childhood in the Victorian countryside. My parents were Scots who arrived in Australia with very little money, to face a depression and the problems of raising a family in the poverty that inevitably resulted. We had one other family of close relatives in Australia, with whom we often lived. In the warmth of close relationships we did not know what it was like to be an isolated family unit. We lived close to nature, I was indoors as little as possible and my main companions when the others were at school were animals. Our simple life-style engendered a feeling of warmth, security, close attachment to the country and the family, and left us with no awareness of our poverty.

All the people around us had lived through hard times in the Australian countryside. They told many of their own bush yarns, spontaneous exaggerations of local events and incidents whose flavour was entirely Australian and fitted completely with my own experiences of the countryside. Listening, I learned the history and geography of the region and knew that I belonged. I was intrigued by the many Aboriginal place names and the white country people's reminiscences of the times when the Aboriginal people lived in the locality. The oldest neighbours could remember having seen Aboriginal people around, but had never had direct contact with them.

Our home life retained its orientation towards my parents' homeland: Scottish stories, folk songs, the occasional piper and British books which assumed an understanding of a countryside totally different from the one I knew so well. My parents were unlike our neighbours in their approach towards education and, in particular, towards music. They disapproved of the educational standards acceptable in Australia at that time and, as far as was possible within the scope of their limited income, provided extras which Australian families tended to ridicule. The most important of these for me was their interest in music.

My first, very strong, musical associations were with the music of Scotland, through which I learned the fundamental importance of music as a means of expression beyond the verbal level. My parents had no need to speak about "home" in the presence of Scottish music — they were there. "Good" music, on the other hand (which they also associated with home), had very little meaning for me, since it bore no relationship to my experiences and had no connection with this land which had its own history embedded in the natural, rather than man-made, features.

The musical life of white Australian country people at this time centred on the weekly community singing (often led by Welsh, Irish, or Scottish people who themselves sought to reproduce the folk music of their homelands). Instrumental music for weekend dances was provided by the local pianists, of whom there were many, and button accordionists, concertina players, mouth organ players and the occasional gumleaf player. (All these folk-type performances began to disappear in my teens.) Little of this folk music filtered into the schools, and none of it was Australian in origin, although it had become Australian by adoption. Aboriginal music was totally unknown.

We attended the nearest government schools, usually alongside children from much better circumstances than ourselves. My formal schooling began in 1940, during World War II. Government funding for education had such a low priority that in some areas schools had been closed through lack of funds, and in one case I know of the local grocer was supplying wrapping paper for use as writing material. In my first year I was in a class of over one hundred children, and what reading we did from the few books available was totally irrelevant to my experiences either as a Scot or as an Australian. Consequently I had no desire to read. By the time I reached secondary school level, however, more finance was available. Our school was one of the first to have a library — an institution until then unknown to me — yet even then educational methodology and content were still largely unrelated to Australian conditions.

For me one of the few redeeming features of this education was the avid interest teachers took in things Scottish. They sought a reinsemination of those experiences which had, presumably one or two generations ago, been part of their own home enviroment. However, this constant looking back at a distant home had the effect of negating anything of Australian origin. There was a general feeling that everything Australian was inferior, everything British superior.

Today, Australia is far more multicultural. Since World War II there has been massive immigration of people from European countries. This has meant that hundreds and thousands of non-English-speaking adults and children have been battling with much greater multicultural problems than I have had to face.

When we could eventually afford adequate music tuition, specialist music study became my aim even though I was openly penalized by the headmaster for "wasting too much time on music". Memorable experiences through performing were of major significance in my personal development. They enabled me to overcome the prejudices others had against me because of my different background, my poor-looking appearance, even the handicap of my interest in music. None of these were important while I was performing, during which time I could be wholly myself (to the best of my musical ability) without expecting recriminations for my atypical behaviour.

As I progressed into more advanced study, I discovered that the music of my Scottish background was not considered music at all. Apparently it was something uncouth and un-mentionable, and the important matter at hand, it seemed, was to play better than one's fellows in order to get the best job. This egocentric attitude was foreign to my early music making, on the strength of which I had chosen a career in music, and I ultimately realized that I had unintentionally made a move which alienated all my childhood experiences. No longer did music act as a higher form in which the con-tradictions of my environment could be integrated; rather, it became a lower process which was involved in splitting apart experiences, classifying them as "good" or "bad" on an exceedingly restricted continuum which was labelled "music", but which actually excluded all but classical Western music. While this shift of values disturbed me a great deal, my teachers showed either a puzzling lack of awareness of it or, worse still, rejoiced at my having at last "made it".

Although theoretically the musical tradition within which I had my advanced training was akin to the one of my childhood, since both at least shared common structural elements, it was the mode of performance and the purposes for which a performance was given that were completely different. While I could happily have accepted these as different, and perhaps even as a different order of musical experience, I could not accept the teaching I received which decided the one to be unacceptable while the other was "good".

I completed my first four years of tertiary education feeling that the most important questions I wanted answered had not yet been asked by my teachers. At this point I was offered the opportunity to study Aboriginal music and this seemed as likely a way as any of coming to know precisely what those questions were.

This was in 1957, when enthnomusicology was not the thriving subject it is now. The *Journal of the Society for Ethnomusicology* was still within its first volume and at the time there were only a few recent publications on Aboriginal music (Jones, 1956; Strehlow, 1955; Waterman, 1955). With the exception of Waterman and Jones, the subject had not been studied in the field by musicians since E. Harold Davies's work in the early 1920s, and that work covered the music almost entirely from the point of view of a Western musician (Davies, 1947).

A period of study at Glasgow University enabled me to combine my interest in understanding my Scottish heritage with the continued structural study of Aboriginal music. It also enabled me to see, in the perspective of a non-Australian environment, the importance of a thorough understanding of local Australian material, and to recognize that while I felt a close affinity with Scottish thought and scholarship, I was first and foremost an Australian and not a Scot.

In retrospect, the whole of my educational experience seems somewhat similar to that of some present-day detribalized Aboriginal people. The analogy covers my early childhood experiences of a culture with values different from those espoused by the school system; irrelevancy of teaching material in that school system leading to a low level of literacy; high emphasis in the home on experiential learning and on music as opposed to the slight emphasis given these areas by the school system; feelings of inferiority in the school environment; desire to know the cultural heritage of traditional forebears; recognition of the affinity of the thinking of the older generation while being unable to relate directly with them; a need to search for a meaningful heritage which recognized both past affiliation and present reality.

Even now, there seems to be little progress being made in Australia in moving toward multicultural education which can accept the background of the student as legitimate experience upon which his or her further education may be built. My choice of movement through Aboriginal music will suit few young people in Australia today. Depending on their own backgrounds, now often of European origin, they will desire specific learning experiences to maintain relevancy; yet the principles will remain similar. Those of my students who have recently studied ethnomusicology in the community to discover their own cultural foundations in a multicultural society have all passed through the same type of experiences as I did.

With no scholars ahead of me to determine the appropriate courses of action, my study of Aboriginal music took a number of different directions according to the problem demanding most attention and requiring resolution at any given time. Trevor Jones and Alice Moyle, who were studying Aboriginal music in other areas at the same time, found themselves in similar predicaments. Originally, it was sufficient for me that I was merely exposed to Aboriginal music and the thoughts that lay behind it. This initial contact through recorded music made in the field by others had a profound impact. It was obvious, even from recordings, that the sense of the significance of any performance was always present in Aboriginal singing.

The first research work that I undertook attempted to answer basic structural questions concerning scales, rhythm, performance practice and so forth. As I slowly assembled information on these, important educational implications began to emerge. For instance, if songs are learned and taught in a specific way, through structures totally unlike those known in Western music, what happens to the child exposed either to both, or to Western music only and forbidden exposure to his own? Such questions opened the way for further research.

This background academic research was of great value in preparing me for actual field contact. Once in the field, working directly with Aboriginal performers, I understood musically what was taking place despite being greatly hampered by my initial lack of knowledge of the language. Nevertheless it was possible to examine such factors as the distribution of particular song styles, and to carry out much recovery work in areas where little or no tribal music was remembered. Interdisciplinary field research into women's ceremonies (Ellis, 1970) gave rise to more comprehensive academic work which gave me a more detailed understanding of the structural nature of Aboriginal music, and the relationship of the structures to the functions which performance maintained within a tribal community.

This work occurred at a time when Australians were beginning to show an interest in Aboriginal culture, perhaps as a counterbalance to the strong sense of ethnicity of some migrant groups who were becoming numerically large. This attitude did nothing to help Aboriginal people, but was, rather, a move to help white Australians to discover what Australian-ness was about. For my part, because of the regulations applied to the available research grants, I had no choice at first but to involve Aboriginal people only as subjects in my research, despite the risk of appearing to endorse the underlying assumption of superiority inherent in many who adopt this approach. Subsequent efforts to overcome this had only limited sucess. One way of attempting to involve Aborigines on a basis of equality was through co-authorship. We attempted this on a number of occasions (see, for example, Ellis *et al.*, 1978), but this led to further problems since those Aboriginal people not directly involved saw the exercise as one in which white people were using Aboriginal people for their own gain.

In order to develop situations where a real contribution

from Aboriginal teachers was possible, much work had to be done in learning what Aboriginal teaching means to white Australians as well as what it meant and means to the Aboriginal people themselves; what it means to the Aboriginal child growing up in the tribal situation to be confronted with European education, and what it might mean to an Aboriginal child in the city having only European education with no access either to Aboriginal education or to education through music.

It also meant looking more widely into areas of music therapy. What does music do in our own system? How does it operate as an educating agent? In what ways could it be used to help bridge the existing gap which prevents great Aboriginal educators from taking their place in our world? For me, learning to perform Aboriginal music in the field was the beginning of my realisation that I was culturally deprived. My higher education may have taught me accurately about my intellectual self, but it ignored my physical, intellectual and emotional wholeness. It had left me segmented and with large parts of my personality undeveloped and lacking integration. My tribal teachers knew this of me, as they know it of most white people, but they did not reject me for what they saw as shortcomings in my personality. They worked patiently and perseveringly, gradually and often painfully exposing me to my own inadequacies.

It was through this experience that I recognized the tribal elders as great teachers. They showed me indirectly that my own culture did not, and perhaps could not, teach me about reaching my whole self; yet, through their demonstration, they showed that they could help me to do this. Their teaching emphasized restriction on too much music making because this causes sickness. (This had interesting relevance to my earlier and continued experience of working with professional musicians.) The concept is based on the understanding that music making has a profound effect on the performers. Music draws together sources of power which, if over-used, cause debilitation. Moreover, it showed me that no education was available to Western musicians to teach them the consequences of their methods of teaching and performing, or to develop skills in their use of music for constructive, nonegocentric purposes within the community at large.

I began teaching ethnomusicology at the time I was recognizing the greatness of tribal teachers. My aim, therefore, was to enable students to go beyond merely studying what other ethnomusicologists had written and the mechanical development of those technical skills then of paramount concern in the academic discipline of ethnomusicology. I aimed, rather, to help them understand the need for a greater awareness both of their own cultural heritage and of their cultural deprivation; and consequently, to develop sensitivity towards other people's culture.

After these self-examining experiences, my aim in teaching ethnomusicology was to encourage students to penetrate into the deepest levels of thought of another culture by examining the communication through music, particularly of matters not normally spoken about. It is at this deep level that interaction without compromise can occur between cultures on the basis of mutual growth in understanding.

possible?

desirable?

Contradictory?

1
Music As Communication

The present multicultural society which exists in Australia provides a tremendous challenge, one which must be met with an education system which seeks to integrate, while at the same time retaining individual cultural identity. In Bateson's terms (1972:65) it is necessary to seek the persistence of groups "in dynamic equilibrium within one major community".

I am aware of the feelings of disorientation that can confront the person who seeks this path of integration and I am equally certain, after seven years' practical experience in the Centre for Aboriginal Studies in Music (CASM), within The University of Adelaide, South Australia, that music provides a vital element in education within any multicultural society. It can bridge various thought processes; it is concerned with the education of the whole person; it can stimulate inter-cultural understanding at a deeply personal level, with the result that a person is no longer a member solely of one culture. The student must break through the limits of his own culture — often painfully — and learn to see all situations from many points of view. This type of cross-cultural learning is available to any person who chooses to study seriously under musicians of high calibre whose culture is different from that of the student. By being open-minded a student can become at one with the thought processes of his teacher, irrespective of the cultural barrier which may exist in all other spheres of interaction between the pupil and his master. After a cross-cultural experience of this nature it is possible to return to one's own culture with eyes and ears refreshed. Then, one perceives bias all around, especially in the Australian education system.

Success is achieved in this kind of learning when the student becomes aware that he is no longer satisfied to live solely within the values of his own culture. He must, however, become aware of the peak of achievement aspired to within any culture. It is through this higher level of learning that cultural disagreements begin to disappear.

I am using the term "culture" to refer to that body of learning and attitudes which a child first receives informally from those in his immediate enviroment. These enable him to establish, early in his life, patterns of thought, or "scripts" in Eric Berne's terms (1972:25), which are constantly reinforced and used by him to process all subsequent life experiences. These patterns are maintained by a group of people (usually a large group) living in close proximity. They can therefore reasonably be expected to be understood by all members of that group. However, what happens in multicultural situations is that these unconscious patterns are at first applied unthinkingly in a situation where the original concept may be unknown, unacceptable or encompassed in totally different form. What is required here is for the individual to become conscious of the cultural patterning of these basic prescriptions, and then to learn how to apply these scripts in an acceptable manner in the new culture. This is very difficult learning and often does not eventuate, leaving the person operating unsuccessfully in his or her new cultural setting.

Variety of musical styles, their uses, and views about the value of music

Music has many and varied uses in each of the communities in which it has been studied, but views of musicians about its nature and significance show a strange basic uniformity despite the fact that a musician from one culture may not even recognize as music the sounds so defined by the musicians of another. Each musician — whether from a Western or non-Western culture — talks about deep human values and regards music with awe, often as a voice from the gods (see, for example, Merriam, 1964:209ff).

Music in nonliterate societies often functions as a mnemonic device and in this and other ways, replaces literature as the repository of important information. This use does not detract from its aesthetic value. The scientifically trained person in Western culture often dismisses music from serious thought because it does not convey factual information. Some music scholars share this view about information communicated through music, as can be seen from the entry under "Absolute Music" in the *New Grove Dictionary of Music and Musicians* (Sadie, ed. 1980) in which it is pointed out that music, to be Absolute, must have no external reference and require no subjectivity. It is regarded as objective when its structure is governed exclusively by its own internal logic. Further, it is generally believed in the community at large that music has no essential function in the operation of the society in which we live (Hood, 1971:12). The existence of pop music and the use of music in advertising seems to suggest that factual information *is* conveyed through Western music and that music can be utilitarian in our society, but these exceptions only serve to highlight the fact that Western music is normally thought about only in aesthetic terms.

Research done by scholars from many different fields indicates that in traditional Aboriginal communities, on the other hand, song is one of the most important vehicles of communication (see, for example, Strehlow, 1971; Berndt and Berndt, 1964:307ff). Through song the unwritten history of the people and the laws of the community are taught and maintained; the entire physical and spiritual development of the individual is nurtured; the well-being of the group is protected; supplies of food and water are ensured through musical communication with the spiritual powers; love of homeland is poured out for all to share; illnesses are cured; news is passed from one group to another. This vital role of music is retained in some form by many

Aboriginal people who now live in the Western society (Brunton, 1982:15ff; Pearce in Isaacs, 1979:41).

Western music does not fulfil many of these functions for white society, as Aboriginal tribal musicians and Western musicians with experience in Aboriginal music can well see. Thoughtful musicians from each culture are aware of the need for, and possibilities of, adaptation if musics so vastly different are to coexist. Yet both sides are limited in their thinking because at best each lacks a comprehensive understanding of the other's music, and more often than not each fails to see the other's performance as music at all.

When I discuss Western music I want to stress that I include not only what are generally considered the great works of art but all areas of music making: light entertainment music, pop, jazz, children's playground songs, music for advertising, recordings of environmental sounds, church music, music therapy and so forth. Indeed, being concerned with the cultural interchange between Aboriginal and white people, I find the sounds of both natural and man-made surroundings important (Schafer, 1977) since both peoples live in this same sound environment. However, it is necessary to remember that such sounds, whether considered part of music or peripheral to music, will be perceived differently by members of different cultures.

Tribal Aboriginal musicians only rarely talk about music. This makes it difficult to contrast the Western view of the two musics with their views. There is literature available on Western music and some authors such as Parry (1925) and Sharp (1907:7) give the older Western musician-scholar's view of Aboriginal music as "rudimentary", "primitive". It is clear from discussions with both Western and Aboriginal musicians that each assumes that no other real music exists apart from that which they themselves practise, and that the meaning of this music is self-evident. It is incomprehensible to each why the other fails to receive this meaning when it is communicated through the traditional, the "only", form of music.

The variety of musical cultures existing in Adelaide, and probably most Australian cities today, is often overlooked by its citizens. There are many peculiar juxtapositions of experience which the average South Australian, for instance, going about his daily round of activities, fails to see.

These come to light in unexpected places. For example, in the parkland directly opposite the main Anglican cathedral in Adelaide, with which we associate traditional liturgical music, non-English-speaking Antakarinja women performed a women's love charm intended to "catch" a man for an unattached Aboriginal woman. Another example occurred when, while addressing a group of students from one of the large colleges of advanced education, I played recordings of music from many minority groups. Although the recordings had been made within a kilometre of their campus, the students thought the music laughable.

On another occasion, when on my way to record an Aboriginal singer, I met many of the members of the fully professional Adelaide Symphony Orchestra who were going to the nearby rehearsal studio. Neither they, nor the Aboriginal performer – who had adapted many of the older songs of his people to partly Europeanized forms – was aware the other existed. In the same way, many of the staff of the university's Elder Conservatorium of Music are unaware that Aboriginal song can be seriously considered as real music, yet the tribal performers are now recognized members of the teaching staff within the university. Further, it is now possible for a tribal performer who wishes to study for a degree in music in the normal way to be able to take his performance subjects in Aboriginal music, yet at the same time, professional musicians are objecting to the inclusion of non-Western instruments as legitimate for practical examinations in schools.

These different values in the immediate environment alert the serious thinker to other previously unnoticed contrasts. The traditional Western attitudes towards music, particularly those of the elite, can be contrasted with the attitudes of members of the alternative movement – the so-called hippies. The conflicts of professionalism can be seen against the socially rewarding aspects of community involvement in music. Rigid traditional approaches to performing structured compositions can be contrasted with the attitudes of musicians who specialize in improvization. Researching another's music is seen as an acceptable scholarly pursuit while respectfully sharing music across cultural boundaries is not.

Within South Australian Aboriginal music itself there are many regional styles which I have detailed elsewhere (Ellis, 1966), but which have no bearing on the general point I am making here. What matters is that by now most of the traditional forms in South Australia (and presumably this applies equally to the remainder of Australia) have been disrupted either by violent means or by the insidious intrusion of Europeanization. Thus, in this state, music from the northwest border areas is the only traditional form still practised.

The actual structures of all Aboriginal music are markedly different from those of Western music. Even in the few areas where didjeridu occurs, the music is primarily vocal. It is built around short bursts of singing, the length of which is governed by the short-term physical endurance of the singer, depending on his capacity to maintain adequate breath control. In Pitjantjatjara music from the northwest of South Australia, each short section of singing, encompassing a specific song text, lasts for about thirty seconds, after which the singers rest and chatter for a minute or so. These recurring small segments of a larger work may be integrated with other art forms to create a ceremony lasting half an hour, or three days, or more.

In Western art-music emphasis is on instrumental music which is often divorced from other media. From this flows a further difference between the two musics, the difference of scale structure. The origins of Western scale structures appear to lie in the acoustical properties of instruments (for instance wind instruments overblow at an octave, or a twelfth, after which they reproduce the original intervals; on string instruments, the octave occurs at the midpoint of the string). In Central Australian music there are no such external measures governing the development of scale structure (Ellis, 1965).

Traditional Aboriginal education systems throughout Australia have stages of learning, each intended to develop the integrated growth of the whole person towards a state of knowledge and wisdom. Tribal teachers maintain strict professional codes of behaviour, which are retained to ensure the accuracy of learning. Many of the Pitjantjatjara teachers have told me that no person will be taught until he shows his preparedness to learn. This then ensures the student's motivation to handle rigorous and painful lessons.

Even in the few remaining areas where tribal music is still taught, these strict codes of behaviour in teaching present many difficulties, particularly with Westernized Aboriginal people. The problem is similar to that which occurs when non-Indian students seek out the Indian *guru* from whom they may learn sitar (see Shankar, 1969:12ff); their inability to respect and revere their teachers in the manner traditionally expected negates what those teachers have to impart. Characteristic features of urban Aboriginal people are their feeling of alienation from all education, and their distrust of any form of authority, black or white. Because of this they will never come and ask any teacher (Aboriginal or non-Aboriginal) if they may learn. They find the very notion of asking a degrading one. Consequently there is a conflict between the traditional code of teaching among tribal musicians and the present-day behaviour acceptable among urban Aboriginal people who want to know more about their former traditional heritage. Aboriginal people who have moved away from tribal affiliations, or whose tribal relatives have all long since died, still make music — but of a very different kind.

The contribution of Aboriginal arts, thought and action to the white community until very recently has been almost nil because Aboriginal artistic expressions are of, and for, the society from which they arise. They belong to the life-style of the executants and are not isolatable products for mass production. Further, the very life-style they portray so tellingly is unacceptable to the majority of comfort-loving Australians.

The nature of musical communication

The first noted enthnomusicologist to emphasize the fact that music is not sound alone was Alan Merriam. His study deals with the social behaviour associated with music making as well as with the patterns of sound used to encode information. He says (1964:27) that "the sounds of music are shaped by the culture of which they are a part . . . Each culture decides what it will and will not call music". He discusses the patterned behaviour involved in music and the fact that unless listener and performer alike agree on the nature of these patterns, there can be no music.

Some contemporary Western composers find the unacceptability of their music so perplexing that they have suggested that an audience is not a necessary part of music: a musical experience exists, and is not a means of communication. A related idea has been documented by Nettl (1973:163), although the analogy should not be taken too far. He states that among the American Indians, the Pima believe that songs exist whether or not they are communicated aurally. According to Nettl, what is required for them to be communicated is a person to "untangle" the songs that are ever-present. However, one presumes that then the songs become comprehensible — unlike the experience of the contemporary composer.

The contemporary composer's perplexity is understandable. The newness of his work, which often shocks the public, is no longer apparent to the composer himself. He has become accustomed to his own new patterns for such a long period before he presents it to the public that he has forgotten where he began. Understanding his own work within a now larger framework of accepted sounds, he is surprised by the public's lack of comprehension.

Meyer's views about music as a form of communication are useful (1967): included is the idea that music requires both a generating source and a receptor. However, many composers have argued with me that music exists whether or not it is communicated; that the music of a score is there, accessible to the music reader, but not communicating in the sense that there is a generator and a receptor, and not necessarily in the sense that it is understood.

One explanation of the reason music may, or may not, communicate has been offered by McLaughlin (1962:285), who points out how we must know the system used for encoding the musical communication. He notes that, while all problems of communication are interesting, the process which takes place in musical communication is "the most fascinating and baffling of them all". He follows the chain from the purely physical vibration to the recognition of the sound in the brain, but this remains a "code without a key". At the point where the message is deciphered, he says, "the scientist loses it. It seems to have gone through the mirror into another world, where our instruments cannot follow. For us, on the other hand, it has suddenly become alive."

Music as a channel of communication

The problem of deciphering the code used in any music is one which is associated with the basic patterns of music, patterns which have been acquired from the enviroment continuously since earliest childhood. Frequently in modern Western society we do not even bother to decipher this code. It is often considered irrelevant compared with the so-called real things of life in a mechanized, commercial world. We tend to regard music as an inessential extra which can be taken or left as required. It is a trimming which may, particularly in schools, be cast aside for subjects considered more important educationally such as mathematics and science. The devotee of classical music in our own society has few arguments at his disposal to discount the charge of superfluousness.

This idea that music is superfluous is contradicted, however, in the adolescent interested in popular music. For him the music enjoyed by his peers is essential all the time: he eats with it, studies with it, takes it to bed with him. To others who are not part of that particular age group, his music may be a terrible noise, a distraction, an irritation.

Some of these curious anomalies in the musical activities of Westerners are highlighted by Blacking (1976:4ff). Speaking about musical activities in worldwide terms, he notes that there must be both social and aural patterns of sound governing musical behaviour in any community. He is puzzled, however, as to why musical ability should be restricted to an elite in cultures supposed to be more advanced, while musical systems which are based on the same intellectual and musical processes in other cultures are generally available to all members, as both performers and listeners. He draws attention to the anomaly in our own society, where the extensive use of music in film, television, and many other situations presupposes that the audience will interpret the patterns of sound accurately — as fearful, passionate or whatever other emotion the music was intended to induce — yet allows that few are musical.

He writes:

"My" society claims that only a limited number of people are musical, and yet it behaves as if all people possess the basic capacity without which no musical tradition can exist — a capacity to listen to and distinguish patterns of sound. (1976:8)

While Blacking is deeply concerned over why we have a musical elite, Merriam (1964:134f) points out that many communities (and he cites examples from Ghana, Brazil and Melanesia) respect their musicians highly, often regarding them as close to the gods. This is not to suggest that the musician's social behaviour is always acceptable; indeed, Merriam hypothesizes that "the musician, in view of the license allowed him, seems to be of such special importance that he must be retained in the society even at considerable social cost".

Whether the music is known and performed by most of the members of a society or only a few, there remains the fact that the music must have within its technical structure patterns of sound which are understood by the majority and which are associated with particular behaviour and emotional meaning. The reverse is also important — that when the patterns of a particular music are not understood, the communication is not regarded as music at all by those who cannot reach this understanding. It then becomes a useless channel of communication.

Music is often said to be incapable of conveying factual information, but many examples seem to contradict this. Lévi-Strauss (1969:18) formulates his ideas on this in terms which relate it to much that has already been said:

> But since music is a language with some meaning at least for the immense majority of mankind, although only a tiny minority of people are capable of formulating a meaning in it, and since it is the only language with the contradictory attributes of being at once intelligible and untranslatable, the musical creator is a being compared to the gods, and music itself the supreme mystery of the science of man, a mystery that all the various disciplines come up against and which holds the key to their progress.

In the following examples information is shown to have been decoded when the only communication channel was music, or remembered accurately when music and words were combined in the communication. These examples represent several different levels of the problem of decoding. In each instance information was conveyed through some aspect of musical or acoustical structure. They contradict the basic Western assumption that music is a useless channel of communication.

In the first, a student of mine happened to observe her neighbour working out of the line of vision of her television set, close enough to hear music but not to understand speech. The woman was a chain smoker. Each time the advertised jingle for the particular brand of cigarette she smoked was presented on the television, she lit a fresh cigarette. She would then put the cigarette out, start other work, and become involved in her conversation and chores. Immediately the jingle was played again, however, she lit another cigarette and began smoking again. This woman was quite unconscious of the fact that she was being reached by music and instructed to carry out a particular action. As a suburban Adelaide housewife she would almost certainly have shared the widely held view in our community that music does not convey factual information.

Another example occurred when I asked an Aboriginal woman with me if she knew the number to ring for a taxi; she immediately sang a commercial jingle which included a phone number for a taxi company. Here, the learning was frighteningly more permanent than anything else this woman had recently absorbed. It brings to mind the potential use of music in political situations, for propaganda and indoctrination.

Studies by performers show that communication of factual information can occur at another level with Western music, but it requires long training to decode this. Specific technical information is conveyed to the performer who is listening. Through the messages of the music alone he can learn where the performer he is listening to studied, what type of instrument he uses, what country his reeds come from, and so on. This is true also of Aboriginal music. Tribal songs which are performed for fun may become widely disseminated from their place of origin, and their meaning may be unknown to the new owners. In a case where such a song has been transmitted further than the language of its text and a collector records it in this new area, no explanation of the text may be possible, but this does not mean the song was constructed from meaningless syllables. Davies (1947:30) gives an example of a recorded song which was recognized when played to Aboriginal singers living sixteen hundred kilometres from the locality in which the recording was originally taken.

My own experience of tribal song-recognition has a special twist to it. While my husband and I were recording children's songs at Indulkana, in the far north of South Australia, the men were unable to resist interrupting a session in order to demonstrate their own vocal prowess. They sang one song after another, but each requested a replay of the recording of his performance before the next performer took over. As well they greatly increased their enjoyment of the occasion by adding sound effects to the performance of others. In this atmosphere of hilarity and exhibitionism I felt it was inappropriate for me to stop the flow by asking for explanations of the songs.

Later, in quieter working conditions at Port Augusta, some

one thousand kilometres south of Indulkana, we asked a knowledgeable elderly man if he could by any chance explain these songs to us. He listened, but as Antakarinja was not his language, he could not "catch on to" these Antakarinja songs. We were about to stop playing the recording when he suddenly said, "That's Tim's song". We asked many questions, but he replied that he had never before heard the song, he did not know the language, he did not know the performer, but he did know it was Tim's song.

As Tim was living at Port Augusta, we were instructed to get him and let him hear for himself. We brought Tim along without explaining our interest, and then played him the recording. He immediately reacted with, "I made it up", to which the first man responded, "That's what I told you when we started". When I asked how the first man had recognized Tim's song when it was sung by Billy, he replied, "He (Billy) copied it off his (Tim's) tune, you see. What Billy was singing now, he sings Tim's way". The characteristics of Tim's music making, when accurately copied by Billy, carried specific information concerning the source of the song.

Throughout this discussion it is necessary to bear in mind the very real difference between one form of musical expression and another. Yet there are features which musics throughout the world seem to have in common. Charles Seeger (1971:391) notes that "music is one of the two traditional means of auditory communication among men, the other being speech". He clarifies this (p. 398) by saying that "music, though not a universal language, is without question more nearly universal in all senses of the word, including world-wide perspective, than speech". Wachsmann (1971:381ff) in his endeavours to locate the universals in music notes that "man has forever postulated . . . that a phenomenon like music is at some level 'one' with the universe"; and again (p. 384) that "music is a special kind of time and the creation of musical time is a universal occupation of man".

There are other aspects of music which seem to be near universal, as a random search of literature on specific cultures shows. A Ghanaian ethnomusicologist, Kwabena Nketia

(1974), himself a competent performer of the music of his own people which he has studied in depth, gives us insights into the nature of music in Africa. Music, he says, is closely linked with other activities, particularly with significant social events. It is multidimensional, being integrated with other arts – dance, drama, and various visual displays such as masks. When the social, political or religious practices change, so too does the music used to express these.

This is similar to the role of music amongst the Aborigines, for whom music performs many different functions, ranging from that in which a person is "sung" (for good or evil) by a powerful individual, to the large group performances which involve every member of the community in an event which reaffirms their allegiance to their tribal land, with its deeply spiritual associations. Once the land is taken by white people, and the government store replaces the old practice of food gathering, many of these songs fall out of use. New singing, for example in the church, is of a different type, even if there has been no direct pressure to force this change. Music is not static; it must change to express the changing life situation of the musicians.

Because performers in most cultures do not talk about what is significant in their music, it is often only through the ethnomusicologist that we come to know some of the things regarded as important by musicians in a particular group. For instance, Cadar (1973:234ff) notes that ensemble music of the Maranao (a Muslim group in the Philippines) has many different functions. It is used as a channel for bringing about solidarity and as a method for learning and practising ethical principles such as that manners must rule behaviour and respect must be shown. Performance, he says, is a "self-compelling stimulus for people to behave correctly", sometimes deliberately aiming to subdue conflicts. At other times music serves as an arena for recitation, singing, dancing and various other forms of expression; as a method for disciplining one's inner self; and as a medium of entertainment and hospitality. He notes, too, that music plays an important role in bringing people together. It allows for various groupings of players; the value of unity is instilled through applauding the group as a whole; the audience becomes actively involved and hence there is more socialization.

Music therapy: a special-purpose communication

In many societies music is used for therapy. Music therapy is generally defined in Western terms as a practical form of treatment to be used alongside guidance from medically trained personnel. Alvin (1975:4) has described it as "the controlled use of music in the treatment, rehabilitation, education and training of children and adults suffering from physical, mental or emotional disorder". Dolan (1973:173) states that "Music therapy is the scientific, functional application of music by a therapist who is seeking specific changes in an individual's behavior". Although there can be no doubt that such therapy is effective, its unique application to each individual patient makes it difficult to observe the actual processes involved.

The writings of Gaston (1968), Nordoff and Robbins (1971, 1971a), and the journals exclusively devoted to music therapy contain much relevant material. Robertson-DeCarbo (1974:31ff) attempts to probe the problems that lie within the sociological, psychological and biological levels of interpretation of this special purpose musical communication as it occurs in Western and non-Western therapeutic processes.

Aboriginal and Western understanding of the use of music in therapy differs. When a tribal Aboriginal musician says she has "sung" the unborn baby, she does not mean she has sung *to* the baby; she means that through the power of song, which draws on the resources of the original creation, she has been able to will the baby to be born. We have no equivalent use for song in our community; no situation where, by taking the sounds of an object, we can have influence over it. Our nearest equivalent use of music is a therapeutic one, where we observe that music has beneficial effects on certain patients with physical or mental illnesses. Nettl (1973: 162f) gives an example from one American Indian community, where persons who are maladjusted go into seclusion to meditate and "dream" songs, with subsequent improvement in their state of mind.

What we have learned through observations of both Aboriginal and white response to music in a therapeutic situation is that the same techniques in the music of several traditions (e.g., the unbroken, metronomic pulse of Indian tabla playing, the unbroken pulse of the beating accompaniment in Aboriginal singing and the unbroken pulse of Ravel's 'Bolero') produce similar stabilizing responses. From this it seems that there are some physiological responses to certain musical techniques which do not depend at all on association for their effectiveness.

Tagore draws our attention to rather different aspects of the therapeutic value of music, when he discusses the whole problem of the swamping of Indian thought by the dominant English education system.

> Our conscious mind occupies only a superficial layer of our life; the sub-conscious mind is almost fathomless in its depth. There the wisdom of countless ages grows up beyond our ken. Our conscious mind finds its expression in activities which pass and repass before our view. Our sub-conscious, where dwells our soul, must also have its adequate media of expression. These media are poetry and music and the arts; here the complete personality of man finds its expression.
>
> The timber merchant may think that flowers and foliage are only frivolous decorations for a tree, but he will know to his cost that if these are eliminated, the timber follows them. (1961:225f)

Tagore stresses the importance of recognizing music and art as essential in overcoming problems of cultural identity. This, he acknowledges, is quite different from the notion of patronizingly tolerating music in our schools and universities.

In general, the Aboriginal people I have observed using music therapeutically attempt to encompass the ailing person within the whole social framework of their community and to spell out in the strongest terms possible the total acceptance of the ailing person, thus enabling a regrowth within the frames of acceptable social behaviour. This may be done in many ways, and no doubt specific herbal cures, which are sometimes involved alongside music therapy in the tribal situation, aid the patient in given ways. However, the process itself, as I have observed it, is primarily one of encompassing the patient with expressions of the total acceptance, both spiritual and social, which is possible through the use of music. Hamel (1979) gives many examples of the therapeutic use of music in his book *Through Music to the Self.* He draws examples from different cultures and postulates that the techniques he has observed in use in the music of other cultures may be applied successfully in our own.

Music education

Just as the notion of music therapy is rather more restricted and scientific in Western thinking than it is in many non-Western situations, so too the concepts about the role of music in education differ between Western and non-Western educators.

Music education in South Australia today can be broadly described as either child-centred, for the general school, or subject-centred, particularly in specialist music schools (normal secondary schools which allow high specialization in professionally-oriented music study as part of the school curriculum). The success of the school music program is believed to lie in its ability to meet both these needs. Many of the earlier justifications for including music in school work (particularly within the system in which the present decision makers have been educated) were that music is a pleasant relief from what are generally considered more serious and useful subjects; a means of inculcating good moral tone and sentiments of patriotism; an aid to religious instruction; a means of introducing breathing exercises which would produce physical well-being, and so on.

More recent arguments (and it is sadly significant that arguments are needed at all) for the inclusion of music in the school curriculum are that music is intellectually equivalent to other school subjects; that music making, particularly in groups, develops the students' skills of communication with others; that it develops individual creativity; that it provides a useful means of occupying leisure time (regarded now as important because of the high rate of unemployment and shorter hours of work).

Music educationists throughout the world have approached the matter differently, yet there are many points of agreement. Ethnomusicologists such as Hood (1971), Nketia (1977), Seeger (1977), who have attempted to integrate what they have learned from Western and non-Western musicians, question much that has happened in music education. For example, Seeger (1977:15) sees three branches of music education, each disagreeing with the other. These are: education of the professional musician, education of the scholar and musicologist, and education of the layman and his children. He also sees (1977:16) a disagreement between the musician as music educator, with his emphasis on subject matter, and the educator in music, with his basic interest in the growth of the child.

Music teachers are now realizing that students need and want to be aware of their larger environment. This is reflected in the material in current music education journals. Articles in the *Australian Journal of Music Education* in 1977 — the same year as ethnomusicologists were writing in this journal — covered such topics as attitudes to music, musical heritage, music in the theatre, specific instrumental or vocal teaching techniques, music on a university campus, the creative process. There were also articles on the relevance of ethnomusicology to schools. In the same year the *Report of the Proceedings of the Third National Conference of the Australian Society for Music Education* covered technical problems associated with teaching and recognition of the musically gifted child, music therapy, Asian and Australian Aboriginal music, adult education and community music, electronic music and so-called school music.

Internationally, bimusicality is considered one important aspect of contemporary music education. Nketia (1977:23) says that "Throughout the ages, the primary objective of education has been the transmission of a society's cultural heritage . . . ", yet he notes that within Western music we make judgments about what parts of this heritage will be transmitted. Some idioms of Western music and entire non-

Western cultures are left out of the curriculum. Describing traditional African music teaching (p. 24) he notes that "traditional music education provides a programme of semi-comprehensive education through its dual commitment to art and society". He sees music very much as part of the social process and bimusicality as an encouraging sign for the future.

Probably the achievement of bimusicality depends on an initial strong awareness of the student's own traditional music. There has been little research done on this aspect, yet many people now have access to at least two musical forms in their daily lives. It is difficult to determine whether the obliteration of indigenous musics on contact with European music is caused by musical or social factors, but it seems clear that unless the indigenous performers have a strong desire to retain their own traditional forms, bimusicality is not practicable.

The importance of the child becoming sensitive to the sounds of his environment has been studied extensively by Schafer (see, for example, his book *The New Soundscape* [1969]). He is one of the few music educators who sees music as an integral part of a child's whole life. He has spent much time researching the sounds of the environment and his book *The Tuning of the World* (1977) contains many ideas about how we react to sounds and how these shape our lives. He also maintains that it is our responsibility to shape the sounds rather than allowing the sounds to shape us.

All this broadening of the scope of music education does not even yet make it like education through music. The two start out to be the same, but increasingly diverge as the education progresses. Music education can be a step in providing the elements through which education through music may occur; the latter is probably a life-long process.

It seems to me that Tagore sums up in his own non-Western way the insight that has crystallized for me out of my own experience with Aboriginal music. Unlike many educators of the present time he was aware of his own deprivation:

In the usual course I was sent to school, but possibly my suffering was unusual, greater than that of most other children. The non-civilized in me was sensitive: it had a great thirst for colour, for music, for the movement of life. Our city-built education had no need of that living fact. It had its luggage-van waiting for branded bales of marketable result. (Tagore & Elmhirst, 1961:53).

2
Experience and Message

There are many theories of learning and personality development, but few refer to the ways in which cultural learning is transcended so that real multicultural development takes place. Among the vast literature, only a few concepts can be found which explain our experience of the way music, with all its diversity, can help people rise above old cultural boundaries to higher levels of human understanding.

Performers' insights into the nature of music

One performer who has given us deep insights into his own culture's view of music is Ravi Shankar (1969:11ff). He lists three words which he considers to be the heart of the Northern Indian musical tradition: *guru,* the teacher; *vinaya,* humility; and *sadhana,* practice and discipline eventually leading to self-realization.

> The choice of the *guru,* to us, is even more important than choosing a husband or a wife. A potential disciple cannot make a hasty decision to take just any teacher as his *guru,* nor should he break the bond . . . once the . . . initiation, which symbolically binds the two together for life, has taken place.

Shankar talks about what happens in a good performance in the following words:

> When, with control and concentration, I have cut myself off from the outside world, I step on to the threshold of the *raga* with feelings of humility, reverence, and awe. To me, a *raga* is like a living person,

and to establish that intimate oneness between music and musician, one must proceed slowly. And when that oneness is achieved, it is the most ecstatic and exhilarating moment, like the supreme heights of the act of love or worship. In these miraculous moments, when I am so much aware of the great powers surging within me and all around me, sympathetic and sensitive listeners are feeling the same vibrations. It is a strange mixture of all the intense emotions – pathos, joy, peace, spirituality, eroticism, all flowing together. It is like feeling God ... The miracle of our music is in the beautiful rapport that occurs when a deeply spiritual musician performs for a receptive and sympathetic group of listeners. (1969:57f)

Shankar regrets that the understanding of the vital importance of accuracy, correctness, humility and appropriate teaching in music is fading out, particularly with the impact of Western students and their disrespect for their teachers.

One of the many great Western musicians who has expressed the desire to use music for the betterment of mankind is Pablo Casals. His whole life was dedicated to the use of music for international understanding and world peace. In his book *Joys and Sorrows* he says:

I am a man first, an artist second ... As a man, my first obligation is to the welfare of my fellow men. I will endeavour to meet this obligation through music – the means which God has given me – since it transcends language, politics, and national boundaries. My contribution to world peace may be small. But at least I will have given all I can to an ideal I hold sacred. (1974:286)

Casals' comments on the power of music are very like those of Shankar, even though the two speak of musics which do not share a common heritage.

To see people gathered in a concert hall came to have a symbolic significance for me. When I looked into their faces, and when we shared the beauty of music, I knew that we were brothers and sisters, all members of the same family. (p. 111)

Why this feeling of rapport should be so strong between sensitive musician and listener, or between two musicians interacting, is discussed in some detail by Mantle Hood. His book *The Ethnomusicologist* provides many insights into the activities of an ethnomusicologist, an important one being the experience of performing music. One of the leading ethnomusicologists in the world, he has been closely involved with performers from other cultures in his university teaching. Concerning these studies in performance, he says:

> It is probably impossible to convey to someone who has never been a performer the extent to which making music together or moving together in dance is a mode of discourse, a mode of communication. It is different from "talking together" . . . probably because music and dance are more abstract modes of discourse than is a spoken language and at the same time are more responsive to concrete and precise communication. A beat in music or a movement in dance either is in time or it is not; the pitch is correct, a quality of movement right, or they are not. For the participants such facts are readily discernible. Two or more musicians or dancers can communicate at this level or expectation, without ever uttering a word, for hours on end. The level of communication established in the process has no equivalent in the spoken language. (1971:218)

These aspects of communication which performers speak about presuppose that the listener is a member of the performer's own culture. Without long immersion in the music concerned, neither listener not performer can achieve the level of insight being discussed. However, even within the music of one culture there seem to be different systems of thought and different ways of perceiving the world, and these differences have a profound effect on the understanding of music.

Different systems of thought

The above comments by musicians highlight the very different system of thought that is used during musical performances from that of everyday experience. Stan Gooch, throughout his book *Total Man: Towards an Evolutionary Theory of Personality,* shows how we each have within us a polarity and favour one of the two apsects of our personality at any given time. This in turn affects the form of communication we will find most satisfying. Gooch draws attention to the existence of this polarity within literature, legend, religion and language. He deals with the nature of consciousness and the "rise to tyranny of Western consciousness". He defines two systems of thought, labelled "System A" and "System B", both of which are potential in all human beings and capable of either parallel or unequal development. The paired word list below gives an indication of the distinction between these two systems as Gooch sees them.

System A	System B
doing	being
objective	subjective
impersonal	personal
thought	emotion
thinking	feeling
logic	magic
detachment	involvement
discrete	associative
proof	belief
scientific knowledge	non-causal knowledge

Gooch is postulating that while we have the choice of which system we will use, in the Western world the majority of individuals belong within System A rather than System B.

What Gooch is talking about in systems of thought, Jung and others speak about in terms of the conscious and the unconscious. Jung is fascinated with those aspects of non-Western knowledge which are non-casual (and therefore, in Gooch's terms, belong in System B). Jung (1965:304) suggests that the psyche at times operates outside the laws of time and space as we conceive of them (as System A thinkers?) and that our knowledge of causality is therefore incomplete.

Both these authors, and many more whose thinking stems from System B as much as from System A, know that both systems of thought are necessary. They postulate that to become a whole personality both must be developed and integrated. Gooch suggests a third — System C — in which this transcendent integration occurs. He lists (1972:522) some possibilities for this three-level system, in which the third reconciles the polarities of the previous two.

System A	System B	System C
male	female	whole
doing	being	alive
thinking	feeling	reasoning
reductionist	associative	creative

He postulates that a well integrated person must develop both System A and System B and then integrate them in System C processes.

Entire cultures tend to develop this same dualism, the majority of members giving preference to one system rather than the other. Rattray Taylor uses the terms "matrism" and "patrism" to refer to the extremes of this duality as expressed in social systems. Throughout his book *Rethink* (1972) he suggests that all these phenomena could be encompassed within an intregrated and balanced social system if children were adequately trained for the task.

Such intregration is lacking in Australia. The knowledge which tribal Aboriginal people consider most important for their existence is non-casual and therefore belongs within System B. What predominates in our own European traditions is System A. Extended non-causal systems of thought (System B) are few in European traditions, but one of them happens to be music. However, since the underlying technical structure of music is mathematical, it belongs within System A and can therefore be experienced as an entirely logical process which conveys factual information of some kind. But music is more than this. The message is often emotional and associative and as such music then belongs in System B. Although Gooch does not mention music, it could be categorized in his System C, being a System A mechanism which can convey both System A and System B information simultaneously.

Figure 1 in the Introduction can now be restated: the continuum "music is not a useful channel of communication/ music is a useful channel of communication" represents attitudes stemming from System A/System B. The cone, "music is both experience and message" represents the integration possible in System C.

Bateson's theory of learning

The problem of the nature of the education and the deep thinking about human values which is represented in Tagore's statements and in those of musicians such as Ravi Shankar and Pablo Casals is best illuminated by Gregory Bateson's theory of learning. Bateson (1972:283ff) describes learning as a process which denotes change. He suggests that "learning" is often used incorrectly to describe situations of habituation which imply no change, or minimal change of response. This he classifies as "zero learning". All learning above zero learning contains some degree of trial and error.

Bateson gives three different levels of learning beyond zero learning, each requiring a change in the previous process. Learning I he suggests is found in extinction of habituation, response to reward and punishment and other areas where there is a change in the previous specific response. Learning II covers most of what we consider learning. It involves corrective changes in the set of alternatives from which a choice is made, a process of learning to learn.

Bateson's theory is most important here because of his definition of Learning III. He cites religious conversion and some processes of psychotherapy as among the few known examples of Learning III. Most of our learning in life belongs within Learning II. It is more or less unconscious and, because it is its own justification, it results in patterns that are almost ineradicable. It is self-centred rather than centred on the larger ecological balance and harmony of all things. For this reason, what Bateson calls Learning III is likely to be difficult or rare. Learning III is concerned with spiritual issues. It requires a profound reorganization of character. Once Learning III is achieved, "the concept of 'self' will no longer function as a nodal argument in the punctuation of experience" (p. 304).

Musicians who speak about their intense experiences of ecstasy, brotherhood and rapport are presumably speaking about a Learning III experience. As Merriam (1964:135f) has made clear it is not always that the musician himself is affected by this learning. But perhaps such depths of experience can only occur when the musician is humbly aware of the deeply spiritual nature of his art. From my experience of cross-cultural education, it seems to me that not only have Aboriginal musicians learned a great deal about achieving Learning III (although not all of them reach this level), but also the very act of attempting, at whatever stage, to study under such knowledgeable musicians brings non-Aboriginals, as well, into a Learning III situation. This learning may subsequently be disregarded should the time of contact be short, but indications from students who have faced this experience are that it has had a profound effect on their personalities and on their activities within their own system.

Bateson's Learning III − the area of spiritual growth− is at the core of what I am talking about when I speak of education through music. Our present education system limits itself to Learning II, and in fact its institutional rules and technical examinations ensure that Learning III, which transcends such things, will be unlikely to occur. Thus, even where music is accepted, it is as music education which is a Learning II process. The Aboriginal child, on the other hand, from the beginning of his education has the example of Learning III constantly before him and expects his own endeavours to culminate in these high reaches if he uses his ability and diligence to master all the preliminary stages of training for personality growth in which music is the central communication medium.

A brief examination of Bateson's theory in relation to musicians helps to explain the obvious discrepancy between those musicians who are noted as wise people in the community from which they come and those who are considered tolerantly to have failed to reach the standards of normal behaviour for that community. The musician may achieve an ecstatic experience from the base of Learning II. This may affect his life very little, or it may affect it either positively or negatively. (The number of fine musicians who would be classed as alcoholics in the terms of our own social standards is probably quite high.) But one should note Bateson's comments that Learning II is self-validating and almost ineradicable. Although the ecstatic experience can be transferred to other areas of learning, either within or outside music, it is the rare musician who follows through the insights available to him from his experiences in music to the point where his life must be profoundly reorganized because of these insights.

Perhaps the importance of music lies in the fact that this possibility of Learning III is already implicit in the Learning II experience (and maybe even in Learning I). It may not be necessary for a musician to move beyond Learning I for his performance to be the agent for other more developed people to make such a move to higher planes. This may explain the point noted by Merriam (1964) that musicians are often excused for inappropriate social behaviour, presumably because of their special importance to their society. (For further elaboration of this theory and its musical implications, see chapter 8.)

Music, myth and spiritual experience

Authors such as Shankar (1969), Casals (1974) and Jung (1965) — who demonstrate from the content of their views, quoted in this chapter, that they have themselves reached Learning III   often have extreme difficulty in expressing what they have to say. Musicians' accounts seem to indicate that only music can express this information successfully.

In the contemporary situation, and perhaps, indeed, in the tribal one, the person (whether musician or not) who has moved beyond the confines of Learning II to understand wider and deeper meanings than those accepted by his peers, must search for and use a different mode of expression from everyday speech. Perhaps it is this necessity to communicate at these levels which differentiates the musician and the great composer from the merely technical exponent of music. And perhaps myth is a comparable form which may be used by the non-musician to explain his contemporary insights.

Lévi-Strauss (1969:17f) sees the two forms of communication, music and myth, as closely related:

> Music and mythology bring man face to face with potential objects of which only the shadows are actualized, with conscious approximations (a musical score and a myth cannot be more) of inevitably unconscious truths, which follow from them . . . When the myth is

repeated, the individual listeners are receiving a message that, properly speaking, is coming from nowhere; this is why it is credited with a supernatural origin.

He has been responsible for the decoding of myths so that those items used to explain the unknown in different cultures can be seen as exchanges of items existing in the myths of other cultures. Maranda (1972:17) sees this exchange of items in myths being expressed in our current advertising:

> Technology convinces us that it can achieve what our forefathers thought magic would do . . . our myths are made of depilatories, royalty, pets, antiques, political ideologies, religion, hair tonics, cinemactors, scientific theories, cars, etc. — enticing avenues to the Paradise of which, ultimately we refuse to acknowledge the loss.

Maranda defines myths (p.12) as "the structured, predominantly culture-specific, and shared, semantic systems which enable the members of a culture area to understand each other and to cope with the unknown". This could as well be a definition of music. Cassirer (in Maranda, 1972:23) emphasizes that myth is metaphoric thinking, and that the simplest mythical form arises only when mundane and everyday impressions are transformed by this metaphoric process. Lessa (in Maranda, 1972:71) carries this thought further when he says:

> Myth does not reveal the whole of a people's culture and design for living, though what is embedded in tradition often leads to knowledge and truth lost to the conscious mind of a people.

My purpose in this brief, inevitably superficial glance at mythology is to show the expressions of Learning III through this form as well as through music. Tolkien, the master of myth in our own time, expresses beautifully the nature of the dilemma of communicating Learning III information verbally:

> The realm of fairy-story is wide and deep and high and filled with many things: all manner of beasts and birds are found there; shoreless seas and stars uncounted; beauty that is an enchantment, and an ever-present peril; both joy and sorrow as sharp as swords. In that realm a man may, perhaps, count himself fortunate to have wandered, but its very richness and strangeness tie the tongue of a traveller who would report them. And while he is there it is

dangerous for him to ask too many questions, lest the gates should be shut and the keys be lost (1964:11).

Why, then, are myth and music important and what is it that they actually convey?

The layered structures of myths, with their multiple cross-references, are seen by Lévi-Strauss (1969:340f) as signifying the mind that evolves them by making use of the world of which it itself is a part. Thus there is simultaneous production of myths themselves, by the mind that generates them and, by the myths, of an image of the world that is already inherent in the mind. He also sees that his study of myth has, in a sense, become his own myth.

In his book *Memories, Dreams and Reflections,* Jung discusses his own experiences of moving beyond conventional realms of thought. His search to express this shows something of its difficulty. He speaks about his own absence of awareness of self in a way Bateson describes as being characteristic of Learning III:

> When people say I am wise, or a sage, I cannot accept it. A man once dipped a hatful of water from a stream. What did that amount to? I am not that stream. I am at the stream, but I do nothing. Other people are at the same stream, but most of them find they have to do something with it. I do nothing. I never think that I am the one who must see to it that cherries grow on stalks. I stand and behold, admiring what nature can do (p. 355).

Moreover, he speaks about his own search for this learning in terms of developing a myth:

> My life is a story of the self-realization of the unconscious . . . What we are to our inward vision, and what man appears to be . . . can only be expressed by way of myth. Myth is more individual and expresses life more precisely than does science. Science works with concepts of averages which are far too general to do justice to the subjective variety of an individual life (p. 3).

His understanding of this need for mythic expression is further underlined when he states (p. 340) that "meaninglessness inhibits fullness of life and is therefore equivalent to illness. Meaning makes a great many things endurable — perhaps everything. No science will ever replace myth, and a myth cannot be made out of any science."

Music and myth are necessary for meaningful existence. Music occurs in all societies. Western man, to a large extent, seems to have lost his myth, which therefore becomes unserviceable as a means of inter- or cross-cultural communication. His limited view of science has replaced myth; yet such a partial appreciation of science cannot give his existence a human, spiritual meaning. Music — along with art, drama and literature — can, and does, reach to the core of man's existence. It has special human significance in enabling us to transcend the cultural divisions and other disintegrations that are the legacy of Learning II.

Why, then, does music generate such intense antagonism across cultures? It is virtually impossible to recognize the expressions of Learning III when these occur outside one's own culturally accepted patterns — in music, language, art or the higher forms of scientific thought. With sensitivity, the outsider may realize that these forms have a deeply spiritual effect on their creators (even if not on him), and this realization may in turn help him to be absorbed into the total experience. To know this spirituality at first hand, with the help of the great performers of the tradition concerned, is an experience that requires many years' intensive training.

It is, however, possible to perceive the existence of such expressions in our own culture even if we ourselves have not reached the level of learning required for their production. In this case, the listener or performer may well become sceptical when he senses the greatness of the works within his own tradition yet fails to have any such deeply moving experiences through contact with other traditions. He may subconsciously feel apprehensive about an experience called "music" within which he is totally lost. He may then feel entirely justified in saying that such spiritual experiences do not exist in those other musics.

Indeed, for him they do not. This problem is increased by the fact that musicians operating at these deeply significant levels rarely speak about their experiences; so he cannot know that musicians from another culture feel that same awe and ecstasy when the works of their own musical heritage are performed, and the same disrespect when they do not understand foreign music.

There may be a further complication. Although it is considered inappropriate to make value judgments about
different types of music, it is also recognized that there are
different value-levels of music within any one culture. The
use of music in advertising, for instance, is related to Bateson's
zero learning, and the great works of our own musical heritage to his Learning III. Presumably this applies in other
cultures as well — musics of very different value-levels
operating under the one general title, "music". A musician
from one culture, then, needs to establish the level of musical
activity taking place in another culture if he is to make any
appropriate differentiations or comparisons within and across
cultures.

The importance of being able to make explicit the depth
of operation of any musical culture today lies in the need for
mechanisms which can step beyond the constantly divisive
factors of different cultures. Those thinkers who have seen
clearly the nature of thought involved in Learning III provide
us with the key to this over-stepping of cultural difference.
Although a person who has reached Learning III perceives
universals (and this can be shown by looking at the statements of the great mystics from many different cultures),
they originally had to develop their thinking through the
media of one specific culture. The people in today's multicultural world who can act as models for higher learning must
have experience in cross-cultural communication. They have
to be able to convey the universals they understand to those
who still operate within the strong limitations of cultural
difference.

Those of us who have not reached this stage of development must necessarily have human examples on higher rungs
of the ladder if we are to be successful in our own long climb.
In South Australia today there are very few living examples
to whom one may turn in this endeavour to climb beyond
the mundane, to overcome the prejudice within oneself. I
know of no such person in my own culture, yet some may
live quietly in seclusion, ignored by an education system
which perceives Learning II as the peak of development. I can
safely say that they are not and cannot be models for me

because I do not know where to find them. I do know, by contrast, that some senior Aboriginal people have attained this level of learning and are prepared to teach me, my students, and my family.

My personal understanding of the profound statements of the great musicians and thinkers whose ideas have been touched on in this chapter is that education through music is of fundamental importance. My personal experiences with tribal musicians from the north of South Australia, and to a lesser extent with musicians within my own culture, heavily influence my view that education through music is concerned with the development of the highest reaches of the personality, both of the musician and of those who are bound to him through the ties of the aural experience. These areas of education are never easy for student, or for teacher. They make a demand on the personality which is at times intolerable; yet it seems that only through meeting this demand can we seriously speak about meaningful education in a multicultural society.

3
Aboriginal Music in
South Australia

In pre-European Australia, Aboriginal music varied markedly throughout the continent. As with Aboriginal languages, large areas had common structural attributes with differences of dialect. For example, from what we now know, the songs of the Pintupi (R. Moyle, 1979) and those of the Pitjantjatjara, Antakarinja, Wongkanguru, Arabana and Kokata-speaking peoples of northern South Australia (Ellis, 1966) are all accompanied only by some form of percussion beating. They are structurally similar in almost all respects, having differences only in such features as vocal range and tone quality. However, this one overall song style appears to be different from the Arnhem Land music described by T. Jones (1956) in which didjeridu is also used. The songs of southeastern South Australia are quite different again (Ellis, 1966). A. Moyle (1967:73) has produced a map of musical regions throughout Australia.

Academic studies in several disciplines have attempted to explain the large number of differing forms which occur regionally in language, material culture, initiation rites and so forth - to show that Aborigines descended either from one group of people originally, or from two or three different groups. Whichever case is true, the specific form of the aural tradition seems to have been moulded by a combination of life factors which meant that although groups were isolated for such daily activities as food gathering, well organized trade routes across the whole of Australia facilitated the continuous exchange of ideas, myths, music and ceremony.

The effect of this is diversity in local form, within the larger unity of common Aboriginal characteristics. The diversity may arise from features such as the "dialect chains" identified by Hale, O'Grady and Wurm (Wurm, 1963), where , in a chain of three languages, the middle one, B, is mutually intelligible to A and C, but A and C are mutually exclusive. Such a chain may run step by step, with adjacent dialects understood by the speakers but with the dialects at the extremes of the chain having little in common with one another. As. a result of this classification of languages into dialect chains the authors consider there are approximately one hundred and fifty distinct languages which were once spoken in Australia.

Part of the reason for the occurrence of marked differences between some local groups is that such adjacent groups practise varying forms of initiation or have markedly different systems of personal relationships such as marriage laws. In these cases little overt communication occurs between the groups. Another factor causing distinct cultural pockets is geographical isolation as a result of some physical barrier which makes communication difficult. An idea of these major boundaries, as well as tribal locations, can be found in Tindale's map *Tribal Boundaries in Aboriginal Australia* (1974), and information on other significant factors such as trade routes, from Peterson's book *Tribes and Boundaries in Australia* (1976).

Whatever the causes and whatever the reasons for these causes, however, it is now clear that not only were there once many different forms of music existing throughout Australia, but that even within South Australia at least three basically different styles of music were once performed. It is not possible to be certain about the details since in many areas of South Australia there is no person living who remembers having even heard his indigenous music, while some old people who have performed for me have done so after many years during which no one took any interest whatever in their songs. Hence there is no way of knowing how accurately the singing style of the area has been represented.

Unlike Aborigines of more northerly regions, South

Australian musicians do not use the didjeridu or any other pitched musical instrument in daily music making. This leaves the researcher entirely dependent on vocal music and the accuracy of the aural memory of each performer for definition of the styles that can now be located.

The three main musical styles in South Australia

The details of how the different South Australian styles were identified are published in several different sources (e.g., Ellis, 1966, 1967). The basic features of the musical styles are mentioned here briefly to remind the reader that the best known form of South Australian music, that of the Pitjantjatjara-speaking peoples of northern South Australia, is unlike the other two in many respects. The most conspicuous characteristics of the music once common in the southeast of South Australia, which was recorded by N. B. Tindale from the last traditional singer in 1937, are: an ornate singing style and free rhythm which is not closely controlled by the structure of the song text; a lighter quality of voice than is found in most other parts of Australia; and a melodic line which quite often rises, and covers a wide range of notes. The style found in isolated parts of northern South Australia, and more often in Central Australia, by contrast uses a very small melodic range, a descending pattern and rhythmic reiteration of the final note. Prime importance is placed on strict rhythmic structures. (There is an additional hybrid form thought to have once existed in the northeastern regions of South Australia which combined the narrow range and strict rhythmic structure of the Central Australian style with the melismas and ascending melodic patterns of the southeastern music. Not enough evidence remains to corroborate or refute this suggestion.)

The music of the Western Desert areas is still being taught to children today. The melody is wider in range than that of the older Central Australian type mentioned above (although some other Central Australian songs also have wide range), but apart from this the two styles are similar. The structural details of Pitjantjatjara music, itself characteristic of most Western Desert music, will be discussed in depth in chapter 4.

Disintegration of traditional forms

In many areas of South Australia no living performers can be found, and there are no recordings which provide information about the indigenous music. There are two main reasons for this obliteration of traditions. The first was recounted to us many times while we were in the field trying to locate performers from particular areas: the mass poisonings, epidemics and massacres of Aborigines, occurring as recently as the 1930s, wiped out entire tribal groups overnight. (For related documentation see Rowley, 1972:36ff, 157f, 161ff, 288ff; and Robinson, 1976:40, 281, 299.) When all the knowledgeable songmen and songwomen of an area were affected, the extremely long process of education through music was inevitably called to an abrupt halt and the entire system disintegrated.

A second cause of disintegration arose when missionaries took Aboriginal children away from their parents in order that they might make their way more easily in the European world. This dislocation of life style and values was equally effective in terminating the traditional system of education.

Close in time and purpose to the missionaries who forbade tribal performing came other white people who constantly ridiculed Aboriginal music. For the young Aborigines, there was no hope of acceptance from those white people who ridiculed traditional music if it became known that they were interested in that music. This more subtle force still works strongly to prevent the Aboriginal youth of today from openly expressing their interest in tribal teaching, and even where the music is still functioning, disintegration is occurring.

The advent of the local store in a tribal district, for instance, makes a marked impact on some areas of the total song repertoire. For instance, in precontact days it was possible for the elders of the group to ensure the continuity of the species of their particular totem through the accurate performance of the appropriate songs. In this way, it was believed, the abundance of the food supply was ensured. These elders never doubted the power of song to influence a wide range of practical situations; any failure of a ceremony to bring about the desired results was attributed to faulty performance.

The function of these increase songs may disappear over-night once the government store is available and tea, white sugar and white flour replace the staple diet of the food-gathering groups. It is only a matter of time before these songs cease to be performed. Similarly, contact with European systems of health, education and medical care all too often bring with them the discontinuation of traditional healing and educational practices and their associated songs.

From birth to death, Australian Aboriginal music is directed towards particular ends. Because those passing on the traditions have full understanding of the importance of music to the community, they pass on their knowledge to the next generation in a way which ensures its accurate preservation.

By contrast, our own Western culture ascribes only marginal value to music. There are several unfortunate results of this, which become increasingly apparent once one establishes contact with a culture where music is more central. The first is that purposeful educational programmes in and through music rarely occur, whether directed towards white or Aboriginal students. The second is that Western-trained musicians working alongside Aboriginal musicians rarely become informed on vital aspects of Aboriginal music which are not found in the Western system. Most damaging of all is the persistence among Western-trained teachers and musicians in thoughtlessly introducing tribal Aboriginal children to Western music without considering or recognizing the cultural and musical implications of this action.

Ways in which Aboriginal music is used

Many of the songs my husband and I recorded were taken at

a time when the traditional expressions which were often no longer relevant to contemporary living had been discarded and forgotten. The fact that I could record mainly love-magic songs from Antakarinja women does not mean that this was the only, or even the most important, song type these women possessed in fully tribal times. It suggests merely what while many aspects of their lives have changed, the women's sexual and reproductive role has remained relatively unaltered.

When I have asked these women for the songs they used in the old times for putting the baby to sleep, they have usually said that there are none used now, and when we enquired about songs used while grinding seed, the old women told us they could recall them being sung, but had never performed them and did not remember them. When we asked about songs performed at childbirth we were often told there were none. However, the following examples indicate that such information is not accurate.

In one of the Antakarinja women's ceremonies which I have recorded in full — a ceremony which is primarily concerned with love magic — there is reference to singing at the birth of a baby. The whole ceremony is an account of the travels of the two ancestral sisters, and it tells of the birth of a baby to the elder one. The other sister, together with women from the camp, "sang" the baby throughout the entire labour and the actual birth. Another reference we have came from an Aranda man (from Central Australia) who knew the correct song to be performed at a difficult birth. He told us that selected, skilled performers of both sexes sang the song to aid in such a situation. He would not perform this song, however, because of its particular power.

Where songs believed to have the power to influence external events still exist, they are not usually performed on request. If they are performed at all, it is either because the power itself has to be called on for an emergency, or because the singer no longer accepts that the song has power. In the latter case, the musical information is of little value, since the attitude behind the performance is entirely contrary to tribal belief, and only the externals of the performance are preserved. This problem does not exist for songs which traditionally and contemporarily are performed for entertainment, with the expectation that nothing other than the happiness of the community will result.

On one occasion, another woman researcher and I were recording a women's secret song from the northeast of South Australia. The very knowledgeable woman who was singing performed all the small songs associated with her own totem, and explained in detail what these signified. We heard the description of the countryside, and the special verses for increasing the totemic species in the area. At the climax of the performance, however, the singer refused to go any further. She explained that if she sang the next small song everyone would get very bad diarrhoea: such was her understanding of the power of the song.

In order to provide a picture of the general scope that music may once have had in the lives of tribal Aborigines throughout Australia, I have drawn on material from the adjacent Pitjantjatjara and Antakarinja. They have only slight differences in speech and no significant differences in music, and since my recordings include both groups (sometimes performing together) I have not attempted to differentiate between them. The following song types are those which occur in the collection recorded between 1962 and 1977, in some cases by myself alone, and in others with researchers from different disciplines. For all its omissions, this collection forms the basis of my knowledge of the music of this northern area of South Australia. Although structural details vary widely between the music of these Western Desert performers and groups in other areas of Australia, the use of music seems to be similar throughout the continent.

Children's songs

Children's songs can be regarded as the first stage of formal learning in traditional Aboriginal societies. It is difficult to find singers who know, or who will perform children's songs in the field, not only because of the natural shyness of the children themselves, but also because any social disintegration tends to disrupt this stage of music learning immediately. When we first started collecting children's songs in the field in the 1960s we found that Aboriginal women in their midforties and over could recall a few songs, and with the added interest shown by researchers they began teaching some of these to their children. Younger adults had not heard songs for children because they were not taught them in their childhood.

There are two types of children's songs: those made by adults for children (Ellis and Ellis, 1973; Kartomi, 1973) or those made apparently spontaneously by children, and preserved by one generation of children after another.

The traditional songs passed on by adults to children, and deliberately taught, form miniatures of adult music making. They retell parts of the Ancestral Dreaming of the locality in which the children live, and serve to teach not only about the history of the area, but about musical form as well. (One such song will be studied in detail in the next chapter.) There are also present-day songs made by adults for children. They are in traditional form but recount contemporary events (Ellis and Ellis, 1970).

In both types of children's songs there is associated physical activity in the form of mime or dance. The songs are concerned with developing the social, physical and intellectual awareness of the child. Whether the songs are made by children or adults, the texts and underlying myth usually emphasize the behaviour the song-maker or song-teacher expects of the song-learner. As well, the children are learning to handle the complex system of communication which operates in the adult Pitjantjatjara world.

Open songs for the whole community

Children may also participate in the open songs which belong to the whole group. These are the open forms of those songs which retell the original events in the creation of the locality, the history, and the essential religious and spiritual attitudes of the people. In these open songs the entire group participates together. Men, women and children join in recounting through song the events in the time long ago, and the observable impact — the sense of social belonging created — is a very important feature. Being present and participating in a performance in which every other member of the group is likewise present and participating has a tremendous impact on the individual, giving him a strong sense of identity.

This heightened sense of social belonging is often used deliberately by the knowledgeable musicians to overcome psychological ills caused by trauma faced by individuals in their own lives. At the same time, the performance of the open songs serves as a major part of the entertainment of the whole group and is thoroughly enjoyed by everyone present.

In the myth which lies behind a song, there are psychological components which become increasingly familiar to the participants as they grow and mature. Initially every piece of information is taken at its face value (i.e., it belongs within Learning I), but gradually the import of specific events becomes meaningful to the more educated in quite a different way from its original childhood interpretation (i.e., it is now interpreted from the base of Learning II). For those older people who already possess the necessary knowledge the presentation of an open song contains implications of secret and sacred information (i.e., they have already experienced it as a Learning III form). Their presence and participation in such an open performance allows them to recall the details of the power of those things they already know from their Learning III experiences. They cannot openly share this with younger members of their group. Nevertheless, during such an open performance, an experience common to that knowledge is implicitly shared by the whole group. In this way all the participants can be receiving vital feedback and undergoing a deeply moving experience which is directly related to their own level of personal growth and understanding.

It has been my observation that one of the most important features of the open songs performed by the community is that the education of the whole family occurs simultaneously. Through this group celebration, all members are challenged to the fullness of their ability — musically, intellectually, emotionally, physically and spiritually.

Closed songs

There are many songs which may be sung by, or in the presence of, only selected members of the tribe. There are a number of reasons for this exclusion of people who may be from another totemic group, or members of the opposite sex, or members of different age groups.

One reason for closing songs to the opposite sex and to a given age group is that they may contain explicit statements about the sexual behaviour of the ancestral participants. Such behaviour is rarely verbalized, even within the closed group allowed to attend and participate in the performance. Explanations of these songs (which in my experience have been women's secret songs) are given in whispers, if at all. Yet the song text may spare no detail. Merriam (1964:190ff) speaks about this incongruity in relation to music in other cultures — those matters which it would be impolite to voice directly may be sung about without causing any embarrassment.

Another reason for songs being closed to some members of the group is that they contain details of the antisocial exploits of the ancestral characters. In these cases there is much verbal excusing during the explanation of such a song. Performers say this is "just singing, not what we normally do". This excuse is now offered when nudity is presented unabashedly in the songs, but also applies to more complicated issues. One song which was known to older men and women was translated as the description a young girl gives of the appearance of her brother's penis after he has been initiated. The senior performer's response to this aberration, and to the hilarity it caused for the other performers, was "Don't laugh. It's not rude here. This is a song". Other antisocial acts (such as murder) included in songs are also explained away on the grounds that this does not happen now . . "it's just a song".

Probably the most important reason for having closed songs is that some, known only by the eldest and most knowledgeable, have power which is obtainable only through the correct presentation of performance. In such cases there is an acceptance that the entire personality of the performer can relate to the creative life-force through the use of song as a connective lead. (A useful analogy is the way an electric lead may be plugged into a power point and release energy which activates objects at its other extremity.) The power released through making connection with these greater forces can be used either for re-creation or for destruction. Unless the passing on of such potent information on how to tap these sources of supreme power is carefully guarded, the danger for the group as a whole is that the persons assuming senior roles may be bent on destruction rather than re-creation.

For these reasons there is a carefully graded and closely guarded system of training which involves prohibitions and exclusions. The individual moving through this process is watched closely by the most knowledgeable people to ensure that at every level his personality attributes are acceptable and his intellectual ability is sound. If the trainee breaks one of the prohibitions, he will be trusted with no more of the information leading to access to these powerful songs. If he continues to develop, he progresses beyond the levels of education we consider basic and, through concentration on music and all that it implies, moves into that level of learning described as Learning III.

The process of learning through music begins when a child sits in his (or her) parent's lap through a performance, absorbing and imitating the musical forms and learning their meanings. The more formal training leading to Learning III starts during adolescence when childhood patterns of behaviour are set aside. The process takes place at the same time as strict discipline (as opposed to the freedom allowed the younger child) is enforced through acts leading to the initiation rites. The outer form of these rites varies from one area to another and is different for males and females, but for both sexes it marks the commencement of the ordered learning of songs which contain important information for the preservation of the life of the entire community. This learning becomes one of the most important facets of the adult life of the individual, one through which he can progress in stature within his society, and one which requires many further years of study. He will not learn the highly secret songs at least until he is about forty years old, and even then he will not be considered remarkably knowledgeable. Ultimately, the individual's status within her or his traditional community is directly related to the number of songs about which she or he is deeply knowledgeable. The elders of the group are those who are knowledgeable about the traditions and about life: the wise men and women. They are the song owners (*inmaku walytja*) and are said to be *ninti pulka* ("having much knowledge"). As they are responsible for the day-to-day observance of the law, they are regarded with awe not only on the ceremonial ground but also in daily life. One such wise man was described to me by a younger Aboriginal man as *wati inmatjaraku pulka*, "a man equipped with many songs".

Multiple forms of the one song

It is possible for the one myth, and the songline representing it, to be presented in a number of different ways. A songline is a mapped form of a song, each small sung presentation being located at an identifiable place. Each of the series of small songs represents consecutive events in the myth. Pitjantjatjara performers speak about *mainkara wanani*, "following the way in song".

There can be a children's form of a particular songline. This form gives sufficient information about the events in the Dreamtime for the child to be able to relate closely to the story as it occurs in the song. The same song may be performed by the whole group together — men, women and children — and then it may have many more of the details of the story within it. In this case the performance does not depend on the abilities of children and considerably more intricate text forms and song patterns can be used. The information is still available to everybody and it consists of of the basic everyday events of the myth being represented.

There may also be closed forms of the same song. I have known of a men's secret song which the men assure me is the same as the open form of the series by the same name, but contains additional verses which would not be known by women and children. I can only guess at how these might be the same, since I am not entitled to be present at the performances or listen to recordings. I have been present at women's secret songs which I have also heard performed openly and in these it seems that some information, particularly that of an erotic nature, is excluded from the open performance of the same song. In other respects the open song seems to be identical with the closed form. It is possible in these cases simply to ignore sections of the story in the open performance, and to behave at an open performance as if these particular exploits had never occurred in the story of the life of the original Dreamtime people being then recreated.

I have also witnessed a women's secret performance in which the participants made reference to the parallel ceremony in the repertoire of the men's secret songs, and which was subsequently performed by the men as an open ceremony, for men, women and children. Each of these forms of the one myth were restricted to those features considered to be the most important for the group attending the performance and at no time were the secret aspects revealed in the wrong company.

The intoned story

All forms so far mentioned involve the selected group in performance together. The story on which the songline is based is unveiled through singing successive small songs (each about thirty seconds in duration) which together represent the totality of events. In the intoned story the musical elements and other features are restricted to the minimum. The story itself is alternately sung in a recognized melodic and rhythmic form by everyone present, and declaimed on one note only, by the principal performer.

The normal sung performance of a myth, through the singing of many small songs, involves everyone present. A person participates either as a member of the group which sings, in unison, the successive small songs unveiling the story in short segments while also performing a beating accompaniment; or as a dancer who represents one of the characters and events of the myth; and/or as a painter who is responsible for ensuring that the body design on the dancers is accurately executed; and/or as a manager responsible for organizing the performance.

To our ears, the intoned story seems to intersperse solo singing and actual telling of the story with brief presentations of one small song. The Antakarinja performers at the one example of an intoned story which I have observed told me, however, that while the small song was indeed "singing", what I understood as the sung form of story-telling was not singing, but "talking" or "sighing". The event, which centred on a single performer, unfolded as follows.

A group of women, myself included, gathered to hear one of the senior women perform a song that none of us had previously heard. She began the performance singing the one small song by herself, with no explanation. None of us knew what the small song meant. It was a very contracted statement about a particular man being killed. Who he was, how he came to be killed, or who else was involved were all factors about which we had no information and about which we did not ask.

When the songwoman had finished singing this she began to intone a story. After she had intoned a little of the story she burst forth into the same small song again for about thirty seconds. Immediately on completion of this singing she began intoning the next section of the story. Gradually, as she revealed section after section of the story, each time interspersing her intoning with the singing of this same small song, we understood one or two of the words in the short text.

We understood these not in the sense that they had been translated for us, but because we started to feel the impact of the central characters and issues in the story. We gathered the import of the contracted statement that was the essence of the text of that small song, and gradually we began to join in the singing. There were only six words in the entire song text and it was soon possible for us to participate in this as the

story progressed. By the conclusion of the story we understood the meaning of each of the words in the sung portion
and with the presentation of that short burst of song had
become aware of the ramifications of the whole of the myth
that lay behind it.

I have often wondered since whether this type of presentation used to be much more common. I was told by the singer
that this intoned story was one of the many that used to be
sung by the old women to their tribal granddaughters at the
time the latter were separated from the group during
menstruation. As such temporary isolation is no longer the
practice, this singing has probably dropped out of existence
altogether.

This type of key verse may be yet another form of the
multiple presentations of any particular myth. Perhaps this
myth was on some occasions sung as an open song, in which
case it would have contained less specific sexual detail; and
perhaps, too, the one repeated verse we heard is only one of
many in the open song. Its explanation to the children
present would then be much simpler than that we received in
the unfolding of the intoned story.

Understanding the song text

The text of each small song of a songline, whether that songline is itself long or short, consists of a very few words which
convey particular meaning. However, the explanation of song
texts is by no means as simple as it seems at first glance. The
process of learning Aboriginal music, from early childhood
through to later years of maturity, is one of integrated
growth which provides the individual with a set of rules
enabling him to develop to his own fullness without oppress-
ing others. It is also a process which presents much of the
information to different ages simultaneously.

For this reason, it is important that different levels of
meaning can be extracted from the same basic material. The
text itself is not separated into discrete words in the sung
form and it is therefore possible to extract different key

words from the one text if it is incorrectly grouped into word divisions (Strehlow, 1971:64). (The nature of the song text is explained in more detail later, as we progress in separating the elements of the song.)

There are often three different levels of meaning in any one song text (cf. Strehlow, 1971:197f). A song text may refer to an event such as the crossing of a creek when the water is running, but there may be a deeper meaning implied in the text itself. It may be possible to decode the text to extract different words and the knowledgeable may well know that to describe this song as one crossing a creek is to present a false front for the real meaning lying behind.

This false front (*inma ngunti*) is the type of "outside" information which is normally made available to children, whether they are present at an adult open performance or singing one of their own traditional songs. The explanation of this same song text for the young adults may contain erotic material, the existence of which was ignored when the teacher offered the explanation to the children. The most knowledgeable people understand that a further level of meaning is possible (though certainly not present in all song texts). It is the explanation which embodies the spiritual essence of the small song, the power which may be drawn forth from a particular place in order to alter the objective world in some manner.

If a particular song text has three such possible explanations, those which are not concerned with the emanation of power from the place described are considered to be false fronts guarding the secrecy of the important meaning. The most powerful songs do not have such false fronts and are exclusive in ownership and performance rights.

Given the complexity of meanings which lie behind one simple song text, it is not surprising that there is a great deal of confusion over the matter of song texts in general. One of the most common complaints the researcher hears from other white researchers (always secondhand, of course) is that the original researcher was not given the real meaning of the song. For the white nonresearchers working on Aboriginal reserves this is frequently elaborated with, "All So-and-so collected was lies". These are statements about the nature of the false front in songs, and about the fact that an explanation given on any one occasion depends on the status of the person explaining the song and also on what he or she perceives as the status of the person receiving the information. If both are of senior status then the most secret information may be divulged. If either is more junior, the lowest level represented by their status will be applied in the explanation.

An incident illustrating these levels of meaning clearly was recounted to me by another field worker. She was having great difficulty understanding the meaning of a particular song text because the singers, when asked privately, did not agree between themselves. First she had a particular word translated as describing the insulation cups on the telegraph poles. One might say she received the modern, general, face value explanation. At a later date she was told this song described a woman's breast; and still later that it described the sacred anthill of that locality. That the shapes were all related is obvious, and in such a case the text probably contained reference to the shape rather than to specific detail of what that shape represented.

The intoned story discussed earlier gives perhaps the best indication of the role of the song text as a mnemonic device. Through the repetition of these few words the performer recalls the essential personal/community interpretation which he or she has been taught. As he or she progresses, the earlier false front meanings have to be relinquished alongside other immature beliefs, yet the text remains, a reminder of growth as well as of all else that its literal meaning implies.

Pitjantjatjara terminology

The terminology used in music also forms part of everyday speech, and the duality of meaning between the technical musical use and the everyday use of the same word provides insights into relationships understood by performers themselves. These terms will be dealt with more specifically under the following sub-headings: onomatopoeia; song, music;

Dreaming, story; singing; dancing; design; melody; rhythm; general performance instructions; and song texts. In this way a wide coverage of various terms is possible.

Field observations made by people outside the culture always contain elements of cultural bias, however careful the observer may be. Examination of the words used by performers to describe musical concepts helps to compensate for this even though it, too, is not free of bias. After all, I usually only find out about the words I know to ask for, and I have great difficulty understanding anything at all about a word which cannot be translated in any way. Given these limitations, this process of working through the concepts spoken about by performers themselves can prove helpful. I have not included all the terms themselves, since these vary from one dialect to another. (Ellis *et al.,* 1978.)

First, however, a few general experiences I have had in the field may help to make these concepts more understandable. Strong associations are built between particular musical items and memorable events which occurred concurrently with those musical items. As an outsider I have acquired several such associations and through these I realize that the Aboriginal person must have many more.

I was working in the field with a linguist at the time of the first relevant event, our interest being centred on women's secret ceremonies. We had recorded part of a ceremony which was associated with elaborate body design requiring a lot of preparation, and the next day the ceremony was to continue. As usual, we went to the leading women and they soon began calling all the performers together. This procedure inevitably takes a long time, and our early call made this day no exception. Those ready to go out to the ceremonial ground waited in a small group with us, and the others continued locating the performers. One of the principal dancers could not be found; everyone discussed where they had last seen her. In a short while they discovered her body. She had died alone the previous night and nobody, until then, had missed her. The shock to everyone was great, and our own position, directly involved as we were, was very awkward since we knew nothing of the correct behaviour under such circumstances.

We sat with the performers, who showed no outward signs of distress, until the required legal procedures had been completed and the white officials had removed the body. At this point, without any warning to us, the seated women rose and began wailing in the traditional pattern. The wailing, known by performers as "crying" (R. Moyle 1979:12) continued throughout the morning. It sounded unlike any other Aboriginal vocal production that I had heard. The pitch was very high — a clear soprano voice — and great prominence was given to the top note of the wail, a note which, in isolation, would have been meaningless to me. After this experience, however, for more than two years, I immediately reacted to this note.

Both the linguist and I were in the field on three subsequent occasions when this particular note occurred (always at the start of wailing) and we both immediately reacted with dread because of the associations which it aroused. The first time was about nine months after the death of the performer for whom we first heard the wailing, when we were working with a group of women in a camp many hundreds of kilometres from the place of our original experience. We were suddenly disturbed by the unmistakable wailing, with the pitch just an octave lower, at the extreme of the tenor range. We were shocked, but the women merely laughed. They explained that the man was "crying" because his wine bottle was "dead" — he had finished all his wine.

The next time, nearly two years after the original incident, this wailing occurred during an immensely exciting performance of a sacred, but nonsecret totemic ceremony. In the midst of a thrilling performance, with over one hundred singers and many dancers, one woman began to wail. I could hardly continue recording, so great was the shock I felt. We later learned that the woman was permitted this expression of homesickness ("crying"), because the song concerned her birthplace.

The third incident took place at about the same time (and at the same place), and occurred because one of the old men of the camp (many kilometres from either of the other camps) was very ill. This time it was clear that we were not the only ones affected by the wailing; the response was immediate, and the news of the man's condition was quickly circulated throughout the population.

There are three significant aspects of these examples. The first is that on all these occasions the pitch on which the wailing occurred was the same: this suggests that the process we know as perfect pitch is in operation. The second is that the extra-musical association with this pitch and its means of production was rapidly established in a situation which was emotionally highly charged. The third is that the concept of musical "crying" is applicable to more events than ritual mourning.

The firmly established meaning of this note and its tonal quality, which had been programmed into me on the first occasion of my hearing it, gradually diminished so that I no longer have the same immediate reaction to its performance. What this experience shows is how such highly developed musical forms can remain unvarying and intact without the need either of musical instruments to ensure accurate pitch or musical notation to ensure accurate reproduction of the total musical idea. The music as a whole, with all its particular characteristics, is indelibly imprinted both on the mind and the autonomic physiology of the adolescent at the time of his first great trial, when he proves his ability to withstand the ordeals of initiation or, as in our case, at the death of one of the group.

For the initiate all the embedded characteristics constitute part of the identification mark of the totemic ancestor with whose song he is closely tied. The association of the total ceremonial (music, dancing, verse, design, etc.) the ordeal, and the newly acquired patterns of behaviour will remain with the young initiate throughout his life.

It is here, then, in the songs associated with the totemic ancestors, the songs which are passed on only as the individual proves his courage and dependability under stress, that we can best find the musical techniques; and we can expect them to change only in unimportant details as they are transmitted from generation to generation. The patterns are permanently established, and conform to a widely distributed system. The examples used to illustrate this process of implantation, which we ourselves experienced, showed also the uniformity of the system over a wide geographical area.

The specific technical meaning within music of the word for "taste" in Pitjantjatjara is also the word for "melody", which we may now see involves the concept of the identity of the totemic ancestor to whom that melody belongs and whose life essence is present during a correct rendition of the song. The term for "singing" is also the word for "laughter" or "playing". (Hence, one may "sing" in happiness, but the expression of grief is "crying", not "singing".) The term for stick beating as rhythmic accompaniment is also the general word used for "hitting". The term for the false front of a song is also the word used for "telling lies".

I have elaborated on some of these concepts in the following sub-sections, but many technical features of the music require detailed analytical explanation for the outsider before the system of communication and the information communicated can be understood. This is never given to a tribal student, since he already knows it from years of earlier background learning. It is therefore difficult for outsiders like myself to come to grips with how such tribal performers perceive their music.

Onomatopoeia

There are indications in the language that much of the environment is perceived as the sounds which that section of the environment produces. There are many onomatopoeic words and these in themselves provide an interesting example of the way the people perceive the sounds around them. Perhaps even more interesting is the idea that onomatopoeic words such as *ru:rmananyi** may be applied to a number of similar sounds. *Ru:rmananyi* was originally explained to me as the noise of swirling water during a flood. It was later translated as the sound a stationary motor car makes when it is continuously revving up. Still later it was the term used to

---

* The colon after a vowel indicates a lengthening as in, for example, the English word "fa:ther".

describe the electricity generator which created serious disturbance for Aboriginal people in the camp at Indulkana. On
yet another occasion *ru:rmananyi* was used for the sound of
too many voices and too much undisciplined behaviour in the
camp. Each of these ideas labelled *ru:rmananyi* seemed to
indicate disturbingly continuous noise. Where there are many
words referring to one particular concept, it seems reasonable
to suppose that that concept provides the name of a class of
sounds, itself an onomatopoeic representation of the type of
sound being classified.

Onomatopoeia is present in the naming of many species of
birds. Each name uses both the rhythm and an approximation of the sound-quality of the call of the bird concerned.
For instance, the owl is called *ku:rku* and the crow, *ka:nka*;
the squealing of a dog is *ki:lmananyi*; and the dull thumping
sound of the emu, *tukul*.

Tukul is a good example of the type of information on
music making which is available through the language. Not
only is it the description of the sound of the emu (and therefore the name of the sound), but it is also the term used for
the beating performed by the women during ceremonies. The
correct procedure for women taking part in any performance
is for them to sit on their heels or with their heels alongside
their buttocks, creating a cavity between their thighs. Over
this cavity they beat with one hand (which is held by the
other hand). The correct sound of this beating is a dull
thump.   In this case, *tukultjingani,* the term used for this
beating, may be described as making a *tukul*-type sound.

There are a few other musical terms which are likewise
onomatopoeic. *Timpil* is the sound of the beating that the
men may do when they use two boomerangs or sticks beaten
together during singing, and *lakalakani** describes the accompaniment to the dancing which requires that the boomerangs
or sticks be rattled very rapidly together.

It is possible to hypothesize that one of the most critical
elements (as indicated by common labelling) in the classifica-

---

* The stroke under a consonant indicates a retroflex — the tongue is turned
  backwards to produce that consonant.

tion among Pitjantjatjara people of all sound-producing bodies, animate and inanimate, is the actual sound normally produced. However, this is not usually so in the case of music. It seems that musical terminology which is not concerned with an actual sound-producing object refers to the relationship of music to concepts other than sound, and these related concepts give us an insight into Pitjantjatjara feeling and thought about the music itself. Strehlow (1971:674f) draws attention to the use of onomatopoeia in song texts among Aranda people.

Song, music
The word most commonly used to describe music is *inma* which encompasses the entire concept of song, music, dance, design. It can be used for songs alone; it can be used for an entire ceremonial performance; it can be used for non-Aboriginal music and, for instance, in the Centre for Aboriginal Studies in Music, the tribal people often talk about *inma walpa* (wind music) when referring to Western instrumental playing on flutes, clarinets and trumpets.

The traditional uses of this word, apart from simply referring to ceremony or the fact that a song is to be performed, include "good" *inma*, "bad" or "unreliable" *inma* performances, an exceedingly sacred and secret ceremony, or a ceremony with a "false front" (*inma ngunti*). *Inma ngunti* are the songs mentioned earlier which are taught to children in the camp and which also have behind them a more profound secret ceremony. The word is also used to define the small unit of musical structure — that which I have so far called the "small song". This is called *inma tjukutjuku** (*tjukutjuku* means "small"). A "songline" consists of many small songs recounting one long myth.

There is also a "good and true" *inma* which is the sacred performance lying behind a false front. There is a "big" *inma*, which is one associated with an important ceremonial site and which has particular power; and there are certain types of *inma*, for instance, *ilpintji* which is the well-known

*   tj = ch, as in cheese

form of love-magic. (e.g. Strehlow, 1971 [many references under *ilpintja*]; R. Moyle, 1979 [many references under *yilpintji*].)

Dreaming, story

Inma does not exist without the Dreaming (the beginning of time and its population and events) which is its source. The main words used in discussing the Dreaming are *tjukur* and *wapar*; the first being an actual dream, or the Dreaming – the time "long ago", – and the second a story about the Dreaming. The song arises from the activities of the ancestors in the Dreamtime-long-past and at the beginning of a song one may hear a performer speaking about "listening to (or thinking of) the story of the song", or "listening to the sound of the Dreaming story".

The word *mayu* may also be used. This is the word for the correct "taste" of a melody belonging to an ancestor and the correct Dreaming "taste" for any given occasion is *mayu tjukur*. This melody may be hummed (*mayu tjukur ngu:ṇmananyi*). As well, there are the same concepts, as for *inma,* of "good" Dreaming, "bad" (inaccurately presented) Dreaming, and a "false front" Dreaming.

It is possible to dream a song as a contemporary event. The description of this process as given by the performers is that a person lies down to sleep and rises in his dream and dances and sings. In this way, by lying down to sleep, then dreaming of dancing, the dreamer can "catch" a new *inma.* This can be remembered in the morning and taught to others. It is still a proper Dreaming, a "true" Dreaming, as it draws on the eternal sources of the original Dreamtime, but it is a contemporary form of this Dreaming.

The ideas of the song/ceremony and the Dreaming story provide the basic philosophy for all that happens in Aboriginal music making.

Singing

The principal word for "singing" is *inkanyi* which may be translated as either "to sing" or "to laugh" or "to play". The idea of "singing" has much greater significance for

Aboriginal people than for us. It implies not only the act of singing, but also the act of causing events to occur through drawing on the power accessible through song. Thus an Aboriginal woman may sing her lover, a skilled medicine man may sing a person well (or ill). The evil connotation of being "sung" is one which is dreaded by Aboriginal people: often a death is attributed to a person having been sung.

To avoid ambiguity with the word *inkanyi,* specifying its musical sense, performers may say *inma inkanyi,* thereby making quite clear that they are referring to singing a song.

There is a term for "singing fat". This, when I have seen it performed, has involved putting the power of the song into a piece of animal fat which is subsequently used to massage people who are ill. There are also terms for one person singing first and the others joining in one after another; for loud or high singing (the one term); for the occasions when harmony results from one or more singers being late or early in moving from one section of the melody to the next (that term may be translated as a "different sound"); for singing together in unison; for singing in a low voice, that is, slowly and quietly; and for singing which is loud but not fast; for mourning wailing; for shouting; for humming or using meaningless syllables as a wordless definition of a melody (*ninaninanyi*); for the vocalized breath intake during singing; for painters and the group of singers during a ceremony, each simultaneously singing different small songs of the one ceremony.

There are also many expressions referring to humming, which is related to the word for "sighing". There are terms for humming the sound of the Dreaming, but also for the humming which is "looking for a hint of the song" — humming a particular small song in order to remember the words. Perhaps one of the greatest errors in performance is to sing incorrect words, and so being able to hum first, which performers describe as "looking for a hint of the song", ensures that the leading singer is able to fit the words correctly to the melody without actually uttering them. Such humming of the melodic outline clarifies the rhythmic definition of the text being sought.

Unity — like
modayin system?

Dancing

The key word for the activity of dancing, whether male or female, is *pakani* which means "rising". Apart from referring to dancing and singing, or to a song which can be used for dancing, there are specific technical terms: for moving along standing on knees; for quivering the thighs and knees; for stamping the feet; for dancing, carrying ceremonial objects; for the jumping motion performed by the women, which leaves continuous tracks in the sand; for the description of other bodily movements such as "head down on one side when dancing". Many of these steps are specific to the dancing of only one sex.

Design

The terms referring to painting designs on the bodies of the performers seem to be fewer in number and are mostly based around the key word *walka* which means "mark" or "drawing". When painting is in progress it is often said that the participants are "drawing the song". There is another term for rubbing out the painted body designs immediately after dancing where it is necessary to prevent identification of the designs, and there is a term for a performer painted ready for a dance. There may well be other terms which belong in this category (see, for instance, N. Munn, 1964).

Melody

The concept of melody is a rather more difficult one to follow. The basic word is *mayu* which means the "taste" of food or the "sound" of the song. There are terms referring to this which mean trying out ("tasting") the tune before starting the first verse; the sound of the song, usually the melody but sometimes also the rhythm; for singing out of tune; for singing the same tune; for being unable to think of the correct tune; for a change of melody within the course of one ceremony; for someone singing wrongly, out of tune or with the incorrect melody.

Rhythm

Rhythm is also a difficult concept to handle since there is no word we have been able to relate it to. The only terms we have found are ones which refer to singing with syncopation; singing quietly without syncopation; tapping out the rhythm of the words of an *inma*; the strong beating to accompany singing; and heavily accented singing or beating.

General performance instructions

There are terms of instruction which are used at a full performance of the ceremony: instructions for everybody to look at the ceremony or for people to close their eyes at appropriate points; for the singers to go back and repeat the previous verse in order to sing it correctly; for the women to put their heads down when they are not to see a particular painted design on the body of the dancer before it is presented simultaneously with the correct musical form and dance step; and for closing the *inma* at one location and then moving on.

Song text

When we have asked the performers how to understand the musical structure they have usually said, "You have to know the words before you can understand anything else". The principal word concerned in discussion of text is *wangka* which means "words" or "talking", and there are terms for the song text itself. Then there are descriptions of song texts which include the number of words involved, a song text which is the same and a song text which is different from the previous one; or an occasion when someone is singing the wrong words.

In the total performance there are many consecutive small songs in a songline, and these each may be described differently according to their type. There are what is known as "travelling" small songs which are identical in every section of the total performance. They may, for instance, describe the crossing of a dry creek bed. On each occasion that they are repeated in the ceremony it may be a different creek bed that is involved but the same song text is used.

Texts often have two halves, as described in chapter 4, (cf. R. Moyle 1979:77) and a link song text uses half of the text of the previous small song and adds a new half, thus tying sections of the ceremony together. There are small songs which "name" important sites in the totemic history of the Dreaming concerned (cf. Strehlow, 1971:452). These are known as "powerful" small songs. There are special small songs performed at the close of each section of a ceremony (cf. Strehlow 1971:141). These are usually repeated to check correctness and to know what the next small song will be. There are small songs which are concerned with painting up for the ceremony. There are terms which refer to humming in order to remember the song text which is presenting a problem. There is a separate term for the final small song at the very end of a ceremony.

The study of descriptions given in words leads only so far in understanding song texts. A fuller understanding is possible by looking at the texts themselves and how they operate in the context of a song line, which is itself the presentation, in a highly structured form, of a myth which may be found encompassed in other structures (e.g., as a story).

The text of a small song conveys basic factual information, and is repeated over and over again in the course of any one small song. The number of repetitions depends entirely on the accompanying action. If a lengthy dance is taking place then the text must be repeated, and the melodic outline with it, for a sufficient number of times to allow the dancers to complete their action. If the small song is just being sung with no other action taking place the text is still repeated a number of times to complete the shape of the melody. For greater detail on this, see chapter 4. At the moment, one example will suffice. The following text, which is quite short, is usually repeated four times in the course of the presentation of one small song:

anpiri nya nya anpiri nya nya
yuru kulpa yuru kulpa

The factual information contained in any one song text is very limited and it is not possible to understand the events in a sequence of small songs unless one knows something of the background of the Dreaming. The above text, translated directly, means "Listen! What is that? Water running".

This particular text comes from a songline associated with the ancestral Zebra Finches who travelled around at the beginning of time. The children's version, from which this small song is taken, describes the Zebra Finch group (who frequently change from their human to their bird form) travelling around in a large circle, returning back to their home camp. At the point in the songline when this small song is performed, the story relates that there are two groups of birds. One has stopped at the deep creek and includes many different birds such as robins and ducks. When they hear the sounds of running water they call out, "Listen! What is that?" They tell the birds travelling behind them that the creek is in flood and the water is too deep to walk across. Next morning they were able to walk through.

To listeners who do not know something of this explanation, the actual song text tells very little. However, to those who know the story, the song text acts as a mnemonic device, reminding the singers of all the events associated with that particular incident in the journey.

Usually, each text describes one geographical place, or an event that took place in the lives of the original Dreaming ancestors. The central characters appear either as animals or in human form. In theory, at least, the texts in any performance of the one ceremony should always be in the same order. In practice this is not so. There seem to be some stable elements and some which are variable. When we have enquired about these we have been sharply reprimanded for asking too many questions.

The story of Miniri/Langka

Even in the title of this songline dealing with events in the lives of the ancestral *miniri* and *langka* (analysed in detail in chapter 4) there is some ambiguity in our information about the ancestor who is primarily involved. The songline is one taught to children by the adults. We have recordings from the field, as well as many made during the lessons non-tribal students have had from the tribal teachers at CASM. On some occasions this series has been named *miniri* (the "mountain devil", *Moloch horridus;* a small ant-eating reptile which is named *ngiyari* in a neighbouring dialect, see Figure 3.1c). At other times we have been told that the songline is known as *langka* (a lizard species, probably "blue tongue"). At other times again we have been told that Miniri and Langka were one. This oneness probably applies to the nature of the myth.

The version most often given in the presence of students at CASM describes Miniri and Langka as brothers in the Dreaming, travelling the same route in ancestral times. Miniri passed through the places first and Langka travelled through them later.

Mountford (1973:59ff) records a similar story from the extreme northwest corner of South Australia, the same general locality from which our versions have come. (The story was told to him by Pitjantjatjara people from further west than those with whom we have worked.) His story recounts how the *miniri* acquired its present-day markings. It is a small, fearsome-looking yet harmless lizard. In the time-long-ago, the Dreaming, Miniri invited all the other small creatures to attend a ceremony at Miniri (which Mountford states is sixteen kilometres south of Moanja in the Mann Ranges). At this time all the creatures were creamy white and they came from near and far to be at Miniri for the performance. They paired off and began to decorate one another for the performance.

Since Langka and Miniri were the main performers they spent the most time over the designs to be placed on them. Time delays meant that the sun had set before they had completed preparations for the ceremony. Some of the participants lit bunches of highly inflammable grass to give light for the continued preparations. However, a breeze sprang up which spread the fire out of control and engulfed all the small creatures. Many escaped unhurt, wearing the

Figure 3:1a Zebra Finches as represented in *Inma Nyi:nyi* (Artist: Josie Townsend).

Figure 3:1b Blue Tongue Lizard as represented in *Inma Langka* (Artist: Josie Townsend)

Figure 3:1c Mountain Devil *Miniri* as represented in *Inma Langka* (Artist: Josie Townsend).

decorations they then had which they have kept ever since. Some were blackened or scorched, and have remained in this condition to the present day. According to the Mountford version, Miniri and Langka escaped with their decorations too, and Miniri also retained his ceremonial headband; and even to this day the *miniri* will attempt to shield his eyes from the heat of that fire by raising his little hands before his eyes should you pick him up.

In our studies, both in the field and at CASM, we were told that the journeys of Miniri and Langka in these ancestral times converged on the one campsite which now bears the name "Miniri". It contains, in this vast, waterless country, a rockhole with a permanent water supply. Miniri is therefore the name both of the place which is central to the story and of one of the principal characters in the story.

The children's section of this songline which we are concerned with represents only a minor portion of the "proper" Miniri songline. After reaching the rockhole, as recounted in the small songs of the children's version, Miniri began another longer journey. The songline associated with this longer journey is kept secret from women, children and uninitiated males.

The translation of the verses of the children's version which we have learned tells about the Bird people watching for the tracks of Miniri in the early morning. The Birdmen passed the old desert oak at the top of the sandhill and saw Miniri's tracks. They searched for him in the scrub without success. Then the Birds saw him and speared him. Miniri ran all the way to his camp with the spears in his back. (This accounts for the spiny back of the present-day mountain devil.) Miniri turned into a flat stone by the rockhole named after him. (No mention is made of the contradiction between this explanation and the secret version which asserts that a further journey took place. This suggests that there may be recognized, but substantial, alterations of the main myth when it is used as a false front.)

The Lizard saw all this from a sandhill further away. He saw the Birdmen celebrating their victory over Miniri, dancing and singing. The Birdmen later met the Lizardman who was carrying on his head a dog whose feet were tied together. The place where Miniri turned into a rock became an important meeting place for everyone. There the Willy-wagtail danced on the hard ground by the cave where the rockhole is located, and the Grubman ate so many ants that he lay on his stomach, bloated, unable to take part in the dancing. When the dancers looked sideways over their shoulders they could see Miniri up there, lying curled up.

Neither the performances we have heard in the field or at CASM have ever gone beyond this point.

Inma langka is the name the tribal teachers most often use to refer to the songline. In it, this series of events is described in many small songs, each conveying one episode (cf. Strehlow 1971:146ff). The correlation of the story of *inma langka* with its musical form not only completes the picture of how a myth is presented through a songline, but also highlights many perceptual and structural features common to the music of Pitjantjatjara-speaking people. We now leave the aspects of music that can be observed from outside the actual music, including the meaning of the song texts, to pass on to an examination of what occurs inside the experience of music making.

4
The Pitjantjatjara Musical System

Perceptual background

Aboriginal music has an iridescent quality. The colour depends on which aspect holds one's attention at any time. The structures, even if completely unaltered, can appear first in one form, then in another. The multiple sets of possible variants around one pattern increase this potential. If outsiders fail to appreciate this, they fail also to understand how a tribal performer perceives, and can be enthralled by, something which seems mundane, simple and primitive to these foreign listeners.

An analytical study helps the person who has not grown up within the culture to overcome this problem. In it, the complex overlay of patterns can be displayed, but it is only when these patterns are subsequently combined in performance experience that they are of more than purely intellectual interest. If the study is both analytical and practical, the great artistry and incredible skills of the performers can be appreciated.

The problem of perception is related to that of recognizing reversible configurations (e.g. N.L. Munn, 1966:494). In suitable circumstances, a light-coloured pattern may be seen with a dark background; suddenly this configuration may reverse and a dark pattern emerge against a light background. Once this reversal has taken place, the original pattern cannot be seen, until a further flip highlights the pale pattern, and the dark one disappears. Only one figure at a time can be perceived, the other becoming background.

Similarly, in a performance of Aboriginal music, one figure in the whole can be aurally identified and then perceived in different relationships to other simultaneously occurring patterns, which become background; then one of the background patterns can emerge as foreground, to be turned around in various ways in relation to its background, only to be replaced by a new focus of attention. With each of these changes, the play of colours is varied. Analysis shifts the time-bound aural form of these patterns to a visual approximation which allows careful inspection of events which otherwise pass too quickly.

Since it is difficult to understand the musical structures in either Western analytical terms or in the context of traditional tribal performance practice, it is as well to consider why the effort of understanding them is important.

Many facets of Aboriginal thinking can be understood by listening to, or reading about, traditional stories such as those found in *Australian Dreaming* (Isaacs, ed. 1980) and accounts of daily living (R. M. and C. H. Berndt, 1964) which make possible a deeper understanding of Aboriginal thought. They provide the framework within which the more highly structured patterns of communication may be understood.

However, this type of information on the life practices of tribal people may not be as important for present-day education and social adjustment of urban and tribal people as the actual forms within which this content is encompassed. Failure to understand this in the past has led at best to ridicule of Aboriginal artistic creations, at worst to educational processes which totally underestimate the capacities of Aborigines for learning intricate information. A balance is possible, where the educator sets out to offer a realistic contemporary learning experience for tribal Aboriginal students in Western schools; yet this does not seem possible if the educator has no access to detailed information on the structures of the traditional communications systems.

Since music is the central repository of Aboriginal knowledge, and because it can allow little structural change of the major formal boundaries without disintegrating, understanding its processes is of significance to any educator, but particularly to those concerned with Aboriginal work. And, of course, the complexity of tribal Aboriginal music makes a mockery of the assumption that Aboriginal children are genetically inferior in their capacity to learn. Music is the main intellectual medium through which Aboriginal people conceptualize their world. McLuhan (1967:41) stresses that if we perceive the same external world through different media then we see a different world. Therefore, we cannot begin to understand the world as it is perceived by a tribal person unless we have a deep insight into the media through which he is observing and communicating. We cannot seriously reach out through education to an Aboriginal person unless we recognize that the environment created by his media becomes, as McLuhan (1967:157) again points out, his means of defining his role within his environment.

The most important facet of the structure of Pitjantjatjara music is its capacity for expansion and contraction of formal units within established boundaries. This expansion and contraction can occur in different directions for different aspects of the overall pattern, yet fixed points must interlock. At the risk of over-simplification, a comparison may be made between Western and Aboriginal music at this point. In Western music, sections usually divide into equal and symmetrical subsections: thus a bar may be subdivided into four equally separated short beats, and once this sub-division occurs (whether into four, three, six or any other number of beats), all subsequent bars are normally subdivided in exactly the same way. Phrases, or groups of bars, are often built of four bars; and larger sections of multiples of four bars. A diagrammatic representation of this type of symmetrical patterning so common in Western music is given in Figure 4:1(a) which shows equal-sized patterns within fixed musical boundaries.

In Aboriginal music, by contrast, a pattern which is repeated throughout many successive verses and which must fall within fixed boundaries of text length, melodic shape and so forth, may be flexible in duration. Figure 4:1(b) uses the straight line to depict the shortest pattern and lines with varying degrees of fold to depict the related patterns of

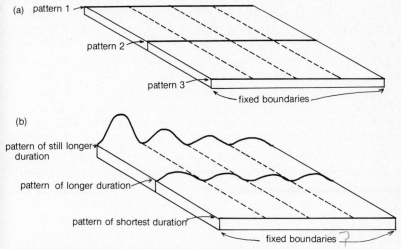

Figure 4:1   Musical patterning within fixed boundaries.
(a) Western music, where patterns are normally the same length as one another and are symmetrical.
(b) Aboriginal music, where duration of patterns frequently changes within fixed boundaries causing asymmetry.

longer duration which must fit within the same fixed boundaries as the shorter pattern. Comparison of these two figures gives some idea of the nature of the difference between Western divisive forms and Aboriginal additive forms.

The structures within music embed patterns of thought which operate outside music, and being able to highlight this difference between the rigid divisive thinking shown in the structures of Western music and the flexible additive thinking shown in the structures of Pitjantjatjara music is important because of its profound implications. The most conspicuous use of this structuring in both musics is in relation to time and anyone with experience in the two cultures involved knows that the concept of time is totally different in each. Not only does the structural information clarify this difference in attitudes to time, but it also suggests a greater capacity for exclusion on the part of Western thinkers and for incorporation on the part of Aboriginal thinkers.

I observed a good example of this difference between Western and Aboriginal thinking in the field when an educator, involved in an administrative capacity in the city with tribal Aboriginal people, visited the area with which he was most concerned. There were general discussions between the tribal people and the administrator, in the light of which, during a friendly interchange, one of the tribal people asked of the administrator, "Are you our brother?" (i.e., Can we incorporate you into our fixed system of tribal relationships since we have the capacity to expand these under special circumstances to *include* some outsiders as a special honour?) The administrator laughed and said, "Of course I'm not your brother. And anyway I must go now as it is lunchtime." (i.e., No, my personal interest in you *excludes* your concepts of interpersonal relationships and of time; I am here concerning your education.)

In this case, tribal capacity to incorporate, which has great advantages in cross-cultural learning, was inhibited by the administrator's culturally-taught negative reaction and non-incorporative processes.

Incorporation such as that displayed in the structure of the music is also present in the flexibility traditionally shown over land usage. Boundaries between food gathering groups in desert areas were retained rigorously until times of disaster (floods, fires, droughts) when it was possible to "fold" the area available for a particular group by temporarily extending the boundaries (but never abandoning them).

This flexibility is also apparent in the structures of kinship, where apparently rigid limitations, when looked at in close detail, become complex forms of extension and inclusion within the fixed limits applying to the system. The extended family, which causes such hard feelings in city living, is an example of the capacity to incorporate many people within the fixed limit of the family circle.

Use of time shows this same flexibility. Tribal people often complain about Europeans who have to operate their daily lives by the bell and have to watch the clock all the time. Tribal division of time — year, seasons, moons, sunrise, midday heat and sunset — always allows for flexibility within these fixed points and does not allow the boundaries themselves to become the limiters of every action. By contrast, we measure time to the hour, minute and second and are bound by such small divisions. Probably all aspects of tribal life one may choose to examine will show this same capacity to incorporate, to add to, to "fold" information in some way so that more may be included within the fixed boundaries when this is required.

However, it is this very capacity to incorporate, to assimilate foreign material, which often brings about disintegration of tribal life. If the boundaries once become strained beyond their capacity to spring back to their original position, permanent damage has occurred. The close sanctions that apply to the teaching of secret songs and to the use of the power these contain is the statement of a fixed boundary which, if traversed by the wrong person, can cause the system to disintegrate from within. Once a knowledgeable person has been admitted to such realms of power, he cannot subsequently be excluded (unless quite exceptional measures are taken).

In such a system, where inclusion is always possible, it is necessary to have strong barriers preventing unhealthy penetration in the first place. Otherwise, too much non-traditional interference may force the system to a point beyond which it cannot recover its boundaries of limitation intact. This unrecognized potential for over-incorporation in tribal/white contact often leads to total breakdown of the tribal system. The urban Aboriginal person, on the other hand, is usually without any traditional boundaries at all, but has inherited structures of thought which call for incorporation rather than exclusion. He is therefore at the mercy of those who choose to manipulate him, since he has no inherent mechanism of exclusion once the boundaries have been broken, and has a strong need to incorporate as much as possible into his own thinking.

In music, the danger of incorporation to the point of disintegration is held in check by the need for many structural elements to have similar boundary points which interlock. Presumably this was the case in traditional patterns of living as well, but as boundaries are eroded, the capacity to locate the essential points at which exclusion must occur is being lost.

Undoubtedly the most disastrous present-day implication of incorporation to the point of disintegration lies in the tortuous wrangles over Aboriginal land rights. Where the traditional concepts can be extended to incorporate mining on sacred land, it is only afterwards that the tribal leaders discover that they have unwittingly allowed themselves to be excluded from the land. Their belief that they belong to the land (i.e., they perceive the land as capable of incorporating them and all others who choose to use it), and not that the land is their exclusive property, causes them to let themselves be evicted from their all-important spiritual home.

Much disastrous change takes place in culture contact because these factors are not understood. To return to McLuhan's point, the media we use provide us with different primary perceptions; and these in turn are affected by the way we interpret what we perceive through these media. And it is for this very reason that understanding the structural implication of tribal music is of such importance in understanding the tribal person's perception of his world. The greater flexibility within tribal systems compared with Western ones can be related to the theoretical discussion of different systems of thought in chapter 2, the incorporative one fitting Gooch's System B, while the Western processes of division and exclusion fit his System A.

Although the perception of environment is potentially a continuum, many authors, Lévi-Strauss in particular, stress the fact that such synthesis does not occur and divisions of the continuum appear as binary oppositions. Within tribal music this binary opposition is between rigid boundaries and flexible internal structures; but there is also binary opposition between music as structure and music as meaning and emotional expression.

At a more superficial level, understanding structures alone can provide analogies in teaching across cultural barriers, and my concern is to show how this is possible through understanding music. Fascinating use of the concept of conservation is illustrated in all the figures which demonstrate the idea of the "fold" as shown in Figure 4:1. I frequently hear from teachers of Aboriginal children that the latter are "hopeless at maths" but obviously they are ignorant of the complex mathematical procedures which occur within musical structures. With their Western educational biases, they themselves are often "hopeless at music" but they have great difficulty in seeing this as a parallel failure of their own educational attainments. Each of these situations is a failure of structural understanding.

At the level of content and meaning, I have had experiences of using education through music which retained traditional structures while introducing new content. In order to do this it is necessary to have a profound knowledge of the original structures and their functions, gradually introducing new content which is not damaging to either structure or function. For instance, a song taught to children, and intended as basic grounding for their future social and intellectual life may well, with the aid of tribal songmen and songwomen, become the focus for introducing notions on the tribally-chosen form of combined tribal/Western living that the community decides is best for their future. A song form originally used as a source of sexual information for women can have a change of informational content which offers explanation of modern contraception (see Ellis and Tur, 1975).

Several non-Aboriginal students of the tribal elders have helped me in writing this chapter. Their assistance has been invaluable since they have come to the study fresh from their own activities in Western music and can see where difficulties of explanation would confuse those with less tribal contact than they have. We all found it necessary to undertake our own individual analysis in order to understand in our terms what was occurring during tribal singing lessons. Students have now contributed their own experiences and the particular analyses they developed, as well as much critical thought on the final written form of the chapter.

The educational relevance of the following material has prompted me to make every effort to represent musical detail accurately and in a manner which is intelligible to the non-musician. In this chapter, the broad analysis of the music has been presented as part of the text, while the detail appears in the technical Appendix. I will be using the following terms with the general meanings given here:

Beating: each small song has continuous percussive accompaniment. This is performed either by each singer beating the thighs (women); or by clapping cupped hands, beating a stick on the ground, or beating two boomerangs together (men).

Ceremony: the performance through song, dance, body design and various "stage" effects (e.g. sudden flare of firelight) of the myth associated with a particular ancestral figure.

Melodic Section: an identifiable portion of the melody of a small song (q.v.) which emphasizes usually only one particular note of those used.

Rhythmic Pattern: the shortest possible statement of the rhythm which is repeated over and over to complete a particular verse. It has many different possible internal arrangements.

Rhythmic Segment: a rhythmic subdivision of the song text and rhythmic pattern.

Small Song: the smallest musical unit recognized in Pitjan-tjatjara music. It consists of uninterrupted singing for about thirty seconds, after which informal chatter and laughter occur (see also *verse*).

Songline: the sequence of small songs or verses which may be mapped to show their geographical location.

Song Text: the word sequence repeated throughout any small song.

Totemic Melody: the melody which belongs with a named songline (q.v.).

Verse: this generally applies to discussions based on the *text* of a small song. The usage is based on that of Strehlow

(1971). The numbering of the successive small songs (q.v.) refers to this textual aspect rather than to the musical aspect. The items in the Appendix (pp. 209-13) are listed as verses 1–17, with the sub-numbering (a) for the first use of the text, (b) for the second, etc. They could also be listed as small songs 1–34. This latter numbering has not been used because the textual information is considered more important than the sequence of items.

It is intention of the discussion to clarify these terms by giving them structural definition. It should be remembered that if such structures can be repeatedly identified in performances, they must form part of the knowledge (either conscious or unconscious) of the performers.

The analysis begins with the ceremony as a whole, then examines the interlocking of the smaller elements within the ceremony. The main part of the chapter discusses the individual musical elements. The technical detail here is relevant not only to the musician. It describes a communication medium which is crucial to Aboriginal thought and through which positive moves to their chosen constructive future may be made by Aboriginal people in Australian society. It is therefore relevant to educators and those concerned with the social and political development of Aboriginal people in the modern world.

Where references have been used, they are not normally to Pitjantjatjara music. Strehlow, for instance, writes about Aranda music, and R. Moyle about that of the Pintupi. Both these musics appear to have close structural similarity to that of the Pitjantjatjara.

Larger-scale interlocking of structures – music and meaning

During an actual performance of a Pitjantjatjara tribal ceremony, what happens, broadly, is an interlocking between those structures concerned with music and those concerned with meaning. In the music there are various layers of events, each with its own significance. There is a hierarchy of elements of time, from the length of the shortest note, which operates as a basic pulse in the singing; the beating accompaniment which links the singing with accompanying dance; and there are rhythmic segments, rhythmic patterns and complete text presentations which are complex combinations of accentuation of syllables of the text, and of long and short notes placed at specific points in the text. (The inner portion of Figure 4:5 shows how these are related, and a glance ahead to p. 110 at this point may help understanding.)

There is a similar hierarchy of melodic elements in the music, which may be ranked by starting with the smallest interval of pitch difference, then moving to melodic sections which tie together both melody and text. The melodies are recognizable as belonging within the larger framework of certain totemic histories; and they in turn all occur within an overall melodic system which begins always with the upper notes of the total range and descends through several reiterated notes to the lowest note of the range; a melodic contour which has been described in other nonliterate musics as a "terraced melody".

These technical musical features are interlocked with extramusical events (such as dances) and information (such as the songtext) which occur simultaneously. For example, while a group of singers performs a set of small songs related to a particular body design (each small song using all the technical features mentioned above) the performers preparing for the next dance are being painted with the appropriate design; and each mark in that design has specific meaning (see Nancy Munn, 1964). All the events (song, design, dance, etc.) are based around a story which originated in the Dreaming and which tells of the time-long-ago.

The music cannot be fully understood without reference to the meaning of the extramusical information with which it is related (but this is not to say it does not have meaning in its own right). The totemic melody can only be understood in the performers' terms when we recognize that the totemic ancestor who is being recreated at that performance is believed by performers to be present in essence within that melody. As far as we know, there are no duplications of melodies within different totemic songs among the Pitjantjatjara. The melody itself has a structure which results from its particular use of the intervals of the musical system. The latter are unlike Western intervals and can be represented only approximately in Western notation (Ellis 1967a). Each of the larger intervals is a summation of two or more of the smaller ones (an additive process). These are combined in the framework of the "terraced melody" (which provides one set of boundaries).

Rhythmic patterns are permanently combined with given song texts. As a result, the rhythm alone can convey the same meaning as the text to which it is tied (Ellis, 1970:91). A rhythmic pattern consists of the shortest segment of rhythm which is repeated over and over again to produce a complete small song. (This is technically known as *isorhythm.*) Often the rhythmic pattern is the same length as the text (which also must be repeated a number of times to complete a small song) but sometimes it is much shorter, requiring two or even four presentations to accommodate the complete text. The pattern, whether short or long, is built of rhythmic cells which also appear as units in other rhythmic patterns set to different texts (Ellis, 1970:148ff). Sometimes, half of a rhythmic pattern (and its text) is repeated in the next small song, thus forming a link between one idea and another.

This makes it possible for many ideas to be communicated simultaneously. For instance, at any given point in the ceremony the painted design on the body of a dancer may have one specific meaning (e.g., "home") and the songtext with its associated rhythmic pattern may have another (e.g., a description of a journey). If the rhythmic pattern is one which has a link to another small song, then the text meaning of the latter is also implied. There may be rhythmic cells which are the same in a number of small songs, but which are coupled with unique rhythmic material in each case. (Then the rhythmic information is less direct and the relationship which exists between these small songs, although present and recognized by the performers, is less obvious.)

To these sources of extramusical information in music

structure are added many features. For example, the melody to which these rhythmic patterns are set conveys information about the "taste", the essence of the totemic ancestor. As well, however, in complex ceremonial performances there may be at least two types of melodic contour which conform to this one "taste". One of these melodies may be used for small songs concerned with painting and the other for all small songs concerned with ceremonial performing of some sort (Ellis, 1970:160ff).

Further, if the story is not already well-known to performers then it, too, may be told during breaks in the singing; but in any case its foundation for the performance is always assumed. The dance may portray a different aspect of the story from that being presented in any other form during the dance (Ellis, 1970:179ff) and the dancers are, for the time being, the living recreation of the original beings inhabiting the Dreaming era (Berndt and Phillips, 1973:34).

In this way many pieces of information are presented simultaneously. The rhythmic pattern and songtext can refer directly to one event in the story, and to others by implication. The body design on the dancers can signify a different aspect of the story. The dance step, which is tied to musical structure through the beating accompaniment, may depict yet another piece of information, while the dancers themselves represent the personality attributes and characteristics of those whom they portray. Melody, as well as indicating the nature of events taking place in the ceremony (painting, dancing, etc.) acts as a constant reminder of the essence, the "taste" of the ancestor.

Figure 4:2 attempts to display these multidimensional characteristics and show how they interlock.

Smaller-scale interlocking of structures — the elements of music

This section is intended to show how musical patterns are interdependent and at which points they interlock. Although the full import (and the limitations) of Figure 4:5 are not yet

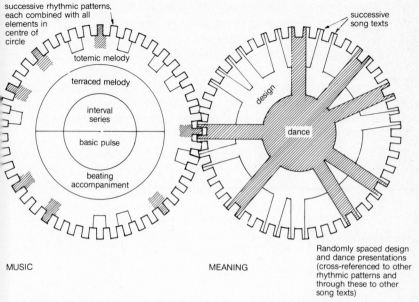

successive rhythmic patterns, each combined with all elements in centre of circle

totemic melody

terraced melody

interval series

basic pulse

beating accompaniment

successive song texts

design

dance

MUSIC   MEANING

Randomly spaced design and dance presentations (cross-referenced to other rhythmic patterns and through these to other song texts)

Figure 4:2 Interlocking of larger-scale structures — music and meaning*.

In the left cog wheel successive rhythmic patterns are indicated by each cog. The shaded ones correlate with periods of dancing, and those merely outlined occur during painting sequences. Those unmarked represent the rhythms of the sung form of the continually unfolded story, verse by verse. In the right cog wheel the representation is the same, with shaded song texts representing those occurring during a dance and the outlined ones during painting sequences. At the point of contact, all elements implied in both cog wheels, through various technical means, are interlocked in one presentation. Immediately after this, as the wheels rotate, less information will be involved as the song text and its related rhythmic pattern do not correlate with either painting or dancing and therefore have no connection with the greater levels of information represented by the inner areas of the right cog wheel.

*This material was prepared in the first place for *The New Grove Dictionary of Music and Musicians* (Ed. Stanley Sadie, London, 1980), and is reproduced by permission of Macmillan Publishers Ltd.

obvious, the reader may again be helped by looking at the hierarchy of elements of time presented in it.

Inma Langka (the song of the lizard) has been selected as the basis of this close examination because we have recordings spanning some ten years as well as many other experiences in performance and tribal music lessons built on this children's ceremony. It serves to illustrate all the important elements, even though they occur here in a reduced form suitable for children and other inexperienced tribal musicians. The recording from which we have worked was made in 1977; some verses on it are not present in other recordings, while the latter contain verses which are not on this recording. We deal, therefore, with a specific performance of Langka and connect here with the background detail on meaning presented at the end of chapter 5.

Positioning of the song text

The songtext of any small song consists of a few words, grouped into a pair of lines and within a line, further subdivided into smaller segments (cf. R. Moyle, 1979:77f). Often the text of these segments is repeated. Each line contains one basic idea. The explanation of these is not given here because of the difficulties of text interpretation (discussed in chapter 3) and of our difficulty in learning about the myth (discussed in chapter 5; Figure 5:2 gives brief details).

There is a standard spoken form which is always given if performers are asked to say rather than sing the text (which they would not do under normal circumstances). This standard version may be given with either line of the couplet as the start. I remind the reader at this point that when I am writing in this and the next chapter about the text aspects of a small song, I will refer to it as a verse. When I am referring primarily to the musical aspects of this same unit, I will continue to call it a small song. The two should be understood as different aspects of the one event.

An example of the standard form of one of the Langka texts (verse 4) is:

> *ngumi ngumi witinu ngumi ngumi witinu*
> *yilingkarkaralu tjana wata waralu*

or:

> *yilingkarkaralu tjana wata waralu*
> *ngumi ngumi witinu ngumi ngumi witinu*

This standard form is not necessarily used in this position in singing. The text starts wherever the song leader chooses, and continues from that point through the full cycle to return to the first word of that presentation; then that cycle and its associated rhythm is repeated.

For example, in the 1969 recording of this verse the text cycle is:

waralu
ngumi ngumi witinu ngumi ngumi witinu
yilingkarkaralu tjana wata

which is sung over and over to the end of the melodic contour of the verse. In each of the 1970 recordings the positioning of the start of the text is almost identical, yet different from the 1969 version:

(a)   *karkaralu tjana wata waralu*
     ngumi ngumi witinu ngumi ngumi witinu
     yiling
(b)   *karalu tjana wata waralu*
     ngumi ngumi witinu ngumi ngumi witinu
     yilingkar

and again each text is repeated to complete the total form of the verse.

In the 1977 recording the position of the text in each performance was identical to (a) and (b) in the 1970 recordings. In those 1977 performances which were not recorded, however, we started this and any other verse in almost any position. Often what happened in lessons with the tribal teacher was that we were instructed to repeat the spoken form of the text, word by word, after the teacher. When we had the stresses on the correct syllables and the pronunciation accurate, the cyclic repetition of the spoken text changed to singing. The cycle was not broken but the point at which actual singing began was the spontaneous decision of the song leader.

Rhythm and text

A small song lasts for approximately thirty seconds (see Appendix Figure A2). Its song text is normally repeated four or five times. The rhythmic segments divide the complete song text, each time it is repeated, into four smaller sections. The rhythmic pattern is usually that amount of music which is required to present the whole text once. It is the smallest rhythmic phrase used repeatedly, cyclically, without alteration. It is never shorter than a rhythmic segment, nor longer than a song text.

The rhythm to which a songtext is permanently tied has long and short notes as well as accented and unaccented ones. The beating in the accompaniment may set up a further pattern of stresses. The constant pattern of stresses tied to specific syllables in the text may sound markedly different when the text is started in a different position, but these accents remain on the same syllables in all performances of the one small song. A different pattern of stresses results from different texts and, like the text to which these rhythms are tied, each rhythmic pattern has a standard form which may not be obvious in a performance.

A particular text such as "*ngumi ngumi witinu ...* " is always sung to the same rhythm. When the text is presented with music, there is normally one note sung on each syllable. A long note (or a pair of notes sung on one syllable) usually marks the end of a rhythmic segment; thus a couplet of the text, when presented rhythmically in a small song, normally can be divided into four segments, each containing short notes moving to a longer one. This division is sometimes obvious in the text because the words are repeated (see R. Moyle, 1979:77f), but at other times can only be detected by the placement of a long note. Thus, in verse 4, the first line can be divided by text repetition even if we do not know that a long note occurs on "*nu*" in each half:

ngumi ngumi witinu / *ngumi ngumi witinu*

In the second line, however, the longer notes emphasize the rhyming syllables "*lu*" which may not otherwise be detected as cadence points.

yilingkarkaralu / *tjana wata waralu*

In some situations these longer notes are themselves subdivided by a slurred descent over two notes. Whether or not this slur occurs depends on the position of the rhyming syllables (see also Strehlow, 1971:90) in relation to the melody at that point. If a descent is required, then the syllable may have an additional vowel to give partial articulation to this slur (Strehlow, *ibid.*, 69). Whether or not the syllables rhyme, or the descending slur has an additional vowel sound, the longer note-value on a particular syllable delineates the end of a segment (cf. Strehlow, *ibid.*, 21).

Thus we see that in most cases a song text, in either of its positions, may be divided rhythmically into four sections; and these elements of rhythm and text are repeated in a cyclic manner as shown in Figure 4:3, with no specific word division occurring within a segment.

Verses 15, 16 and 17 (see Appendix Figure A1 (d) for Verse 17, p. 213) of the Langka series we have studied have texts which divide into three segments rather than four. One line divides as normal into two segments, but the other shorter line has no division, whether implied by long notes, text repeats or by rhymes.

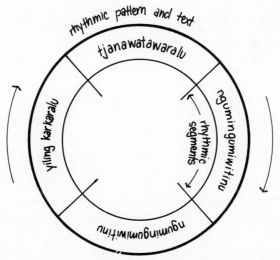

Figure 4:3 Repetitive elements of verse structure: text and rhythm.

Within the rhythm itself there are many elements which are repeated. In learning these texts and rhythms, the student is rarely aware of the division into four segments, but is aware of repeated rhythmic material. These repeated identical rhythms constitute the rhythmic patterns of the small songs. Normally, the rhythmic material of segment 1 is repeated in segment 2, and likewise the material of segment 3 is repeated in segment 4. When reduced, this requires notation (and learning) of only two segments to complete the four-segment text. Sometimes, however, the rhythmic material is not repeated in such a way that its learning can be reduced to a smaller statement; it must be learned as a complete (four-segment) pattern. At other times the rhythmic pattern consists of only one segment, which must be repeated four times to complete the text (see Appendix Figure A1). Shorter or longer rhythmic patterns than the usual ones with two repeated segments tend to contain rhythmic material which is crucial to the development of all other rhythms. Thus, learning these rhythmic patterns — the shortest notated forms of the rhythm required to be repeated over and over to complete a small song — also teaches about the most information-laden rhythmic structures involved in the ceremony (see also Ellis, 1970:156f).

Rhythmic segments from different small songs appear to use similar rhythms. This, too, is important in learning and remembering. However, this similarity may disappear if the precise duration of the beating is taken into account. Then, segments which otherwise seemed similar can be seen to be quite distinct from one another (see Appendix Figure A3).

Duration

One feature which remains virtually unaltered over the eight year span of repeated recordings of the Langka series is the duration of a particular text and rhythmic pattern in successive performances (see Appendix Figure A2). In some verses the duration of the text varied as little as 0.1 of a second in all available recordings; more usually the variation was about 0.4 of a second. In only one case, a very long text, was the difference in separate recordings as great as one second. This constancy of speed seems important.

Within the whole performance, the duration of successive texts may differ. Further, segments within each text may be of different lengths from one another. The duration of the whole of a particular small song may not be the same when this small song is repeated. This is because of the variable lengths of the beginning and ending of the melody; it is the speed of performance of rhythmic patterns which retains its constancy, as mentioned above.

Compression and expansion of duration in melody occur as a result of imposing a given melodic shape on rhythmic segments which differ in duration. The beating accompaniment remains at a stable speed throughout the performance. The fast, equal-division beats are separated by 0.4 of a second and the slower beats by 0.8 of a second.

This makes it possible to use the regularly-spaced beating in diagrams to show exactly how much "fold" is necessary to incorporate added duration into, for instance, fixed melodic movement. It is easiest to show this if only two rhythmic segments are compared. In one position of segment 3, the melody always moves from F sharp to E. By choosing examples that are markedly different in duration, it is possible to show how this regular change from F sharp to E requires a fold in the diagram to incorporate the added size of the longer segment. In segment 3 of verse 8 there are 4 beats giving a total duration of 1.6 seconds for that segment.

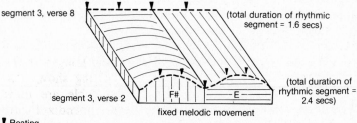

Figure 4:4 Changes in duration over fixed melodic boundaries in the same rhythmic segment of two different verses.

In segment 3 of verse 2 there are six beats, thus the total duration of the segment is 2.4 seconds.

This difference in duration is extended over the whole small song; yet even looking at one segment (approximately one sixteenth of a small song) the necessary fold in duration over the fixed melodic material can be seen (in Figure 4:4). It is this process which has been used to produce the major diagram of the Appendix — Figure A9.

Beating accompaniment

The beating pattern is locked to specific syllables in the song text which never vary with different performances of that text. Occasionally, the rhythmic pattern and complete text must be repeated once before the beating falls on the same syllable as before. In this case, the beating pattern is actually twice the length of the text. As well, as mentioned above, beating acts as an independent duration marker which is not variable with other changes.

There are two types of beating accompaniment. One is a regular pulse which is repeated, unbroken, from its commencement just after the start of a small song to the end of the performance of that small song. The second type is one which has unequal divisions, the first being the main beat, and the second an echo, close to it, which may be omitted in some performances. In the latter, the main beats are separated by twice the length of time of the regular beats in the former, and the shorter, initial beat is the more strongly accented of each pair. Any particular rhythmic pattern is tied to only one of these beating accompaniments. Apparently these are not interchangeable even though, theoretically speaking, this is possible.

Alignment of the four segments of the rhythmic pattern shows the similarity of structure of all regular Langka verses, but alignment by the duration of the beating shows that patterns which otherwise appeared comparable are quite different in relation to one another (see Appendix Figure A3). This relationship or dissimilarity shows depending on the parameter to which the listener's attention is directed.

Rhythmic patterns and rhythmic segments

There is a fixed association between a particular song text and a particular rhythmic pattern. To speak of one presentation of the text implies both verbal and rhythmic aspects. In a small song, these together must be repeated the required number of times to complete the melodic shape. The association between song text and rhythmic pattern remains constant. In each subsequent performance of that small song, however, the relationship between text presentation and melody may change.

A rhythmic segment usually contains a quarter of the song text, but segments may not be of equal duration. Even when they are of equal duration each may contain different rhythmic cells. A rhythmic pattern may be the same length as a rhythmic segment, in which case the two terms are synonymous; it may occupy one line of the text (two segments); or it may span the entire text (four segments).

The rhythmic segments in Langka are more constant in shape than the rhythmic patterns. Each text divides into either three or four segments. In other ceremonies studied there are further possibilities for segment division. There may be six or even eight segments in one text (see Appendix Figure A4). The importance of understanding the structure of rhythmic segments lies in their significance for melodic shape.

Rhythm may carry factual information. I have gathered, from field experience, that performers may learn the specific meaning of a song from the rhythm of the text so that either the text or the rhythm can convey the same information. The suggestion that this is possible arose when I was recording a long Dreaming songline which crossed a number of tribal boundaries, and I was playing back a recording of an earlier portion of the song to a singer who lived in a more northern area and who did not know the dialect of the recorded performance. He constantly maintained that a particular small song on the recording was about a claypan and that he knew it quite well. It was only careful analysis of his version which determined that he was drawing his conclusions on rhythmic and not linguistic grounds. In fact he did not understand the song text as such, because it differed from his own. As well, the speed of the performances differed, as did the singing style. What the two versions had in common was an identical rhythmic pattern.

This suggests that a sufficiently penetrating study of the music of Pitjantjatjara and neighbouring tribal groups could provide a catalogue of not only the various totemic melodies recognized by performers, and a map of the locations of various small songs, but also lists of rhythmic patterns conveying widely understood and quite specific meanings.

Melody and duration

It is through the rhythmic segments that the melody and the text are interlocked. Each melodic contour, which covers the length of a small song, has three main sections. The first section identifies the upper main notes; the second section, if relevant, contains the main melodic descent; and the third section identifies the final note. There is a fixed relationship between the rhythmic segments of any small song and the second section of the melody. This crucial middle section of the melody normally occupies four rhythmic segments. The exception occurs when the entire text consists of only three segments, in which case the whole text will be presented in this melodic section. However, where a text divides into more than four rhythmic segments, it seems that only four occupy the central melodic section. Since the segments are often not of equal duration, melodic structure has to be such that it can be constantly compressed or expanded in time without losing its essence. This time alteration occurs from one small song to another as well as in successive performances of one small song. In the latter case this results from a rotation of the text on the melody.

In all performances, each small song is started by the song-leader. Other performers join in as they are sure of the structural requirements of that small song. The song-leader commences apparently at random: he may start at any point in either of the two lines of the text. In the Langka series the line of the text following the one on which the song leader commenced is the one which starts the main descending section. For convenience I will call this the "descent line"; it may be either line of the song text, depending on the song-leader's whim.

This necessitates flexibility in text/melody relationships. The best way of locating the descent line is to note on which words the most important points of the melody fall over any performance of a particular small song. These important melodic points are the upward leaps — often immediately preceded by a breath. Most upward leaps bring the first word of either line of the song text to the highest note; this line becomes the descent line; and the rest of the text then follows in the correct melodic descent. (This seems to be related to R. Moyle's discussion (1979:89ff) of descending melodic passages "on the near side" and "on the far side".)

The first step in understanding in detail what is happening with melody is to analyse and isolate melodies that performers say are the same to show the sameness of their structure and likewise to analyse and illustrate clearly where performers say the melodies are different. This may seem easy. However, many of the melodies which seem remarkably similar to us are identified as different by the performers themselves. There is a problem in identifying the structural bases of what performers mean by same and different melodies. One of the easiest ways to hear the essential nature of the melody is to play at fast speed the tape recording of a long series of verses with the same melody. Then the outline of the song is compressed and all variations are removed.

It is possible to have melodies which cover the same general sequence of notes in quite different times; and these, performers say, are the same. There are also melodies which seem to us to have the same shape and follow a similar sequence for the same length of time, yet cover a smaller range of notes; these, performers say, are different. There are intermediate forms, too, in which the difference is not easy to identify.

In the Langka series we have been examining in this chapter, the melodies of the small songs throughout the ceremony are virtually identical, and are said by performers to be the same, yet to look at any small song in musical transcription is to find it differing melodically in many respects from the preceding one. These differences can be removed in analysis by aligning the melodies correctly, and by ignoring differences of duration (see Appendix Figure A6).

In the long songlines that tell of the Dreamtime ancestors, the melody is supposed to cross tribal boundaries and follow the ancestors' original journey. It is difficult to identify the essentials of performances of the one song in different areas and to be able to say without hesitation that the same melody is used. It seems that the interlocking of either three or four rhythmic segments of the text with the middle section of the melody, the commencement of which is identified by a breath and an upward leap, provides the key to recognition of this essential melodic movement which identifies "same" and "different".

In the Langka series the middle section of the melody always occupies one complete presentation of the text (i.e., usually four rhythmic segments, but sometimes three). As the duration varies from one text to another, so also does the length of time spent in melodic movement through this descending section. Also, in any one text, the three or four rhythmic segments may differ from one another in duration; this adds a further element of time change. (The sameness, particularly in melodic section 2, is shown in Figure A9 at the end of the Appendix).

Melodic structure and text

Text is significant to the structure of any performance of the totemic melody. It has already been stated that melodic movement occurs within three main sections. In the case of the Langka songline, this includes a characteristic descending passage as section 2. There are also subdivisions of the melody, each represented by one presentation of the text. In Langka there are five such subdivisions (see Appendix Figure A9), the first and last presentation of the text, however, being incomplete.

Each subdivision has specific melodic characteristics. In the first presentation of the text, the movement is from upper G or F sharp to upper E; often there is singing in harmony which discontinues once the position of the descent line in the text is clearly understood. The second presentation of the text remains around upper F sharp and E until almost the end of the text, then descends to G sharp. These two subdivisions form melodic section 1 which identifies the main upper note; it closes with a musical marker (in this case the rapid descent and usually a rest for breath) which indicates that melodic section 2 is about to commence.

The third presentation of the text and melodic section 2 are synonymous in Langka, and probably in small songs of most other songlines. This melodic section is always signalled by a musical marker such as an anticipatory slide in pitch or a rest, or both. This marker occurs not only at the start of the section, but often also at the close. In this case, melodic movement is from the upper main note to the lower main note. It is this movement through melodic section 2 which is important for identifying "same" and "different" in otherwise very similar melodies.

The fourth presentation of the text in Langka always contains a break for breath which is immediately followed by a rise in pitch and a subsequent return to the lower tonic. The fifth presentation again contains divided parts. Basically it consists of repetitions of the lower tonic with a few inflections which often do not agree in positioning from one singer to another. These last two subdivisions occupy melodic section 3, which serves primarily to identify the lower tonic.

In the Appendix, Figure A9 shows the melodic form for each of the presentations of the text of nine verses of Langka. The musical notation of the basic form appears in Figure A7.

When a new small song is sung, or when the same one is performed with the text rotated, using a different descent line, these broader melodic features shown in Figures A7 and A9 remain essentially unchanged by the consequent changes in duration. These characteristics give an indication of the musical basis for the definition of a melody as perceived by the performers.

A particularly interesting aspect of text/melody relationship is found in some closely related Aranda (Central Australian) small songs. Here one sometimes finds examples with more than four rhythmic segments in the text. Then, the characteristic melodic descent of section 2, with a marker at the beginning and the end, still covers only four segments of the total pattern; and section 3 of the melody commences with the remainder of the text.

Several examples appear in other of my publications (Ellis, 1964:70f, 77 & 84). In each case the melodic descent of melodic section 2 of that songline is marked by a rest for breath both before and after these crucial four rhythmic segments, and the text is left incomplete until well into the next melodic section.

Melodic identification across tribal boundaries

Understanding that the essence of a melody is contained in the central melodic section, normally over four rhythmic segments — and that this characteristic area of the melody will have musical markers such as slides, breaths or rapid descent immediately before its commencement — has enabled us to compare melodies across tribal boundaries. Without knowing how to align melodies correctly within one region so that their most crucial features can always be extracted (and heard) as the same, it is impossible to trace common melodies when Dreaming songs cross tribal boundaries. The information contained here has enabled us to make comparisons of recordings of melodies which previously sounded quite different to us, but which were claimed by the performers from these differing tribal groups to be the same (see Appendix Figure A8).

Conclusion

It is the smaller-scale interlocking patterns which bring about the feeling of iridescence referred to at the outset of chapter 4. Through skilful performance the interplay of patterns can highlight changes in perception which are overwhelming. The apparent casualness of the entire performance, in which one small song follows another, seemingly at random and at a time chosen by the song leader, does not in any way prepare the outsider for the pounding impact of the ceremonial climax during which all technical features are held tightly together, interlocked in such a way that the incorrect place-ment of one small element would cause the disintegration of the entire performance. Through correct interlocking the power of the ancestor, being drawn out of the earth by the strength of the song, is present. To lose this power through error is unforgivable.

All these interlocking features of the Langka series are represented in the inner portion of Figure 4:5, but like all the preceding figures it can show little of the iridescence experienced by the performers who perceive the constant interchange between the various facets of the performance. This portion of Figure 4:5 does show, however, that the only point at which all features change simultaneously is at either side of the main melodic descent — melodic section 2 — which may therefore be presumed to be of unchanging and crucial importance to that particular song. At all other points one or another feature changes; in this way many potential breaks in the structure are masked and continuity ensured despite multiple divisions.

Because the representation of these features has become increasingly flattened in order to show how various facets interlock, the figure appears to be symmetrical. An attempt to overcome the deficiency of such a flattened model has been made in Figure A9 of the Appendix. Figure 4:5 while showing how all features interrelate, cannot indicate the perceptual changes which result either from change of duration in one aspect of a small song as against the same aspect of the next small song, or from the "flip" which occurs when the listener's attention is drawn first to one aspect of the formal structure then to another. This change in relationship between foreground and background patterns changes the awareness of the entire structure.

Lévi-Strauss (1969:16f) maintains that music uses time to obliterate time. He sees music as using time-ordered structures to disorient the listener's sense of linear time:

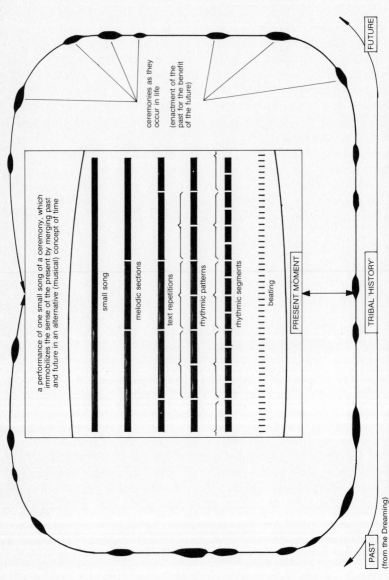

small song

melodic sections

text repetitions

rhythmic patterns

rhythmic segments

beating

a performance of one small song of a ceremony, which immobilizes the sense of the present by merging past and future in an alternative (musical) concept of time

ceremonies as they occur in life

(enactment of the past for the benefit of the future)

PRESENT MOMENT

TRIBAL "HISTORY"

FUTURE

PAST
(from the Dreaming)

Figure 4:5 Diagram showing the hierarchy of time elements in tribal music and life.

while within the bounds of the time elements inside a musical composition, the listener is outside the limiting confines of chronology. King (1974:107) summarizes Levi-Strauss's view on this by stating that "music allows an immediate and more economic view of life totality giving at the same time image and scheme (structure) in a reduced model with an acceleration and condensation of the totality".

In tribal life in northern South Australia, music certainly contains this capacity to obliterate time. The presentation of the ancestor in ceremonial form links past and future simultaneously with the present. From the smallest element of the fixed duration of the short notes in the song text, through the beating duration, the repeated rhythmic segments, rhythmic patterns, text presentations, to melody and small song — each using its own time scale and capacity to incorporate added information, and each a series of intermittently emphasized patterns such that first one, then another occupies the centre of attention — a ceremony which combines past and future is produced. Figure 4:5 represents the placement hierarchy of these elements as they occur in tribal life in the form of a complete ceremony, one of many ceremonies during which the past, present and future are brought together.

The figure also draws on the analogy used by McLuhan (1967:114) when he speaks of the simultaneity of many experiences through myth. He likens myth to a prism which "refracts much meaning to a single point". This compression is increased in the sung presentation of a myth: from the overlaying of many patterns, each with its own reference points linking it to the myth, the verse of the moment simultaneously conveys different levels of meaning, and much information at each of these levels.

5
The Tribal Music Lesson: Education for the Whole Personality

The tribal teachers firmly believe that simply talking about music does not lead to real learning, and that in any case it has nothing to do with music itself. They feel that the only way to learn their music is to perform it. While this is the same as the view of Western music teachers, it contradicts academic procedure which emphasizes an understanding based on verbal and analytical skills. The process of actually learning tribal music is demonstrably different from the process of learning about it, and not surprisingly, those university students who have attempted both find the end results of each remarkably different.

In this chapter it is important to compare the Pitjantjatjara processes of teaching traditional music to tribal children and adults with those which occur now when tribal Pitjantjatjara people teach non-Aboriginal students. The traditional teaching aims ultimately to foster the spiritual insights and personality development characteristic of Learning III (see chapter 2). In focusing on the human meaning and spirituality that is potential in music making, this teaching goes beyond ordinary formal education (Learning II). All tribal students are well aware of this higher goal, whether or not they have the capacity to attain it.

Where tribal teachers are training white students, the aims of the students are overtly much more technical in nature. These university students are studying for a specific purpose, perhaps merely to complete an assignment in the subject of Pitjantjatjara music or to learn more about Aboriginal people.

They focus their attention on a lower form of learning than that of the tribal student in his home environment; but this difference may not be understood by the tribal teacher in the contact situation.

Non-Aboriginal students' response to traditional Aboriginal music lessons highlights points of difference which these students find surprising. Before lessons they had not anticipated such markedly different methods and results from those with which they are familiar in Western music lessons. All the student descriptions in this chapter are written by non-Aboriginal people who have been involved in tribal singing lessons at CASM within The University of Adelaide under the direction of fully qualified tribal teachers. Usually the students have not previously met Aboriginal people, but most have spent some time before they started lessons at CASM studying the known technical details of the music they would be learning and listening to recordings of performances.

All the students comment on their feelings of complete confusion and disorientation at the outset of these lessons, a state which often continues for many months and sometimes for more than a year. They quickly learn to follow the hand-beating, but rarely pick up the flow of the melody or relate the sound of the song text to the words, which are written down for their benefit if the tribal teachers insist on this. The following are one student's impressions:

During a teaching *inma* at CASM the men sit on one side of the circle and women are directed to sit together on the other side. The women kneel and beat into their laps with one hand on top of the other, while the men clap their cupped hands together. Both methods of beating create a hollow sound. The beating is an essential accompaniment to the singing as the elders find great difficulty in singing, without beating, a verse that is normally accompanied by beating. They find themselves out of time with one another. When the beating accompaniment takes the rhythmic outline of the echo beat, the beginner is instructed only to perform the main beat.

The singing has a very hard nasal quality and often the downward movement of the melody leads to very low-pitched passages. Alternatively when the women sing an octave higher the sound is very shrill and piercing. Despite this the level of energy that goes into the singing and beating is quite astounding. For some verses the beating is intensified, and the syllables may be heavily accentuated by using the diaphragm muscles forcibly to expel air. This, coupled with the long phrases, becomes very "breath-taking" and may account for the shortness of *inma* when students are participating fully once they have mastered the pronunciation of the words. Each verse of a song is begun as a solo by a song leader or a person appointed by him. The soloist often does not begin the verse on the same word each time, but, even after he has sung only a few syllables the rest of the group can detect the point at which he has started the verse. The texts of the verses are repeated once the whole group has begun singing, allowing a cyclic type of pattern to emerge.

While lessons in a tribal situation occur intensively over a restricted period of time (perhaps two or three weeks) then not again for some time, lessons at CASM occur at regular intervals. The tribal teachers spend two weeks of every month in Adelaide and at least two sessions each week are held with non-Aboriginal students. Students work with tape recordings of the sessions during their teachers' absence. Teachers themselves roster their visits to Adelaide so that none of them is away from home too often.

The role of terminology, analysis and practical work in CASM

Chapters 3 and 4 cover the aspects which students can learn in theory from analysis and from traditional terminology. In the case of terminology, for instance, becoming aware of a word which isolates a particular feature of the song enables the non-Aboriginal student to hear the feature being named, and subsequently to imitate it more reliably. The naming of events according to similarity of sound (for instance the sound of the emu and that of the women's beating) provides an insight which is not dependent on cultural experience. Thus we know the type of sound that should be produced, even if we cannot achieve this technically.

However, there are not many facets of tribal song which can be understood so easily during singing lessons. There is little verbal instruction. The senior tribal person present acts as the model and all students must follow his lead, whether or not they understand what they are doing or why they are doing it.

The text and its associated rhythm are always presented together. They are not easily isolated and when a student asks for the text to be spoken it is usually presented in its metric form, with no clear starting point or word division. Text and rhythm are repeated over and over again. Although the performers themselves may be aware of a first word the new learner has no indication which it is. It is disguised by the fact that the performer varies the starting point from one verse to the next, and also by the cyclic nature of the text presentations. The student can only start the text by imitating the song leader, joining in the group singing as soon as he can.

Often the new burst of singing starts at a point that follows on from the end of the last repetition of the previous verse. However, it may take a student a long time to discover this simple fact and until then he is in a state of continual confusion about the structure and the nature of the text. (Note that in these lessons in the city no non-Aboriginal person intervenes to explain such problems unless he or she is specifically instructed by the elders to do so.)

Melody also is learned by imitation. This is noticeably the most difficult aspect for the non-Aboriginal student, and our inability to "catch" the melody is a constant source of amusement to our teachers, who reserve several very telling comments for continued failure. A student who has done a great deal of analysis comments as follows on these difficulties and the help analytical work can provide:

> The first lesson was very confusing. One could pick up the flow of the melody and attempt to hum it and the beating was fairly simple to imitate, but the words and their rhythm were very hard to follow. It was not until the Langka analysis that I realized the words were sung to the same rhythm, and that beating fell on the same syllables; and it was not until this analysis that I could predict the rise and fall of the melody. The non-verbal approach of the elders to teaching us was in very marked contrast to our own music lessons, but one nevertheless felt under their complete guidance however subtle or hard to follow.

While we learned a great deal about Aboriginal music from these sessions, much of this could only be clarified by having alternate analytical and practical lessons. Through performing we learned a great deal about Aboriginal music which could not be appreciated from analysis alone: the physical/ emotional involvement and the constant personal scrutiny associated with performing. At the same time performance alone would not have clarified for us many of the features that we understood theoretically. Gradually, as a result of learning what was predictable analytically, we came to be able to anticipate the reproduction of the essential elements in sound. Although I was responsible for teaching all the academic aspects of Pitjantjatjara music, this role was disregarded by the tribal teachers during actual singing lessons, where I was a student among students.

Learning the myth

We were never told the story behind a song that was taught in CASM unless we specifically asked what the song was about. This factor highlights the difficulty we faced if we abided by the tribally traditional practice of not asking any questions. We were expected to enter into the master/student relationship, accepting the masters' personal dignity and authority which then became the key to our further learning. Often, however, we wanted to know why or how a certain thing occurred, and asking this invariably led to difficulties.

On some occasions in the tribal situation new performers are given the story prior to the performance of the song. At other times the story unfolds itself during the performance of a song. Another way is to have an explanation given by a senior performer during the lulls between consecutive verses in performances. Sometimes no explanation at all is given during the performance and only some time later are the new performers informed about the myth lying behind the performance.

One instance of the difficulty of understanding caused by the taboo against asking questions was of interest to us all and was closely noted by the students since I was the principal offender for having been seen by the elders as having questioned the authenticity of their comments (although this was not my intention).

We had, prior to this event, learned the verses of Inma Langka as they are listed in the Appendix. The following detailed commentary by students present at the lesson describes what took place:

During the two sessions before the recording was made we were given the same verses in the same order except that during the first of these, verse 17 was left out, and verse 14 came at the end after verse 16. Also, during the second session, a false start to verse 4 was made after verse 10. After the first session's singing, the song-leader, our teacher, drew the following diagram and we noted the explanations from him and the other elders. (See Figure 5:1)

After the second session's singing, the song leader prepared the following diagram (see Figure 5:2), drawing the line first and then the small circles. He told us these circles represent stages in the journey that the song describes, each circle corresponding to the place at which the incident, described (or rather implied) by the corresponding verse, happened. He gave the "key words" identifying each verse and these we added to the diagram.

We asked the men to sing the verses through while we tape-recorded their singing. After they had sung the 17 verses, Dr. Ellis

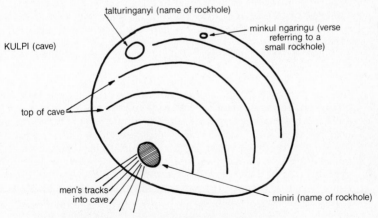

(*talturinganyi* appears in verse 14; *minkul ngaringu* in verse 13;
miniri in verses 11 and 12)

Figure 5:1 The cave containing the rockhole Miniri.

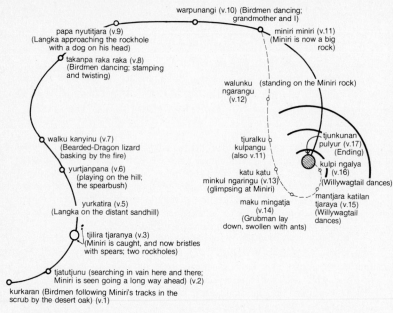

warpunangi (v.10) (Birdmen dancing; grandmother and I)

papa nyutitjara (v.9)
(Langka approaching the rockhole
with a dog on his head)

miniri miniri (v.11)
(Miniri is now a big rock)

takanpa raka raka (v.8)
(Birdmen dancing; stamping
and twisting)

walunku ngarangu (v.12) (standing on the Miniri rock)

tjunkunan pulyur (v.17) (Ending)

tjuralku kulpangu (also v.11)

walku kanyinu (v.7)
(Bearded-Dragon lizard
basking by the fire)

kulpi ngalya (v.16)
(Willywagtail dances)

yurtjanpana (v.6)
(playing on the hill;
the spearbush)

katu katu minkul ngaringu (v.13)
(glimpsing at Miniri)

yurkatira (v.5)
(Langka on the distant sandhill)

mantjara katilan tjaraya (v.15)
(Willywagtail dances)

maku mingatja (v.14)
(Grubman lay down, swollen with ants)

tjilira tjaranya (v.3)
(Miniri is caught, and now bristles
with spears; two rockholes)

tjatutjunu (searching in vain here and there;
Miniri is seen going a long way ahead) **(v.2)**

kurkaran (Birdmen following Miniri's tracks in the
scrub by the desert oak) **(v.1)**

Figure 5:2   A map of the verses which appear in the Appendix was given during a singing lesson. The "key words" given on this map are those that were given by the tribal teachers.

began rewinding the tape in order to play it back to them and check the sung order with the map order to discover which was correct. Unfortunately, they signalled for her to stop rewinding before the verse "*ngumi ngumi witinu . . .*" (v. 4) was reached. This meant that they did not hear it replayed and therefore did not realize that it was not represented on the map.

As they listened to the tape they corrected the map. Throughout this process it was becoming evident that the song leader was annoyed with the diagram and at having to change it.

Dr. Ellis then began asking where she should put the missing verse "*ngumi ngumi . . .*" on the map, but received no direct answer. The leader listed the verses in the order that they should appear, but without mentioning "*ngumi ngumi . . .*". At this point we probably should have played the recording of this verse so that he could hear it had been sung, but instead the leader began giving us a sharp reprimand. We had begun to ask some questions about the meaning of verses but were told that the "chalk had gone wrong" on the map (meaning that we had re-drawn it incorrectly), and that because we could not even place the verses in the correct order, we did not deserve and would not be able to handle any further information.

By this stage everyone felt upset. Clearly we had failed in our relationship with the master musician. Our purpose in attempting to recheck confused information had been to ensure that the order was acceptable to the performers before we started analysis. Since we felt that an analysis which was made from a performance which was not acceptable to them was of little value, it was therefore necessary from our point of view to check as thoroughly as possible those points where contradictions occurred between repeated performances. If, for instance, verse 4 did not belong in the series, the analysis could not produce useful information by including it. If, on the other hand, the map was faulty, exclusion of verse 4 from the analysis may well have invalidated the results. We discovered, however, that these were entirely Western notions which were of no concern to our tribal teachers. The dilemma was summed up by one student as follows:

> The incident serves to illustrate the importance of realizing and appreciating the different concepts that are in operation when learning from and in another culture. I certainly felt some resentment at having been told that we had redrawn the diagram wrongly, could not get the order correct, were incapable of handling more information, and had too many questions to ask! However, in such a situation this resentment must be put aside, as airing it, or hasty uncalculated action, only harbours more misunderstandings.

We often experienced a sense of failure in our interaction during these lessons. It was then necessary to look closely at the way the teaching occurs in the tribal setting, and even though we were usually unable to duplicate such a situation, since neither our own purposes for learning nor the context in which the teaching was taking place was traditional, we felt we comprehended the misunderstandings better as a result of the comparison.

Tribal statements about the traditional music lesson

Tribal people described through their interpreter how they understand the process of education through song learning in their own cultural environment from the point of view both of teachers and pupils.

The tribal teachers under whom we studied repeatedly emphasized that no tribal student is ever taught unless that student sees the need to learn and expresses interest in being taught. This may appear to contradict the process of taking boys forcibly for initiation. However, it is clear that this step was not taken until the boys intended for training had shown their readiness to benefit from it. An account given from the point of view of the boy himself can be found in *Australian Dreaming* (Isaacs (ed.) 1980:186ff.)

At every stage, the tribal teachers told us, the teacher waits for the student to be motivated rather than forcing the student to apply himself. Once involved in the learning process students are continually assessed by the elders, sometimes unobtrusively, in their daily situation. The visiting lecturers from Indulkana who work at CASM indicated in discussions that deliberate assessment is carried out by talking with the student. When the teacher feels that the student responds appropriately in conversation and observes that his or her behaviour in the learning situation indicates a relevant maturity of awareness, the student is taught more comprehensive information about and through songs.

The elders, when assessing, look for qualities such as preparedness to listen without questioning and intelligent response to the teaching that is given. The student shows his or her readiness to learn by being prepared to follow the model of the master teacher and seeking him out for help. It is at this very point that a major cross-cultural dilemma arises for the non-Aboriginal student, since an academic approach, particularly one involving analysis, is built on questioning. And it was here that I failed in the incident quoted earlier. As this case shows, the traditional response is that further information is withheld until the student acquires better study habits. Then more information can be taught.

The visiting lecturers stressed that it takes a long time for their children to develop within their own system. The tribal teachers never get angry with a student who is really trying to learn but they do consider that once the student is aware of the expectations of the teacher, he must abide by these to the best of his ability. If a student has difficulty in grasping information, he is told to stop for the time being and "come back tomorrow and we will start again". The teachers do not tire of the constant repetition that this process of teaching involves. They require only that the student is motivated to learn, shows his enthusiasm and does his best at that time.

If a tribal student is motivated to learn and has the ability, but is not progressing because of psychological factors, the traditional doctors treat him. Once he recovers he proceeds through the system at his own pace.

A Pitjantjatjara musician who worked with us at CASM for some time, told us (Ellis and Ellis, 1973:229ff) that as a small child, even though he had watched many performances, he learned only an odd small song here and there. At about six or seven years of age boys were selected by the older men to learn one of the children's songlines. Because they had not seen or heard it before they did not understand the words at all. Each night, for many hours, the older performers sang the one verse over and over to the boys until they could catch it. Song, design and dance were all presented, but the first thing the children learned was the correct beating accompaniment, which involved learning to select a stick with a good sound and to beat correctly on the mound of earth so as to produce a resonant thump at the correct time. (We have been told by other tribal people that children often learn dances first.)

This performer's rate of learning was one verse in three or four days. Each was learned until it could be sung quite fluently, and after that, verses were taught more frequently. He told us that as children they often had to do without food while they were learning songs in a formal situation. Their teachers considered this deprivation to be beneficial to their speed of learning.

Early in childhood music learning is entirely informal. Often the child sits on a parent's knee and feels the throb of the performance, and absorbs the sounds of adult music making. At the same time the child also absorbs the atmosphere of the entire performance. Later, when he encounters the difficulties of more formal learning, this supportive atmosphere becomes a strong motivating force. For the moment, the informal exposure to music may also include learning songs from other children. Whatever the source of the learning a child is always encouraged and praised for his attempts. While learning informally, he is constantly being reinforced to develop motivation for more formal learning.

Small children on the ceremonial ground also take part in the performance by beating with the others, but as well they may get up between the actual performance times, in those lulls in the disciplined activity, and sing what they can of the melody and do what they can of the dancing. The children are allowed to play around at dancing and singing in such cases, provided the ceremony is not an important or powerful one.

This early music making seems similar in process to the informal level described by Bateson as Learning I. It is concerned with learning to feel what the music is about and informally learning to discriminate between acceptable and unacceptable performances, even though all are equally reinforced. It has little intellectual component. In chapter 4 I spoke about the levels of meaning in song texts; the first is related to this early learning. Song texts, like everything else in this childhood learning, are taken at face value.

As children grow and reach the age of puberty they attend either the men's or the women's secret ceremonies. At the women's ceremonies I have observed, the girls commence participating in much the same way as described by the Pitjantjatjara musician quoted above. At puberty, however, they receive more formal instruction. The first thing the girls are involved in is the correct beating on their thighs while kneeling in the (very tiring) position which gives the greatest resonance when the thigh is slapped. This is one activity that they can be involved in immediately. Sometimes a younger girl is selected to partner an experienced dancer in one of the dances. This too she can manage by carefully watching the leading dancer (or her partner if only two dancers are involved). The reactions of these young girls on their first visit to the ceremonial ground as serious students indicate that they are very bewildered by all that is happening: with the speed of the performance, the heightened emotional intensity, the technical expertise of the performers. It is not until they have been on the ceremonial ground a number of times that they behave with any ease in the situation.

For the boys, initiation is the period when they first learn to apply themselves entirely to the business of formal learning, and at that time songs are taught by constant repetition. This teaching is usually combined with physical deprivation and pain (see, for instance, the description of song learning at this stage given by Strehlow, 1947:100–112). All these serve to make the new learning permanent, indelibly embedded in the thinking of the young men. This process of indelible implantation of the features of the totemic songline, with its implications for every facet of living, is of great significance to each individual. It enables music to be used as a powerful force throughout life.

The significance of melody in tribal music makes it the one element which must be permanently fixed and identifiable under innumerable conditions of change — of text, rhythm, duration and so forth — as shown in chapter 5. It is the essence of the ancestor. Its implantation in the mind of the young initiate seems to be similar to the experience my coworker and I had with the semipermanent fixing of the pitch of the mourning wailing when the dancer died.

In tribal situations where performers may be present at the singing of a song from another tribal area, it is melody which enables them to identify the ancestral associations of the song. The differences in melody from the songs of one ancestor to those of another are often almost insignificant to us, but they are important and must be learned accurately by constant repetition. The melody, once learned, can act as a mnemonic device recalling for the initiate all the psychological elements of his formal learning both now and throughout the rest of his life.

At this level also, all learning is done by imitation and the teacher imitated is always a respected person and an able performer. If a song is unfamiliar to any performers, they do not join the singing immediately, but require some time to acquire the technical features of the song. They must also wait for permission from the song owner before they may participate.

There are times when specific verbal instructions are given to less experienced performers. An instruction which may be issued when the sequence of verses is incorrect or when other errors are creeping into the performance is translated from Pitjantjatjara as an order for everyone to "look at the *inma*" (that is, concentrate inwardly on its correct form). There may be an instruction to "close your eyes", thus improving this inner concentration. These instructions are used to enhance the imitative process, not to replace it.

However, this imitative learning at, and after, initiation is never the same as the unstructured learning of early childhood. Now the student comes to learn about what he has previously learned. In Bateson's terms this is Learning II, which involves a more formal and cognitive approach. Bateson's definition (1972:293) — "change in the process of Learning I, e.g., a corrective change in the set of alternatives from which choice is made" — applies more to the change of understanding of the meaning of the songs and their implications for living than it does to the technical structure of the songs.

The latter certainly becomes more complex in some respects, but all the basic techniques required to master it have already been learned at a younger age. Now, however, the experience is not what it appeared to be in Learning I; it cannot be accepted at face value. As he proves himself worthy, the student is told about deeper levels of meaning that were not known to him earlier. He is told that what he learned as a child was a "false front" for what he is now learning; and the latter, he knows, must not be openly discussed. The elements of secrecy impress on him the importance of his new learning. Strehlow (1971:298 and 1947:46ff) notes that these false versions occur also among Aranda people.

Whether it is the tribal teacher, the tribal student or the outside observer speaking about learning tribal music at this level, some points never vary. One is that constant repetition is essential to thorough learning. Another is that the authority of the knowledgeable elders — "the people knowing many songs" — must in no way be challenged. Yet another is that the student must be motivated to accept the elders unquestioningly as the models of master musicians and wise people, while at the same time learning the strictest self-discipline.

In Bateson's terms Learning III, as represented in the meaning of a tribal song text, embodies the spiritual essence of the song, the power which may be drawn forth from a particular place in order to alter the visible world in some manner. Bateson cites religious conversions and some forms of psychotherapy as among the few known forms of Learning III. By achieving power through the correct knowledge of music and by disseminating this appropriately, the few tribal people who achieve this level are indeed changed persons. They have about them dignity and assurance, quiet power and a deep understanding which often transcends cultural barriers. (This is perhaps the most unexpected information learned by non-tribal students.)

It is this peak of learning that is the ultimate goal of the traditional music lesson. It is known to exist and to be the goal toward which all able students will aspire. It is the personal power to which one aspires at this level that has to be guarded so carefully by the custodians of the tradition. And achieving this level of learning is also achieving a state of integrated personality development.

Tribal statements about lessons in the city

The tribal teachers, when making comments through their interpreter about the work at CASM, did not separate their remarks on how they taught from those on how we learned. Initially they taught white university students in the same way as they taught their own children. They often found this frustrating. The elder in charge of teaching in Adelaide until 1978 said:

> All of us are teaching the students true songs and the language, and the students can't understand it properly. We got the girls to beat in the correct way and taught them to sing and talk Pitjantjatjara.
>
> The students are going to sing later. They were singing last time

we came, and when we come again we might hear them singing the same songs, the songs they wrote in their books. The songs they were singing are all on paper. When we come next time the students should be singing really well. We sing the song with them now, but next time they should be able to sing it on their own. If the students learn well, the next visit we will sing a different song, two or three, so the students can sing along with us . . . (*Tjungaringanyi* Vol. 1, No. 2:3)

Another of the teachers commented:

A lot of students are not learning properly yet. They only know a little. If they sing the one song for a long time the students will start to pick it up. All the students could sing together with us if they learned properly. When they learn properly they can sing on their own without us. They can teach others if they learn properly. (*Tjungaringanyi* Vol. 1, No. 2:6)

By this time, the tribal teachers had resorted to always using some form of written information for students and expected them to learn the song texts thoroughly from the information written in their note books. They recognized that without this visual prop white students were unable to remember. This did not happen in the first year's lessons; the problem then was solved by teaching fewer verses.

Students were told by the elder that they must listen very carefully and always repeat the words of the songs and other words of vocabulary after them slowly at first, little by little, word by word, gradually becoming faster, until they were able to pronounce them correctly.

You can only master the tune by listening very carefully and con-centrating while we sing for you. Then you can join in, softly at first, gradually louder. Close your eyes and do not look at others. Your concentration will then not be distracted and you can listen more intently. You must be patient and not expect to learn a great deal in a short time. Think of learning a little properly rather than half-learning a great deal. Our children take three years to learn these songs, singing around the campfire every evening.

White students' statements about the processes of learning tribal music

The following is a composite statement built from many

comments by students concerning what they learned about their tribal teachers and the methods they used (see also Buxton, 1976).

> The music was not the only thing that overwhelmed me on that first day. The authority and dignity which these men carried on their faces and in their mannerisms instilled in me a great respect for them which poised on the edge of fear.
>
> The fundamental demand from the tribal teachers has been that I am motivated to learn. While I was in the singing class I also saw the great advantages of group learning. I also realized that the interaction between student and teacher is most beneficial when the two sing together. Further, the development of senses other than those used in reading a text book were beneficial. All these techniques of teaching could usefully be applied to Western education. The elders' teaching skills were superb. They expected self-discipline at all times. This expectation was imparted non-verbally. They taught by example. They themselves were intensely involved in the performance they were imparting to us.
>
> They taught by rote. They did not emphasize mistakes but waited for the student himself to observe what was wrong. Not only were they patient in repeating material as often as necessary, but they were ever ready to praise and encourage no matter how small an improvement had been made. I have never forgotten what was learned when we worked without any writing. What appeared to be mindless repetition with no understanding behind it turned out to be a deep and effective learning process. We realized, as we studied more, that Aboriginal education equips a person to live and survive in his physical enviroment, to deal with human relationships and to make sensible and sensitive judgments on other people and situations.

All students have, at some time or another, commented on how much they learned about the dignity and great teaching skill of the tribal elders. While this respect is equally possible in a field situation, there is a large difference between a field worker recording "informants" and the same person seated as a student of the master musicians. The learning is correspondingly tinged with much greater awe.

Student comments made it clear that while they had entered the course for a specific purpose, always one which would fall within Bateson's definition of Learning II, they frequently learned things they had not expected and which caused them to question their original intentions in undertaking the study. These factors suggest that the strong component of Learning III did not bypass them altogether, even though it is rarely found in our own culture and was here presented to them in an alien one.

> I found that I had to become more self-examining in order not to offend my teachers. This close contact with cross-cultural studies taught me what it must feel like to be a person from a minority group. I was constantly facing people of great skill in a culture alien to me in which I was attempting to become proficient. I now have an appreciation of the feelings of disorientation that can be caused through being caught between two cultures.
>
> I watched the young tribal teachers who came down with the senior people, and I saw their enthusiasm when they were in close proximity to the great knowledge of their elders. I thought this type of experience was important for all young people in any culture and I saw it as analogous to my own situation as a university student.
>
> The elders sometimes became frustrated when we were unable to learn a verse quickly. No matter how hard we tried, they considered that we were not concentrating well enough. Laughing, or a gruff manner illustrated their exasperation or frustration at our inept efforts. It can be very effective medicine for the student. It made me feel inferior and incompetent all over again. I completely lost my sense of myself. This forced me to face up to my sense of inferiority and to persevere and ultimately grow through this appalling sense of inadequacy.

There was one major point of difference between students working under the elders at CASM and a comparable experience they may have had in a field situation. At CASM they were able to reach into an alien culture without the oppressive fear of committing an irretrievable error. This is quite unlike the field situation in which the field worker must always ensure that he observes the rules of those around him, often at the price of his own sense of identity. In CASM, we were able to meet on mutual terms: during singing lessons the rules that applied to study under the tribal teachers were observed, but in other aspects of daily work the elders were happy to learn the rules we applied in various learning and administrative situations. This provided a mutual exchange of experience which appears rarely to have been achieved elsewhere.

The senior students, summing up their experiences of

working with the elders, said that they had learned a great deal about education through music which was quite new to them, despite the fact that they had studied music education within other parts of their university course. Music education had taught them how to teach music, but had ignored the social significance of this task. It had neither taught them who their students were nor set about asking why they were teaching music at all. In the contemporary world where the school student is likely to have been influenced by a mass media culture quite different from the music studied by students of music education, they now consider that the knowledge of who students are is of crucial importance to communication. The experience of learning in another culture highlighted for them the inadequacies of teaching in our own.

The traditional music lesson in today's world

For the tribal person, music is an essential part of life, a force without which his known world crumbles. Learning music is a means of entering the highest reaches of his culture's intellectual and spiritual development. Whether or not an individual is capable of progressing through the entire process of learning, his awareness of the fact that some of his own people can do this is a security to him in a world which is otherwise frequently bewildering and sometimes outright hostile to him. Without this security his sense of identity collapses. With it, he has before him a means of education which will develop his individual abilities to the full (provided he makes the necessary effort) and will at the same time develop his whole personality.

Learning Aboriginal music under the direction of tribal teachers would be valuable for any thinking person in today's multicultural world. There is a need not only for the uninterrupted traditional teaching, but also for adapted teaching using similar methods, aiming at the same goals of personality development but reaching Aboriginal students whose life style is an acculturated Aboriginal/white one.

Such adapted teaching may be essential for the survival of the whole tribal education system.

The negative aspects of the lessons at CASM centred mainly on the absence of appropriate environments. The learning would have been greatly improved if some of it had occurred within the tribal territory. For various reasons, however, our frequent attempts to organize student trips to Indulkana always foundered, until late in 1982. Either the elders were free when the students were not, or permission to stay at the reserve could not be granted when both were available at the same time. This was significant because the actual physical environment related to the songs is often unknown to students who have never visited the desert regions which the Indulkana men and women come from. It is then impossible for these students to visualize or to have any feeling for the countryside depicted in the songs. Similarly, the absence of social impact is a serious limitation. Meeting the elders in the city, seated around tables drawing designs on paper, important though it is, is very different form carrying out the correct social procedures for meeting them in their own homeland.

Another negative we found was the use of literacy-based teaching methods, disadvantageous for learning about a process which traditionally was entirely oral. In the first year of teaching at CASM the elders taught in their traditional way. They soon learned, however, that we were unable to absorb aural stimuli as quickly as visual, and so they began insisting that we write down the texts of the songs. This led to a series of false assumptions on the part of our teachers. They thought that if we could repreduce tha song texts from our written notes this meant that we knew them. This was far from accurate. We may have known them in the sense that we could repeat them, but we did not have them, along with their rhythm and melody, indelibly committed to memory. Those of us who had the privilege of being involved in the first year's lessons found that we never forgot the few small songs that were taught to us forcefully, and without any reference to literacy whatever.

This change from oral to visual teaching is a good example

of the problem of incorporation to the point of disintegration mentioned in Chapter 4. Here the change to the visual approach, seemingly a simple incorporation of a different technique, in fact erodes the essential elements of the teaching which are all aural. To avoid such a damaging shift requires a change in Western students' attitudes towards amounts learned in a given span of time. For Western students, quantity is much reduced as soon as the visual component is removed from the teaching. This is frustrating also for their tribal teachers. On the other hand, incorporation of the visual component reduces the quality of the learning by ignoring the whole area of aural memory on which the traditional system rests.

Another problem of the lessons in the city is the absence of spontaneity. In a tribal situation a performance will take place at sundown provided that the weather is suitable, the firewood available, the people present. This allows a flexibility which is totally absent in a more rigorously-timetabled schedule that has to enable students to meet other university demands. There can be no choice of the right moment, the right group of people, the right atmosphere. The performing has to occur at the allotted time, irrespective of who is present and whether or not they feel like performing. Confusion also arises because there are mixed sex groups at all lessons. (This is unavoidable because, as it happens, there is usually only one male student at a time, who is often unwilling to have an individual lesson.) This creates difficulties with teaching since the men traditionally taught the boys, and the women the girls. For purely economic reasons it is only possible to bring four tribal performers to Adelaide at any given time and sometimes these are all men. Then, the female students have extreme difficulty "catching" the melody since they cannot sing in unison but have to sing in octaves. This difficulty disappears when women teachers come, but then the songs are usually not intended for men to sing at all.

As I have had lessons both in the field and at CASM I am more able to compare these different experiences than are most CASM students. I found that it was much easier to learn the structural elements of the songs away from the other pressing difficulties of field work within an alien culture. In the field other things disturbed my concentration too much for me to be able to devote full attention to learning songs effectively and efficiently. (Not the least of these was the need to produce taped evidence of my field work in order to maintain research funds.) These disturbances are unknown to city students.

On the other hand, the true performance on location has tremendous impact; no matter how short-lived the performance, its deep significance is always apparent. This the city students miss. The involvement of the performers, and their unfailing assumption that once I had witnessed a "correct" version of a ceremony I would be forever committed to its preservation, provided a background to my learning. This is unknown to the student who has no field experience. In November 1982, a group of students and the ethnomusicology tutor from CASM spent nine days at Indulkana. This visit stimulated many performers of *inma*, an infrequent event these days. The tribal teachers were excited that this happened and requested many more such visits of tribally trained white people coming to Indulkana to study with them. It further increased their motivation for coming to Adelaide to perform and to teach white students. For the students, the experience proved to be profoundly thought-provoking and exciting, and expanded their experience of learning to cope with culture shock.

The fact that Aboriginal teaching techniques cater for every individual -- allowing each student to develop to his full potential at his own rate of growth -- is a revelation to every person who has close contact with the work and this alone is justification for the city experience, despite its limitations. It almost seems that the cross-cultural aspects of the work are secondary to this important discovery which students make about themselves as whole people, and about the divisiveness of our Western education system. And despite the difficulties which may arise through the adaptation of traditional teaching techniques to a contemporary situation, the fact that this can occur at all seems encouraging for the survival of traditional tribal teaching within the domains of an alien culture.

Non-tribal music

The Centre for Aboriginal Studies in Music works not only with tribal people, but also with the people who have come from areas where there is no longer any tribal music. These non-tribal people still choose to identify as Aboriginals and their music making also has significance in its own right. (Some of them also are now choosing to become students of the tribal elders, alongside white people.)

Although my discussion of Aboriginal music has been drawn exclusively from South Australian material, the general concepts are similar throughout Australia. Only the detail changes from one area to another, not the process itself. The loss of this traditional education system, using music as its central form of communication, has been a severe blow to non-tribal Aboriginal people who now find themselves caught between two worlds, each of which claims a sophisticated system of learning and each of which, by means of many exclusions, denies them the right to be part of its system. It is toward this destructive educational problem that CASM has been directed.

6
Aboriginal–European Culture Contact

Contemporary Aboriginal songs are useful in tracing both the cultural disintegration and positive acculturation that has resulted from Aboriginal contact with other cultures in Australia. The different types of songs depict present life styles ranging from the full, tribal to city living.

Music is a very personal experience but also one which is shared by the members of groups who make it. The songs described in this chapter are mostly individual expressions through which the performer voices the feelings of his own social group. They provide an insight into the history of racial contact directly from the point of view of the performer, and consequently they are invaluable to the educator seeking a clear understanding of contemporary Aboriginal aspirations. Listening to history through song is similar to examining a musical system through examining the meaning of its own technical terms (see chapter 3). It provides perspectives which are not influenced by the outside observer. The songs themselves stand as evidence of the singer's hopes and fears, irrespective of the analytical frame within which they are placed.

Most of the information for this history through music was collected in the field by my husband and me during the 1960s. We have maintained close contact with urban and tribal musicians since that time, but rarely with people living on the outskirts of country towns. However, the eighteen years from the start of our collecting to the time of writing is a very short span of time in the history of a people. The times sung about in the first part of our collection are the times when the present teenagers were born; and in most cases they remain accurate representations of the world as seen by Aboriginal people today.

During the time of our field work among non-tribal Aboriginal people there were many Europeanized songs in the current repertoire. These highlighted emotional reactions to social conditions. Although some were obviously of American origin or influence, their existence in the repertoire underlined their significance to the singers:

> Every nation has a flag except the old black coon,*
> I wish I was a white man instead of an old black coon.

Others were specifically Australian:

> White fella put the fences across the country
> Jacky sits and laughs all day.
> He don't care what becomes of the country,
> But Jacky like to take it that way.

The texts of such Europeanized songs express Aboriginal views of the most pressing problems posed by their transition from tribal life to close interaction with white people.

Careful listening to the subjects of Aboriginal songs teaches one a great deal about the diversity of Aboriginal aims and aspirations, life-styles, fears and the causes of their depression. From this information it is possible to create a table of cultural generations, showing how far people claiming Aboriginal descent today have moved away from an understanding of tribal education through music.

These generations, when viewed from a cultural rather than a physical point of view, show a wide spread of affiliations. Some Aboriginal people who are born of tribal parents in a tribal area may be brought up in institutions which allow no tribal contract whatever; others, though not recognizably Aboriginal and physically far removed from tribal relatives have nevertheless retained a deep interest in and association with tribal life. And it is possible to meet white people who have had more tribal education than younger tribal Aboriginal

---

* A resented white term (of American origin) for Aboriginal people.

Table 6:1 Table of Cultural Generations

Cultural Generation	Musical Expression	Contribution to interaction between Aboriginal and white people
1. Fully tribal – no concession to European thought	Tribal	Can advise on who is tribally qualified to teach; and what levels of interaction can occur between tribal and non-tribal people; teach their own traditions
2. Fully tribal – wish to help in Aboriginal/white relations	Tribal	Are prepared to teach Aboriginal and non-Aboriginal students under the direction of members of Generation 1; teach their own traditions
3. Limited tribal knowledge – living in European situation	Western music and a small amount of tribal music	Can help interpret for tribal people and become students of tribal people
4. No tribal knowledge but deep respect for tribal ways; can recall seeing performances but did not not learn	Aboriginal folk-type songs; "coon" songs; hymns	Are interested in helping with non-tribal Aboriginal people; may want to study in Western institutions and to teach white students about the problems of cultural loss
5. No tribal contact at all but still maintain respect for tribal people	Western; occasionally Aboriginal folksongs	As for generation 4
6. Urban or reserve dwellers with no knowledge of any Aboriginal heritage and no respect for it, or for Western traditions	Western popular music	Often use the political arena to express marked antagonism to white people; show little understanding of tribal people's needs
7. People concerned about their own disciplined education, but with no opportunity to develop through tribal education. Almost indistinguishable from their white colleagues (often physically unrecognizable as Aboriginal)	Western popular music; sometimes a knowledge of Western classical music; pseudo-tribal music (i.e., self-taught and therefore lacking any component of education through music)	Proceeding with the serious business of professional training in the Western world; sometimes, within this training, making contact with tribal people

people who sometimes denigrate everything tribal and seek to be accepted as white people irrespective of how dark their skins may be.

Many Aborigines are caught in cultural conflict. Some part-Aboriginal people want to return to some form of tribal patterning in their lives. Others want to associate closely with their non-tribal relatives while still attempting to become acceptable in the white community. At present these aims are incompatible because many members of the white community regard any association with Aboriginals as an indication of inferiority. Table 6:1 identifies seven different subcultures into which today's Aboriginal population may be grouped through the musical expressions used by each cultural generation. It also suggests the contribution each group may make to the total community.

Cultural Generations 1 and 2

Under fully tribal circumstances music is inextricably woven into everyday life. There is no facet of life that has not been perpetuated in song and there are no important events in the life of the community that do not have songs associated with them. The sacred songs, which are preserved meticulously, also serve as a means of education. Through the most secret of these it is possible for the singer to convey feelings which could not be uttered in words at all. Through song he knows that he can draw on powers that will re-create and regenerate life around him (or destroy it if this is his intention).

Both men's and women's secret songs have their particular functions in the society. The women's songs play their most important role in relation to human procreation, while the men's culminate in the secret increase rites that ensure the tribal food supply. Song is also a very satisfying entertainment. It provides release after an exacting day's hunting and food gathering. Men, women and children can all create songs about the events which concern or amuse them most. The members of Cultural Generations 1 and 2 are part of this fabric of music and life, differentiated only by the greater awareness in Generation 2 of the need for incorporating more from without in order for the system to survive under alien domination.

Once tribal performing is discarded, there is almost never a comparable creative form of communication available to an Aboriginal musician. Those people with whom the detribalized musician comes in contact are generally unaware of the creativeness of tribal music; by introducing music of lesser quality (later discussed as common music) as if it were greater, they have a damaging effect and preclude the creative development of new idioms.

Creativity in tribal music, unlike Western music, rests on newness of insight — inner interpretation without alteration of the outer form. The originality of thought which allows the traditional concept to grow and take on new colour occurs only after long immersion in the conventional process. The illumination of creativity arises (apparently spontaneously) after much thought around the subject of the creative act. It is based on an already existing technique which has been studied for a long time.

Tribal music is technically complex and allows scope for virtuoso performers. It combines minuteness of detail with expansive structures. It is a music which embodies the physical, intellectual and spiritual being of the performers in a oneness with all life. Its preservation is meticulous since the complexity of the interlocking of structures precludes any major alterations without the entire system collapsing. The iridescence of the structures allows the one performance to be perceived at many different levels of learning.

Cultural Generation 3

When detribalized people first move away from their own social group, they often moved to the outskirts of country towns (Rowley: 1971), living in shacks built on, and out of, the contents of the local rubbish dump. They came directly from disintegrating tribal groups, often from cattle and sheep stations which evicted them from their formal tribal lands.

They were later joined by disgruntled former residents of reserves or missions who had grown tired of having their lives prescribed by white people. As Rowley also notes (1971:12) in all areas these fringe dwellers had considerable independence of spirit despite the fact that they often lived in squalid conditions. Some of the inhabitants of these clusters of shacks had fairly constant jobs, some only seasonal employment, others none at all. (The social conditions of fringe dwellers to the present day are described in scholarly literature, but are more tellingly depicted in novels such as Trish Sheppard's *Children of Blindness*, 1976.)

In some country towns in South Australia, where there is a large congregation of semi-tribal and fringe-dwelling people, there have been major government-sponsored programs established which are Aboriginal-centred, catering for Aboriginal activities. These programs show some promise of providing a focal point for these lost communities. But at the time of our work at least one country town in New South Wales solved the problem of unwanted fringe dwellers by first warning the "blacks" to move on and then, if the warning was not heeded, by bulldozing down the shacks that these people had built.

In a country town in Victoria, the openly expressed anti-white feeling of the fringe people was invariably justified by recounting the events of the mass poisonings which they claimed had taken place some seventy years previously (see also Rowley, 1972). We were told by local people that these particular poisonings were perpetrated by means of bags of poisoned flour which "accidentally" fell from loads in transit. The local Aboriginal people later found these bags of flour, took them back to camp, cooked damper, then shared it with everyone. In this way entire camps were wiped out overnight.

The social history contained in the musical output of these fringe people indicates a number of social divisions, each with its characteristic musical expression. There are fringe dwellers originating from tribal groups, some of whom retain a knowledge of tribal songs and perform them; some with only disconnected pieces of information about tribal musics. Other fringe dwellers have no tribal connections at all. They live in a predominantly white environment, speaking English as their only language, but often have a large repertoire of so-called coon songs or of folk songs which refer to their own living conditions.

The repertoire of tribal songs among small detribalized groups when we were recording was limited to those songs which were known at the time of leaving the main tribal group. Where this restricted repertoire was found by the performers to be inadequate, they composed new songs in the tribal idiom. These new songs were guarded by their composers for fear of ridicule and were rarely performed in front of Aboriginal people not belonging to the immediate group. Further, these songs usually were not passed on to others and therefore many have disappeared with the death of the aged performers. These new songs are among the few original tribally-based creations of detribalized people. Not many of them have been recorded.

The very last remembered features of tribal life among non-tribal people appeared in our experience to be isolated words in the original language. It may have been the restrictions from both white and tribal people on the performance of certain tribal music which caused it to disappear before language; or it may have been the difficulty of understanding song language; but it may have vanished first because of the widespread ridicule of tribal music.

Further adaptations of tribal music occurred beyond the closely guarded songs composed in the tribal idioms by newly detribalized people. We met fringe dwellers who had been taught these adapted forms of music by members of the previous generation. These songs were already outside their tribal context, but contained elements of tribal music or language. Only occasionally was there anything in the texts which was specifically tribal, and never anything which had been newly added by the present performers.

Luise Hercus (1969:90ff) gives translations of many of these songs in her monumental recovery work of the tribal languages in Victoria, carried out during the 1960s, when only isolated individuals could speak remnants of their own language. Contrary to the practice of tribal performers, there was rarely any form of rhythmic movement accompanying these songs. The singers had reverted to the tribally-based task of preservation (about which they frequently spoke) without the need now for meticulous observation of the tightly locked traditional techniques. Often the musical intervals had lost their tribal characteristics and had been converted to European forms. However, the broad melodic contour, and many other characteristics, remained recognizably tribal in origin.

The performers of these songs valued the knowledge they retained, not realizing that, all too often, it had undergone a drastic change from tribal music. They recognized the great harm that had been done to their people by the loss of the unique forms of expression which they knew would disappear when they died, and such knowledge usually gave rise to bitter conflict within these individuals. The singer, while wishing his songs to be known, often at the same time refused to perform them. He resented white people for having interfered with tribal life, and tribal people for not having passed on more of their knowledge to the younger people. He regretted that he had taken little interest when he might have learned more and he deplored the lack of interest among younger generations of his own people.

Cultural Generation 4

At the time of our field work it seemed that once tribal music is discarded by the Aboriginal performer, this same level of musical experience is not achieved again (however, see chapter 7). Initial contact between tribal and white people is very often through a church mission. Mission attitudes in the areas in which we worked seem to have been consistent: almost without exception they aimed to wipe out all tribal customs (see also Berndt & Berndt, 1964:428f). There was a regulation at many of the missions where we recorded which made the performance of tribal music an offence punishable by expulsion.

Some of the newly detribalized people told us they stayed

on missions only for the sake of their children. They felt that their own way of life was disintegrating anyway, and believed that the younger generation would benefit from the education offered by the missions and, as a result, would be better able to take their place in a white society. Musically, the offering from the missions was (and still is) limited to simply hymns sung either in English or in the local dialect to the original European tune.

This music, alien to the performers, represented an enormous transition from one system to another. Those who succeeded in grasping the new system often did so at the expense of fluency in their own. To this was added the mission-imposed sense of guilt about performing their own "heathen" songs. The tribal performers then found that hymns alone were a poor substitute for the wealth of musical tradition they had left behind. (This is not to suggest that there are not Western hymns which have a deeply spiritual value for Western Christians; but neither quality nor the possibility of deep understanding were represented in the simplistic hymns many missionaries took to Aboriginal people.)

On all reserves today there is further contact with Western music through the record player, transistor and cassette recorder. Country and Western music is the most popular listening (see also Pearce, 1979:41ff), and in many places, the most popular type of performance as well; but we were told by performers that in the past this too was prohibited by some missions.

Songs sung in English by the fringe and reserve dwellers give clear indications of the tensions caused by the contact situation. Many of these songs have come directly from American sources and performers say they learned them from recordings. Some are parodies (of both music and text) used to express the Aboriginal person's view of white people:

> Last night I had a funny dream as I lay half awake,
> Old Satan came to my bedside and me He began to shake;
> He shook me long, He shook me strong,
> He shook me clean out of my bed.
> He grabbed me by the collar, He looked me in the face,
> And what do you think He said?

"There's gold in the mountains, there's silver in the mines,
They'll all belong to you, Uncle Bill, if you only will be mine."
He took me to the window. Look! The moon was shining bright,
The hills and the valleys all around looked pleasing to my sight.
"All these will be yours", He said, "If you'll be my general when
                    you're dead."
I grabbed Him by the collar, I looked Him in the face,
And what do you think I said?

"Get you gone old Satan, you've come for me to kill.
You can fool all the white folks with that tale, but you can't fool
            old black Bill."

There are a few older Aboriginal people whose parents learned white Australian folk songs while working on various outback stations. The "younger" people (now in their seventies or so) still perform these folk songs which are often retained by them longer than by the country white people whose folk idiom they originally were. This largely because, to the present Aboriginal singers, the songs are expressions nearer to their own life experiences than popular songs of today.

I have rarely heard a love song from a non-tribal performer. This is in marked contrast to the importance in tribal music of the secret love-magic songs. The nearest to a love song that we recorded from a fringe-dwelling singer was:

Git along Eliza, git along,
Git along Eliza Jane.
Git along Eliza me own true love,
I'll never get drunk again.

Oh! I'll never marry a Chinese girl,
I'll tell you the reason why;
They'll take me to the Chinese camp
And smoke the opium dry.

I'll never marry a white girl,
I'll tell you the reason why;
She stretches her neck as long as a crane
And you can't tell when she's gonna die.

I'll never marry a black gin,
I'll tell you the reason why;
Her nose is always runnin'
And her chin is always dry.

The monkey and the nigger
Were sitting on a pale.
The only difference I could tell,
The nigger 'ad no tail.

Often the songs are descriptions of places:

Now me Daddy says that an angel came one day
And built the sweetest spot on earth.
That's why I never roam to Omeo,
Or to Yarrawonga, no, not I;
To Crowajingalong, to Kootamundra, no you're wrong.

Wagga Wagga, Gundagai,
Now there's a place to hang your hat,
There's a welcome on the mat.
That's where I long to be.
Everybody knows where the Murrumbidgee flows,
But the Murray River's good enough for me.

Hilton Walsh

The singers in Cultural Generation 4 still have respect for tribal ways along with their own independence of spirit. The songs are sometimes related in concept to tribal songs, while musically they seem at first to be almost entirely Westernized. However, concurrently with the writing of this work, Marylouise Brunton, a postgraduate researcher at The University of Adelaide and teacher at CASM, has been researching the musical structures of these songs. The analysis shows that there are interesting musical links back to tribal structures.

Within this tradition songs are still being maintained and newly made, but the expression of love of homeland is more intense in tribal songs than in the detribalized expression in the above songs. A few years after recording the song about the Murray River we were present at a spectacular tribal performance. It was an open song, sung by everybody present in the camp at Indulkana at that time (members of Cultural Generations 1 and 2). The history being represented was that of the Kangaroo Rat who travelled through that locality in the Dreaming. There were many points in the song where the journey of the main character took him to places representing the life essence of other Dreaming beings, and when this occurred the relevant characters were depicted both in the song text and the accompanying dance. The two Grub men came past and the old man in the distance chopped down the great tree in order to get the Eaglehawk which was nesting in its high branches.

At one particular point in the ceremony one of the women began the ceremonial wailing normally reserved for marking the death of a member of the group. Her piercing wail could be heard clearly above the hundred or so singers who were engrossed in the presentation of the Dreaming characters. There was a hesitation, then performing continued with renewed vigour. The experience was deeply moving, shattering and exciting, all at the same time. I later learned that the place mentioned in that verse was not only the home of the Dreaming character then being sung about and represented in the dance, but also this woman's birth place. She was entitled to wail in this song because she could, through this, express her homesickness and her love of the place of her birth.

Whatever home may have been — a few branches placed together for shelter, or a corrugated iron humpy built from the rubbish dump — it was important, then, because the soil of the homeland and the close affiliation with the natural surroundings has deep meaning to tribal and non-tribal Aborigines alike.

Cultural Generation 5

At the time of our work in the early 1960s people who came to the city from missions, or from the fringes of country towns in order to obtain employment, were producing almost no music of their own. Their energy was absorbed in attempting to be like their white neighbours. In the early 1970s songs began to be heard in the city and some of these are now available on LP discs. Now, in the 1980s, Aboriginal rock bands are active on the commercial circuit, and all their music is composed by the performers (Ellis, 1979:36).

There are songs covering the problems of the city dweller which, like those of the fully Western repertoire of the fringe dwellers, are often accompanied by guitar; in the city they are sometimes sung in parts using Western harmony. One theme frequently heard makes explicit the anguish of discovering or losing relatives who have been taken away by police, welfare or missionaries, and placed in foster homes or institutions. Another theme is the city experience as seen by the Aboriginal person. Cherie Watkins, a welfare worker who played an important role in the musical revival in Adelaide, wrote this song about her people:

> Come listen all you Nungas,*
> Come listen to my tale,
> Of our poor downtrodden brothers
> A-rotting there in gaol;
> They've committed no real crime,
>
> Apart from being black;
> Some don't know why they're in there
> And will probably go back.
> But prison's nothin' special
> To any Nunga I know.
> The white man makes it prison
> Most everywhere we go.
>
> The white man's way is hard to follow,
> When you're used to tribal law,
> And so before you know it
> The cops have got you for sure.
> And then from just the one arrest
> Seven convictions can be got,
> So the poor downtrodden Nungas
> Are sent to gaol to rot.
> But prison's nothin' special . . . (etc.)
>
> We'd really like to find out
> Just how to apply for bail,
> But then we cannot raise it
> So it's back again to gaol.
> That's where my story started
> And probably will end,
> So don't be too down-hearted,
> At least we don't pretend,
> And prison's nothin' special . . . (etc.)
>   Cherie Watkins

She also sings about the social problems in Adelaide where the main Aboriginal meeting place within the metropolitan

---

* A local word for an Aboriginal person, adopted by the people themselves.

area was, at the time of making this song, a hotel in the city. This area was closely patrolled by police. The music was composed by Cherie and the text written by another urban Aboriginal, Cyril Coaby.

> In the heart of Adelaide city
> There's a place we know so well.
> Some say it's just like heaven,
> But others call it hell.
> In the day-time and the night-time
> If you're passing through skid row,
> You'll always find a Nunga
> Who's got no place to go.
>
> And if you happen to be drinking
> In the lounge or in the bar,
> There's every type of Nunga,
> They come from near and far.
> You can meet your own relations
> Or find a long lost friend.
> Some say they won't go near there
> But they'll be there in the end.
>
> And of the inmates at the watch-house,
> It's nine times out of ten,
> That they will be arrested
> In that same old place again.
> And it's said if you're a copper
> And you haven't made a pinch,
> Just take a walk down that way,
> No worries, it's a cinch.
>
> But no matter what they say or do,
> People try to run it down.
> It's still the Nunga's own retreat,
> The only one in town.
> It's in the heart of Adelaide city,
> A place we all know well.
> Some say it's just like heaven:
> The Carrington Hotel.
>
>   Cyril Coaby and Cherie Watkins

Cultural Generation 6

In the past many children were taken away from their parents once they came to a mission, and were forced to live in dormitories. They were often taught to be disrespectful of everything done by their parents. The parents themselves soon learned, through contacts both on and off the mission, that white people had no appreciation of tribal music or anything it implied. After a short while even their own children laughed at it.

This attitude of contempt still remains. It is widely held among non-tribal people who, unless prompted by political motivation to state otherwise, wish to disown any connections with what they perceive as the stupid mumbo-jumbo of some dirty old derelicts. Our first experience of introducing a tribal singer to urban Aboriginal people later brought forth the comment from the tribal man that the city people all behaved "as if I was a savage". He thought this immensely funny ("poor things"), but the ramifications of this attitude are far-reaching.

The feeling that traditional Aboriginal culture is primitive and inferior will take a long time to disappear from the thinking of non-tribal Aboriginal people. Appreciation of tribal music, for instance, runs contrary to the expectations white people have of "right" and "good" behaviour or "beautiful" music. This causes intense conflict for those Aboriginal people who must choose between a close relationship with their tribal relatives or acceptance in the white community. The loss of sense of identity is greatest among those who still value the tribal traditions yet must survive in the urban community.

Cultural Generation 7

Aboriginal people are now much in demand for teaching Western school children about traditional life patterns, beliefs and experiences. There is usually no attempt on the part of the school to ascertain which cultural generation the Aboriginal speaker comes from, about which he may speak knowledgeably. The Aboriginal university graduate may quite unrealistically be expected to speak on tribal life, as if from a base of personal experience. This has led to further anomalous situations.

For instance there are now a number of completely Europeanized Aboriginal people who have heard tribal songs or didjeridu playing, or have seen boomerang throwing, and who attempt to reproduce these skills to display their so-called tribal knowledge, usually for commercial gain. Their musical performances are completely Europeanized (often including vibrato, which occurs nowhere else in Aboriginal singing), and the performers have no knowledge of the significance of the songs. The interpretations are uncreative and contain none of the positive values of education through music. Unfortunately, today these pseudo-tribal singers can have a marked effect on white people's understanding of Aboriginal music.

The Aboriginalized white person (Cultural Generation 8?)

Although I have not included this group in the Table of Cultural Generations, white people who have absorbed a great deal of Aboriginal thinking and skills can make a marked contribution to the understanding of Aboriginal people in today's society. It would be impossible to name the many dedicated white people whose acculturated actions belong within this category.

One example is the contribution of singer Ted Egan. Through his own gifts as a Western folk singer and his long exposure to tribal Aboriginal music, he has created protest songs (among other forms) which, to the delight of Aboriginal people, present Aboriginal ideas in a composite Westernized/ tribal idiom entirely understandable to white audiences. Some of these songs can be heard on his LP discs.

Implications of Cultural Generations for education

Given this diversity of cultural aspirations, modern educational programs for Aboriginal people face enormous problems. There are many white casualties of our rigid and inflexible education system, and there are even more when the system is applied across cultures without thought of the particular needs of the groups to be "educated". There is a vast amount of material available to educational planners today which results from an awareness of the culture of origin of the students to be taught. In *Tinker, Tailor . . . The Myth of Cultural Deprivation* (Ed. Nell Keddie), for example, the authors draw attention to the importance of allowing educational material to arise from the culture involved. Labov stresses the cultural vitality of non-standard English while other authors in this volume discuss the oral culture that all children possess, noting that it is all too often suppressed in the process of passing on techniques of reading or writing, which themselves imply political and value shifts often not realized by the teachers.

Many researchers have located traditional material from white children, the existence of which was either unsuspected or denigrated by these children's teachers. Ian Turner (1969) provides good documentation of Australian children's lore, while I. & P. Opie (1967) have done the same with English children. Bartók and Kodály established a whole school of music education on the foundation of their own Hungarian children's folk songs. In music, researchers such as Nketia (1977:23ff), McAllester (1972:17ff), Seeger (1977:15ff) and Hood (1971) have written about the significance of cultural influences for music education. Nketia in particular stresses, from his own personal experience, the importance of bimusicality.

This type of cultural awareness cannot occur in Aboriginal Australia until educators understand the implications of the different cultural generations from which their Aboriginal students come, or the significance of the culture-bound expressions of children and the value of folklore for education.

In a different context Freire, in *Cultural Action for Freedom* (1973), shows how the cultural alienation of a dependent group causes them to become alienated even from their own thinking, since what they imagine reality to be like is very different from the way they actually live. Freire seeks to make literacy a process by which the "culture of silence" can find an instrument to voice its growing self awareness. This voice must have authenticity if it is to overcome the inevitable repression which, Freire points out, follows the emergence of a people working to break their submissive silence.

Implications of music for education

In all these writings about cultural alienation, including the many that have relevance to the growth of the Aboriginal person in Australian society, there is rarely any mention of the importance of music. (This, of course, is not the case in the works of the few music educationists mentioned above.) This can only be a reflection of our own underestimation of this important form of cultural expression. The sensitivity of all these writers as they reach to the core of a people's thinking is unquestionable. Yet this very sensitivity is all that is required to hear the voice of the many members of "cultures of silence", as the silence is broken through their own songs. Merriam's information in *The Anthropology of Music* seems not to have filtered through to these areas of education at all. Discussing the importance of music as a safety valve in any society, he writes:

> an important function of music . . . is the opportunity it gives for a variety of emotional expressions – the release of otherwise unexpressible thoughts and ideas, the correlation of a wide variety of emotions and music, the opportunity to "let off steam" and perhaps to resolve social conflicts, the explosion of creativity itself, and the group expression of hostilities. (1964:222)

Merriam and other ethnomusicologists often draw attention to the fact that it is possible to "get off with" singing offensive ideas which would be unacceptable if they were spoken. For instance, Blacking (1976:50) shows how South African Venda music can be used as a safe, constructive mode of social communication: "You do not 'go to prison' if you say it in music".

Thus, music can offer a mode of expression which corresponds with the real, rather than imagined, experience of oppressed members of "cultures of silence".

Definition of qualitative differences in music

Given this role of music in any situation of rapid culture change, an important problem which must be faced is the authenticity of the musical expression and its value to the performers as a vehicle which can act as a safety valve. One of the main problems we have been discussing in this chapter is the replacement of the vital tribal musical traditions with inferior musical forms when European contact has taken place. To state this unemotionally in musical terms we need suitable terminology which can be applied across different cultures.

It is useful to think of music as socially accepted patterns of sound which may be learned by the individual growing up in any particular society and through which all of the individual's musical expressions will be communicated. At this level, musical experience belongs within Bateson's Zero Learning (habituation) or Learning I (unreflective learning). These patterns become associated with particular behaviours, and with the emotional and spiritual meanings which are learned alongside them, thus raising the level to the intellectual involvement of Learning II and the spirituality of Learning III.

In the idioms of popular music, the associations are different from those of classical music. These two forms may be differentiated by examining the type of training required by the performers. Popular music, by its very designation, suggests there is little change in structure once the songs have achieved their popularity (Adorno, 1941:17f). This in turn means that popular music making requires little further intellectual effort once the basic patterns are known. It may always belong at the informal, unreflective level of Learning I. And in popular music it is rare to find experience that leads on to the spirituality of Learning III. However, professional performers of various forms of common music require similar disciplined rehearsal procedures to those of professional musicians in other idioms (i.e., they must work at Learning II level).

In classical music composers are constantly seeking to

develop, expand, contract or restate basic patterns, which requires considerable intellectual involvement of its devotees, and particularly of its performers. This kind of distinction, based on the level of learning involved in the music making, can be made in many cultures and defines what I call "common music" (using Learning I only) and "cultivated music" (involving as well at least Learning II and potentially Learning III). Common music is that which is within the performing reach of children, untrained in music, who have learned the basic patterns of musical sounds informally from their social surroundings; it belongs in Learning I. Cultivated music is that which requires training under a master musician; it can reach the pinnacles of human thought.

When such definitions are applied to Western music, separation is not the same as between popular and classical music. For instance, all unthinking congregational singing, community singing, some folk singing and some popular music are in the category of common music; while jazz, which requires sophisticated performing skills and long training, is in the category of cultivated music. Blacking, in *How Musical is Man?*, provides a different view of the same distinction when he says: "There is a difference between music that is occasional and music that enhances human consciousness, music that is simply for having and music that is for being" (1976:50).

Loss of musical quality in culture contact

In any culture contact it is important that the quality of music remains the same irrespective of other changes — that common music retains its wide availability and somehow copes with the culture contact structurally, while cultivated music retains its status as an intellectual and spiritual force. If a society which places primary emphasis on cultivated music is overwhelmed by a society which places primary emphasis on common music, serious cultural deprivation will occur. In Australia, tribal Aboriginal musicians maintain a cultivated form of music and the majority of white people with whom they have contact know only common music. The latter have often imposed their common music on tribal people, leaving them with an inadequate vehicle of expression.

Government reserves have recently been superimposed on former missions; and at the same time white attitudes toward traditional performing have been changed a great deal as a result of research that has taken place. Teachers going out to these reserves are taught to be respectful of tribal customs and not to attempt to alter them. Even now, though, it is not widely realized that it takes an Aboriginal singer many years to become an expert musician in his own community. We fail to see that the most educated person in tribal eyes is the one who has had the longest musical education, an education which encapsulates all his required learning in society. He is "the person knowing many songs" — the wise one. He has passed through all the categories of learning mentioned earlier and has reached the heights of Learning III.

Such people can teach us a great deal. However, in contact situations, instead of using these knowledgeable members of Cultural Generations 1 and 2 (see Table 6:1) white society has tended to turn to members of Cultural Generation 3 to assist. This is always easier, since the concepts of this generation are more Europeanized than those of Cultural Generation 2. But what they can offer is lower level bridging than that possible through Generation 2. This is because Cultural Generation 3 usually has very limited education in both systems; their musical knowledge is of common music in both cultures. They often have no experience beyond Learning I.

Who is knowledgeable?

Early in 1973 I was working in the field attempting to identify the most senior songmen located within the vicinity of Indulkana. When I had listed fourteen of these tribally educated people I sought to find out how they were earning a living, since this is indicative of our system's attitude towards them. Of the fourteen, seven were receiving old age pensions, five were receiving unemployment benefits and only two were employed. One of these was employed by the University of Adelaide in CASM, and the other was a rubbish collector. Thus, only one of these fourteen knowledgeable musicians was receiving any professional recognition in the white community. Much the same could be said for the knowledgeable women, although at the time I did this particular work most of those known to me had left Indulkana. Some of the younger, tribally qualified women were involved in activities with the health workers and the school.

The history of the development of Indulkana Aboriginal Reserve shows that with the increasingly close proximity of the two cultures from 1967 onwards, major conflicts in ideals and values became apparent. At the start of our work there, the settlement consisted of traditionally built dwellings and people practising most aspects of tribal living (which was, nonetheless, disintegrating). By 1973 there was a large white staff with all the paraphernalia they required, which has since included airconditioning and the power generator which was sited in the vicinity of the Aboriginal camp but, being over the hill from officials' houses, was therefore out of earshot of white staff. In 1973 I took as the epitome of this value conflict those things which has been shown to be of such significance to the tribal people as to cause conflict to the point of death threats. As there had then been several serious disruptions in the camp this information was relatively easy to locate and to recheck with both Aboriginal and white residents.

The first serious conflict arose from the assumed misappropriation of a song. Charges of "selling" secret songs were made (i.e., recording these for financial return, thus desecrating sacred material); and a very stern attitude was taken toward this. It was only because the tribal person concerned was supported by his traditional protectors, who guaranteed that he had done no such thing, that he was allowed to go his way in the tribal world again. The second conflict arose over the ownership of a car.

By regarding these two items — the ownership and

responsibility for *inma* and through this responsibility for the entire system of education through music; and the ownership and responsibility for a car – as the key points of the conflict of systems, it was possible to understand much more of the processes in motion. In Figure 6:1, *inma* is shown as the key point of a circle representing tribal traditional values, and the car as a key point of a circle representing the culmination of our Western system of education as seen and experienced by the tribal people in Cultural Generations 1, 2, and sometimes 3.

This conflict is essentially one about values and human meaning – about "quality". Through ownership of *inma* one can achieve the upper limits of Learning III. Through ownership of a car . . . . ?

If there had been more thought applied to the nature of the culture conflict that arises from the superimposition of two such drastically different value systems, much of the worst of the educational conflict could have been avoided. The left circle of the diagram could have been used as the model for the introduction of new concepts. This model is similar in the music education of almost all cultures and its wide acceptability might suggest something about its usefulness in cross-cultural situations. In this instance, since the march of Western materialism seems inevitable, its more damaging impact may have been reduced by providing acceptable professional recognition for the leaders of the tribal education system, thus maintaining that system in balance with the Western system.

If a model is taken which is built specifically upon literate thought then serious problems can arise when it is used for non-literate students. This is not to suggest that literacy should not be taught; rather, that it can be taught within a master/student model, as shown in the left circle of Figure 6:1, in the same way as traditional tribal singing is taught. It permits conservation of the system while changing the content; but it also makes very high demands on the school teacher.

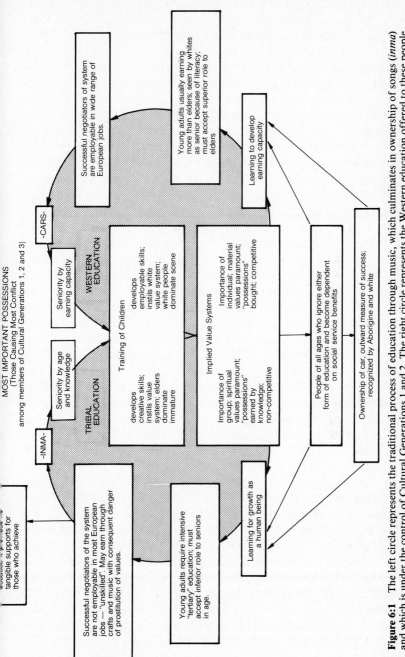

MOST IMPORTANT POSSESSIONS
(Those Causing Most Conflict
among members of Cultural Generations 1, 2 and 3)

-CARS-

-INMA-

WESTERN EDUCATION

TRIBAL EDUCATION

Seniority by earning capacity

Seniority by age and knowledge

Successful negotiators of system are employable in wide range of European jobs.

Young adults usually earning more than elders; seen by whites as senior because of literacy; must accept superior role to elders

Learning to develop earning capacity

Training of Children

develops employable skills; instils white value system; white people dominate scene

develops creative skills; instils value system; elders dominate immature

Implied Value Systems

Importance of individual; material values paramount; "possessions" bought; competitive

Importance of group; spiritual values paramount; "possessions" earned by knowledge; non-competitive

People of all ages who ignore either form of education and become dependent on social service benefits

Ownership of car, outward measure of success; recognized by Aborigine and white

Successful negotiators of the system are not employable in most European jobs — "unskilled." May earn through crafts and music with consequent danger of prostitution of values.

Young adults require intensive "tertiary" education; must accept inferior role to seniors in age.

Learning for growth as a human being

tangible supports for those who achieve

Figure 6:1 The left circle represents the traditional process of education through music, which culminates in ownership of songs (*inma*) and which is under the control of Cultural Generations 1 and 2. The right circle represents the Western education offered to these people and to potential members of Cultural Generation 3. The overlap causes confusion as a result of which many individuals drop out of both systems and depend on social service benefits.

The impact of Aboriginal music on white society

This musical history is not concerned entirely with the impact of Europeanization on Aboriginal culture, but with the reverse process as well. However, Aboriginal culture has had very little effect on the white community. Aboriginal music is not a product for popular consumption. It assumes, as part of its existence, total involvement, whereas the Western world tends to regard music, like most things, as a consumer product.

There have been no attempts in Western music to modify this difference in approach to music, and few attempts to absorb Aboriginal culture into Western art forms. Where these have occurred they tend to be superficial, simply throwing in an Aboriginal component without necessarily understanding it. The evolution of a suitable musical idiom which combines elements of both cultures has so far been slower than that process in art. Rarely does an Australian musician seek to acquire a serious and sympathetic understanding of Aboriginal music. Possibly the synthesis can only be achieved by an Aboriginal who has learned enough about European music as well as his own. The fusion of ideas that has occurred in the spheres of painting and sculpture indicates that Australian music may have suffered a loss at both cultivated and common levels.

Roger Covell, in his book *Australia's Music* (1967:71), notes that many musicians would deem it impossible to consider Aboriginal music as any sort of useful tradition for Australian composers who come from a hitherto exclusively European tradition, and have nothing in common with the idiomatic sources of Aboriginal music. He remarks (p. 73) that the influence of Asian music is much stronger on Australian composers than is that of Aboriginal music.

Despite Covell's negative view, however, some Australian composers have attempted to synthesize Aboriginal musical idioms with their own. James Murdoch, in his study, *Australian Contemporary Composers* (1972), shows this influence for a small number of composers: John Antill, Clive Douglas, Peter Sculthorpe, James Penberthy and George Dreyfus. The effect is little indeed. Sculthorpe has drawn on Aboriginal legends as a source of inspiration and, in his 1977 work "Port Essington", uses an adaptation of a melody occurring on one of A.P. Elkin's recordings of Arnhem Land Aboriginal singing. He feels, nevertheless, that Aboriginal music has nothing of melodic or rhythmic interest which is of any significance to the Western mind (Murdoch, 1972:165). Crisp (1979:49ff) has given a more recent account of Aboriginal influences on Australian composers.

In contrast to these Australian composers, the British musician and composer Peter Maxwell Davies spent time during his year of residence in Adelaide in 1966 acquainting himself with the on-going research into structures of Central Australian Aborigianl music. He found

> a most highly developed art/ritual music, totally unlike anything by which I would presume to *judge* it, and which influenced my formal design greatly in the orchestral work I was then writing. (Murdoch, 1972:*x*)

The creative examples I quoted earlier in this chapter, of adapted song texts set to adapted tribal music and performed by partly Europeanized Aboriginal musicians (or partly Aboriginalized Western musicians) are important in this context. They seem to be the most adequate forms of adaptation taking place between the two musics. Their existence raises many questions relevant to the role of music in the contact situation. Can we hope for widely acceptable adaptation of Aboriginal music when the social conditions this music reflects are themselves unacceptable? Should Aboriginal musicians be encourages to give up their own musical styles and join us in music making? Do we realize that they often know more about the importance of music in a community than we do? Are we to encourage them to retain their own music, which is important to them but unacceptable to us, given that it has often been responsible for their cultural isolation in the community? Or are there alternatives?

The role of the Aboriginal Arts Board of the Australian Council

In 1970 the Australian Government established the Aboriginal

Arts Advisory Committee of the Australia Council. Originally it consisted of six Aborigines and six experienced white workers in Aboriginal arts. Formed under the inspiration of Dr. H. C. Coombs, it was intended to stimulate activity by Aboriginal performing and creative artists. Under its stimulation, many traditional and Europeanized Aboriginal groups came to be known to the general public, through live performances, films and books.

After several years, it was formalized as the Aboriginal Arts Board of the Australia Council and all its members are now Aboriginal. It disburses funds to promote and develop Aboriginal arts and crafts, and makes literary grants to Aboriginal people, enabling them to write their own personal histories and, in some areas to preserve in written form traditional material such as language. Much of the work of CASM has been financed through the Aboriginal Arts Board.

This formalization of Aboriginal performing has had a tremendous impact on work opportunities for traditional artists and urban Aboriginal people interested in the performing arts. The board sponsors both traditional and Europeanized forms: traditional dance groups and modern jazz ballet; traditional and Western music (both cultivated and common); traditional bark painting, and batik work, pottery and contemporary painting. It assisted in the presentation of the sextet by George Dreyfus, a white Australian composer who wrote the work for the University of Adelaide Wind Quintet and a didjeridu player from northern Australia. This group of six performers toured internationally, programming the work alongside the more traditional repertoire of the wind quintet.

These recent developments have made the general public more aware of Aboriginal artistic endeavours. So far, it has had little impact on our own performing artists and only slightly more on our composers, but these developments from Western artists might be expected after a longer period of exposure than has been possible from the short but momentous life of the Aboriginal Arts Board. Perhaps, too, given time CASM will make its own contribution to overcoming the loss of qulaity that has in the past been so marked in Australian cross-cultural contact.

7
The Centre for Aboriginal Studies in Music — CASM

Philosophy and background

The long-term aim of CASM, during the time I worked there, was the develpoment of a department within The University of Adelaide which was wholly staffed by Aboriginal people qualified either in their own traditions and elected by their own tribal leaders, or in Western academic work and in music.

The reason for attempting to establish such a centre was to provide professional recognition and status camparable to that given to outstanding Western musicians for Aboriginal people whose skills were exclusively within traditional Aboriginal education. At the same time it would provide a more culturally-meaningful educational experience for non-tribal Aboriginal people. It was considered that staff of this centre could teach both urban and tribal Aboriginal music at the required level of excellence for tertiary students, as well as undertaking research to develop educational techniques geared to assist Aboriginal people.

In reality, however, the likelihood of achieving this long-term aim in a few years is remote, not only because there are many conflicting aspirations among the members of different cultural generations of Aboriginal people, but also because the work of CASM covers a wide range of academic interests. These include ethnomusicology, with its emphasis on many non-Western musics and on methodology, and music therapy of both tribal and Western origin. Each of these subjects occurring in the context of CASM can be seen as a facet of education through music.

There are a number of non-Western examples of the use of music in education of people living in multicultural situations, and they all place emphasis not only on excellence in music itself, but also on the importance of education through music.

Paynter (1982:89ff) speaks about education through music in our own culture. He mentions the relationship of this concept to "wholeness" (p. 27) and to experience. He also writes about bridging the gap between music in school and music outside school. He states that the main purpose of this musical activity is the "symbolic seeking after order and integration" (p. 92). However, I have more than this in mind in writing this chapter.

My non-Western music teachers have taught me how music can be used as a means of personality growth which highlights my own strengths and inadequacies and provides positive mechanisms for working at these thereby reaching greater awareness of my self. My own experience in music has taught me how to apply this understanding within the context of my own culture and the music which expresses the central values of that culture (see Chapter 8).

Rabindranath Tagore established a university near Calcutta in which all the teaching is through the arts — music, dance, drama and poetry. Tagore himself was a very famous Indian poet, musician, teacher and philosopher who built his work on that of his father, Maharishi Devendranath Tagore, who originally established the school as one for boys of all castes. Rabindranath Tagore chose this site for his work, which he started as a school intended to bring to the surface of the thinking of the students the simplicity of life. At the same time it was also intended to tap the roots of the spirit of traditional Indian thought and teaching. It gradually expanded from the all-boys school of the early 1900s to a program which uses, among its other subjects, a large amount of education through music within a particular cultural context. Interaction is both between different Indian cultures and between these and non-Indian ones. Multicultural balance is achieved by devoting a given period of time exclusively to one culture. During this time, all students and staff become the guests of one particular cultural group and study their performing arts. They accept their traditional modes of conduct and immerse themselves in this specific life-style. Then the next group takes its turn. The name of this university — Santiniketan (Abode of Peace) — makes clear the intention of its founder.

A similar example is found in the Professor J. H. Kwabena Nketia, the ethnomusicologist and music eductor who used his own personal experience as an African musician and his training in Western music to form the Institute of African Studies at the University of Ghana in Legon. There, both traditionally-based and Western-based teaching takes place.

The Institute of Papua New Guinea Studies is another similar enterprise, founded by Professor Ulli Beier in 1974. Professor Beier had previously undertaken similar work in Nigeria and was a member of the Aboriginal Arts Advisory Board when the first work of this type was being attempted in Australia. The Institute of Papua New Guinea Studies (Report, 1978) is strongly research-oriented, with the specific intention of enabling a national identity to emerge by understanding what it is that is common among the diverse cultures involved. This search to reveal common elements of the cultural groups combined in Papua New Guinea also helps increase understanding of the nature of existing differences. The institute publishes two journals, monographs, discussion papers and collections of traditional poetry and folklore, all of which are directed to the people of Papua New Guinea rather than to the academic world. It has also established archives of traditional material: written records, published and unpublished; photographs, films and sound recordings. It involves as many traditionally knowledgeable people as possible in research into their own cultures, regardless of their academic background. These are but a few examples of the use of music as the point of integration in educational institutions in various cultures.

The idea of developing a centre such as CASM is not new in the Western academic world either. Mantle Hood for many years used the advantages of this type of experiential education to develop the teaching of ethnomusicology at the

University of California, Los Angeles. In 1958 he was responsible for the first appointment of a traditional performance
teacher. He was interested not only in the importance for
Western students of the opportunity to study under skilled
performers from different cultures (and he speaks from
experience with close to fifty cultures represented by visiting
indigenous performers), but in the effect that learning about
other musics has had on these visitors. He feels that recipro-
city in music making allows these musicians to develop a
greater awareness of the value of their own tradition as well
as finding points of relationship with other musics (1971:
371ff).

In 1974 I observed at first hand a program using the inter-
connection of African/black American and white American
music, which was the work of Barbara Lundquist in Seattle.
At that time she had developed education through music in
the secondary schools and had achieved an exciting level of
performance of traditional African music among secondary
students. She applied her own learning experiences under the
guidance of African teachers to the teaching of Western
music. Her students in one case were black American university students. I attended one of her group piano lessons
for these adult-beginner piano students and have rarely heard
such exciting music. Each of the students knew only a few
notes on the instrument, yet together they produced music
which was thrilling for everyone present.

The best documented program involving education
through music is the work of the Hungarian school of music
educators, particularly Kodály. He stresses the importance of
music for the development of the whole personality, and
deals sensitively with the development of contemporary
education through the use of the traditional folk idioms of
Hungary which he and Bartók researched so thoroughly. He
states in an article originally written in 1941:

> In music we possess a means not only for a general development of
> the human soul but also for an education towards becoming Hung-
> arians, a means that cannot be replaced by any other subject ...
> Taken separately, too, the elements of music are precious instruments
> in education.   Rhythm develops attention, concentration, deter-

mination and the ability to condition oneself. Melody opens up the
world of emotions. Dynamic variation and tone colour sharpen our
hearing. (1974:130)

More recently there has been research done on specific
aspects of the non-musical results of musical experience. For
instance, the study by Karen Wolff (1978:1ff) deals with the
non-musical outcomes of music education and shows how,
under certain circumstances, significant positive changes in
self-concept were found among children studying instrumental music. Wolff's review of this field mentioned the
research work of Michel and Martin (1970:127) with
problem boys in an elementary school. These authors noted
that the development of musical skill may be an aid in
increasing the self-esteem of disadvantaged problem students,
and consequently may generalize to increased self-confidence
in other tasks. This is shown as advantageous not only in
problem situations. As the work of educators such as Kodály
shows, there is great potential for the use of education
through music with above-average children.

In relation to Aboriginal people, music has an advantage
which may not apply in some of the cases already mentioned.
As one deeply respected, old urban Aboriginal woman
explained to me, "Music gets right to the heart of our
people". Their primary patterns of thought are mostly not
those of the systematic, divisive Western type, and because of
this Aboriginal children have great difficulty comprehending
teaching based on the processes of thought Gooch identifies
as System A. They have had to experience a shift in their *way*
of thinking as well as in the content. Yet this sharp split is
not necessary. Music offers an educational channel related
closely to their present, and to their former tribal practices.
It is also accessible within the Western system, particularly
since urban Aboriginal music is based on Western idioms. It
provides the possibility of education through a traditional
medium in a changed environment.

For all these reasons I saw CASM as important not only
for the tribal teaching, but also for providing specially
developed educational programs for urban Aboriginal people
who wished to become involved in music making in the

community as a whole, and had never previously been given the opportunity. I felt that one of the short-term aims of CASM was to provide training in selected areas of Western music (those most closely related to non-tribal folk traditions but adaptable to professional training), using tribal techniques of education through music to make this training available to urban Aboriginal children and adults who had no traditional tribal background.

In doing this it seemed important that techniques did not dispense with the tribal ideals of education for all ages simultaneously; if a separation occurred this would certainly increase the problems for urban children and their parents. For this reason a three-pronged program was developed to encompass tribal traditional music, education through music with urban Aboriginal adults and Western instrumental teaching for urban Aboriginal children.

As examination of similar programs elsewhere shows, there is nothing unique about CASM — but by early 1983 it still had no Australian counterparts. In CASM there is interaction between tribal and urban Aboriginal people; between knowledgeable Aboriginal teachers and non-Aboriginal students of the university (there are still only a few Aboriginal students at The University of Adelaide); between Aboriginal and non-Aboriginal workers at CASM and visiting performers from Africa, India, Iran, Bali, Japan and many other countries.

I worked within CASM and its predecessor, The Program of Training in Music for South Australian Aboriginal People, for its first seven years, having been responsible for its foundation. The Program commenced in 1971 and CASM was formally established within the University in 1975. Former students who have studied there are now able to develop techniques which have not previously been attempted, and apply them in the contemporary situation at CASM. It may be, therefore, that much that seemed important while I worked there is no longer relevant. For these reasons this is not an account of CASM at present, but a discussion of its history and the philosophy behind its work, which moves to a personal account of my experiences in my own multicultural growth.

Brief history of the establishment of CASM

The Program of Training in Music for South Australian Aboriginal People began in 1971 and the results of these first few difficult years have been regularly documented in reports (Ellis, ed., 1971–2); and more recently, information has been published in the bulletin from CASM, *Tjungaringanyi*. The title of this bulletin means "coming together as one" and was selected by tribal people. The regular comments on day-to-day details in these rather inaccessible sources mean that statements are available from those directly involved.

Once finance was granted to commence the three-pronged program, my first approach for assistance in the Aboriginal community was to the all-Aboriginal Council for Aboriginal Women in South Australia. Their field officer, a locally well-known Aboriginal woman, took the newly appointed urban music officer (white) to visit many families she considered to have suitable environmental conditions to enable children to benefit from instrumental tuition. She explained to the families the nature of our work. After visiting a number of different homes we also made contact with the Port Adelaide Central Methodist Mission Aboriginal Project. This group, which included a number of experienced white professional people and which had a strong connection with the Aboriginal families in that locality, volunteered to provide backing facilities and encouragement for any Aboriginal children from the Port Adelaide area who chose to participate. The members knew of a number of children who, they felt, could benefit greatly from musical tuition.

Two criteria were used to select the original group of students. First preference was given to darker-skinned children. The music officer from the program discussed this with a number of Aboriginal people concerned and all agreed that darker children come up against much greater prejudice and are consequently in more urgent need of assistance than those with lighter skin colour. The second was the degree of enthusiasm shown by the children themselves. No musical aptitude tests were used for selecting children, both because musical aptitude tests are unreliable even where there is no cultural disparity and because it is not necessarily the most musical who will benefit most from musical tuition, although presumably it is the most musical who will proceed furthest in the professional sense. Eventually, after a great deal of discussion with many people, Aboriginal and non-Aboriginal, twelve children between the ages of nine and sixteen were selected. Of these original twelve in 1971, not one was playing an instrument by 1977.

Progressively it became less difficult to select children as the work became better known. As people heard the children playing they began asking if their children could learn. Acceptance of students was them limited only by the number of instruments available. These, initially, were clarinets, trumpets and flutes, instruments with wide scope for many different kinds of music making in Adelaide. Children were taught in groups of four.

These students entered that section of the program which later became known as the Adelaide Aboriginal Orchestra. The other two parts of the program were the Institute of Narrative and Music of Aborigines – I.N.M.A. – (an experiment in applied ethnomusicology designed for urban adults and intended to encourage an interest in tribal music); and involvement of tribal musicians both through the Indulkana Inma Centre and in university and school teaching in the city. These three sections united in CASM after four years, although they all worked together in the Adelaide community.

The Adelaide Aboriginal Orchestra

The Adelaide Aboriginal Orchestra as such developed by accident rather than design. It arose as a teaching device to deal with the problems that occurred in introducing Western musical instruments to urban Aboriginal children. Classes were started with the twelve Aboriginal children from the metropolitan area, and three white teachers from the School of Music which belonged within the then South Australian Department of Further Education. The techniques used in teaching were gradually developed through experimentation, discussion and practical experience; the painful experience of failure, and the exhilarating experience of success.

Music camps came into this last category. These served a vitally important social/musical function. They enabled students to work at music for a continuous period of time (maximum two days) without disturbance from other sources, and were regarded by members of the orchestra as among the most important events in their calendar.

Traditional Western teachers who had not lived through the development of the orchestra, and were still questioning the greater freedom used in teaching within the orchestra, found it difficult to overcome their conventional concepts of progress through scales, exercises and the standard instrumental texts. The music camps therefore also served important functions for any such newly-recruited tutors, enabling them to expand their experience and understanding of music education as it was being applied within CASM.

Urban adults

At the outset of the work in 1971, many urban Aboriginal adults either felt ashamed of their own tribal traditions and heritage or had given the matter no thought at all. By encouraging them to listen to performers from other cultures around them, I hoped to reduce this alienation and help them assume some responsibility for the preservation of their own heritage.

Port Adelaide was a good location for this work as many visiting seamen were interested and ready to help. The Seamen's Union assisted as did shipping companies in Port Adelaide. Seamen from many countries – Malaysia, Philippines, Korea, Sweden and Indonesia – often came and performed to Aboriginal groups or allowed Aboriginal field workers to record them. This work had a marked effect on the world view of these Aboriginal people. Through enabling them to compare music from other countries with tribal Aboriginal music, this work partially succeeded in breaking down the urban Aboriginal barrier toward tribal Aboriginal people.

This particular work was terminated when the largest race riot in recent Australian history broke out in Port Adelaide between seamen and Aboriginals, the basis of the original altercation being prostitution. However, the institute formed for the music study (I.N.M.A.) continued and there has been a lasting impact on urban Aboriginal attitudes, not only towards other cultures, but also towards the Western music the children in the Adelaide Aboriginal Orchestra had been learning. In the latter case, members of the urban adult group have become involved with instrumental students by suggesting some of their own folk-type songs for repertoire, thus helping the tutors to achieve the aim of education of all ages simultaneously.

Tribal involvement

I chose Indulkana as the location for interactive work with tribal people because of the extensive field contact that I had had there. Many tribal people at Indulkana were willing to participate in interactive work and anxious to be involved in activities which, they hoped, would encourage younger tribal people to continue their traditional education. As with urban adults, tribal views of the world were then limited to their own known culture and to the actions of white people in their immediate environment.

Several skilled musicians, Western and non-Western, were appointed at Indulkana with the specific aim of broadening the tribal people's world view through introducing recordings, visual material and live performers from other cultures. This certainly did stimulate interest among the local tribal people, both in other Aboriginal traditions then unknown at Indulkana and in non-Australian people. It was at this time that senior performers from Indulkana began teaching non-Aboriginal people in Adelaide. This teaching was seen to be in the same category as the information from other cultures which filtered into Indulkana: people were going out to the larger world to tell others the importance of their own traditions. It was a reciprocal process.

When the non-Aboriginal workers appointed to help in this teaching left Indulkana they were replaced by a senior tribal man who has held this position ever since. He has stimulated the teaching of tribal children's songs as well as being fully involved in his own traditional activities. Further, he has constantly explained the nature of the work in Adelaide and is responsible for selecting those who come to teach. One of these other tribal teachers, on his first visit to Adelaide, said through the interpreter:

> I came for the first time and was ignorant about what the men did here. I didn't know what was going on here when I first came. I understand now what the old man is doing. I want to come again.
>
> We teach the girls dancing and singing together. We sing and students sing with us. We will only sing one song first and after that we don't know what we will sing . . .
>
> When the students learn properly they will sing as well as they can make their own music. They will sing then without looking at their books; they will sing in their minds.
>
> (*Tjungaringanyi* Vol. 1, No. 2:8)

Approaches to The University of Adelaide

By 1973 there was already a marked change in Aboriginal people's views of themselves. This was noticeable throughout Australia, but those who worked within the three segments of this music program were among the leaders in South Australia. They strongly expressed their need for better official recognition within the university, being at that time accredited a position only as part of my research work. This, they felt, placed them in a degrading position and was quite contrary to the aims of the music program.

Some of the urban Aboriginal people prepared a letter which was later quoted by the Vice-Chancellor, then Professor G.M. Badger, in his document to the Education Committee, entitled *Aboriginal Music* (1974). The letter stressed the importance of CASM remaining within the university as an institution "to allow us to continue our growth without too many pressures being put upon us"; it stressed, also, the importance of interaction between Aboriginal and non-Aboriginal students and scholars, and referred to the isolation an Aboriginal person feels when entering any educational institution alongside other students with better educational backgrounds.

By way of explaining this request, it is worth quoting a typical conversation which could then be heard between

Aboriginal workers within the program, and other urban Aboriginal relatives or friends. It went something like this:

"Where do you work now?"
"At the university."
"What as? A cleaner?"
"No. I'm working in music."
"Who are you kidding?"

This type of reaction always caused hard feelings, because the aspiring student then had to accept the ridicule of his own people for attempting to "be like white fellas" rather than fulfilling his own cultural stereotype.

Together with members of the Aboriginal Arts Board, the Aboriginal people involved pressed the university to accept the work of the Program of Training in Music for South Australian Aboriginal People as a legitimate teaching establishment within the university. As such it was designed to continue the work of the training program, and also to provide access to university staff and facilities for Aboriginal students who were not qualified in the traditional university sense. The Aboriginal people pointed out that there had never been a single Aboriginal graduate from The University of Adelaide, and that many of their people felt that universities were "white elephants" which failed completely in making any contribution to the education of Aboriginal people.

The document written by the Vice-Chancellor and passed formally through all channels within the university was a landmark in Aboriginal/white educational interaction. The Vice-Chancellor consulted tribal people in the field and spent much time with tribal and urban Aboriginal people in the university before presenting his statement. He was aware of the nature and the very great difficulties of this educational exercise and his vision had a marked effect on the emergence of CASM.

In April 1975, the Council of the university, with financial assistance from the Aboriginal Arts Board, formalized the establishment of the Centre for Aboriginal Studies in Music. They officially recognized knowledge gained through tribal education and granted the status of visiting lecturers to tribal teachers. They also recognized the importance of the traditional knowledge of some urban Aboriginal people and granted them appropriate status.

Progress since that time has been considerable. By 1977 CASM was able to present many full length concerts and weekly lunch-hour programs, drawing on the orchestra, the smaller ensemble of the most experienced players (all Aboriginal) and tribal performers, non-tribal singers, solo instrumentalists, and performers from other minority groups in Adelaide. Since 1977, when I left CASM and returned to an academic position within the university, many professional rock bands have emerged (Ellis, 1979:35f). The recent (1981) award-winning film "Wrong Side of the Road" gives an Aboriginal viewpoint of two of these bands, "No Fixed Address" and "Us Mob".

The standard of CASM student performances has increased dramatically over the years and concerts are spontaneous and enjoyable. The experience of performing in front of people seems to transform the students. They learn to develop their presentation and to speak in public. There have been many examples of students who, once they commenced to play an instrument with any success, improved both in their school work and in their participation in non-Aboriginal situations.

A review of one of these concerts gives a good idea of the atmosphere of performances in 1976:

> It was a varied and entertaining night, with a real sense of communicated enjoyment on both sides of the microphones ... An event such as this provides one of the most meaningful points I know of for communication between tribal and urban Aboriginal and white people. How can you fear or hate someone when you have sat alongside him being refreshed with music?
>
> (*Tjungaringanyi*, Vol. 1, No. 3:7)

Courses at CASM

The courses available at CASM at the end of 1977, all of which were open to Aboriginal students, were divided into three different sections:-

Section A provided courses for Aboriginal people who wanted an interesting educational experience through music without worrying about examinations and qualifications. This section was concerned with work with adults and with children, all of whom had considerable difficulty fitting into Western traditional educational organizations.

Section B offered courses to Aboriginal people who wanted to be qualified to enter music as a full-time profession. The students here had almost without exception come into CASM through Section A, moving by choice to an increasingly professional orientation.

Section C offered subjects for university students studying for degrees in music and arts.

Since 1977 this basic format has continued, but with less emphasis on instruments which can be used in classical music. Consequently, the Adelaide Aboriginal Orchestra has been discontinued. Primary direction of effort in Section B is now toward professionality in performing and composing Country and Western music and Rock. Section C remains essentially unaltered.

Aboriginal students at CASM

Sections A and B had, by 1977, reached about ninety Aboriginal students. Some stayed only a short while but forty-five remained for at least one complete year's tuition, and the longest standing student, now approaching professional level in the general community, had then been studying for six years.

I did not see the production of professional musicians as the sole, or even the prime aim of the work of the Adelaide Aboriginal Orchestra although this would certainly have been possible. Rather, I saw the orchestra as more concerned with allowing people to discover through music their own potential and to start using it within the culture they choose to live in. After a time in CASM students often seek to move into different areas of education or accept and hold permanent employment in fields outside music.

Of the forty-five students who by the end of 1977 had stayed with CASM long enough for the work to have some impact, twenty-five were still involved in their own education. In the group of employable age, forty-five percent had been in their present job for more than two years and a futher ten percent were newly in their first jobs. No details were available for twenty-five percent of this group because they had moved away from Adelaide. The remaining twenty percent were unemployed or involved in home duties. Although figures are not available from the Aboriginal population at large, experience indicates that the stability in this group of students and former students is well above average.

Aboriginal Students in Section A — Courses for Interest

In this section the main work was through the Adelaide Aboriginal Orchestra. However, students of Sections A and B could sit in on any of the other sections if they wished to do so.

Techniques Used in Teaching

The teaching techniques which ultimately emerged as most important for Aboriginal students first coming into CASM combined both tribal and Western practices. Those based primarily on traditional tribal methods involved repetition and imitation (in the orchestra this was simultaneously visual, in the sense that students could imitate the fingering of another player, and aural, in that they could play by ear, having heard the note played by the person next to them); strong leadership in the form of competent musicians who played alongside students rather than standing aside teaching them (this is related to the tribal practice of singing alongside the younger performers); and the personal care and concern of the teacher.

In the techniques developed from Western music several tutors, myself included, attempted to use creative music, but very rarely was this successful.

"Creative" music is a term widely used in music education to describe those activities within music which are concerned with making new music for students to perform. Since Aboriginal music (both tribal and urban) is primarily a re-creative activity, this educational approach (see Paynter 1982:137) had mainly negative impact. The work we did was based on that of Schafer, who states, "It is the duty of every composer to be concerned with the creative ability of young people. But he has to be quick to catch it." (1965:33).

Because these experiments did not provide firm musical boundaries which were understood in the urban Aboriginal community, they seemed to create anxiety in the students. This may disappear with greater exposure. One piece was successful and performed a number of times despite strong initial opposition. It was built on a tale made up by the Aboriginal players and then reproduced in sound while someone from the orchestra narrated the story. Slides of illustrative paintings, done by the players themselves, were shown during the performance. Apart from this successful experiment, the experience of creative music with any but the most able players increased anxiety levels and was there-fore detrimental to the work.

The role of the conductor (and white teacher) has always been difficult at CASM since there is no tribal concept of a conductor as such and nothing within non-tribal Aboriginal music making which is remotely similar. For instance, whereas in a tribal performance the song-leader's role is that of initiator and co-performer, in the Western tradition the conductor's function is to superimpose his interpretation on that of the other performers. There is an added difficulty in that the conductor of the Adelaide Aboriginal Orchestra was necessarily a non-Aboriginal, and the nearest model urban Aboriginal people see in such a role as this is the "boss". We experimented with many different solutions to this problem — the conductor playing as a leading member of the orchestra; conductor as conductor; Aboriginal conductors — and so far none of these has been wholly satisfactory. Groups playing with no conductor have similarly experienced difficulties.

Originally there was no thought among students that practice or work on their own was necessary. They expected to be involved only for the time of the actual interaction. Furthermore, there were no facilities either at home or in the accommodation supplied for CASM, for supervised practice. Lack of motivation for individual involvement was not limited to music, but seemed characteristic of all that these children attempted.

It was here that I benefited from the previous work of the Port Adelaide Project, particularly the example of the craft workers. The local Aboriginal children attended craft work each Sunday afternoon, and through the medium of a project involving the making of coffee tables, a series of graded tasks was developed by the white leaders. Initially the leaders did almost all the work, making the tables beforehand and leaving the children to arrange and glue ceramic tiles on the top. The children were enormously proud of these tables they had "made" and the immediate return for their minimal activities motivated them to apply themselves to more comprehensive tasks in later sessions. Gradually the children did more and more of the making, the teachers progressively less.

The three tutors who were working with urban children in the music program at first attempted to teach in the same way as they would have taught white children who were strongly motivated to learn. There was at this stage no correlation between the ideas of the craft workers and those used in the music program. At the end of the first year of teaching, each flute player was able to play only four notes. On request they could together play a melody from these four notes, each playing one note of the four at the appropriate time.

Soon the teachers realized that a technique such as this could be developed for children on their first day. Thus, like the craft workers, the teachers originally did all the work, arranging, conducting and showing the child how to play just one note. Each child had to concern himself only with playing this note when pointed to, yet through interaction with other, better players he immediately became involved in the production of a piece of music. A possible extension of this was harmonizing melodies by using only two notes; then the more experienced players could play the melody (usually by ear) and the beginner of the day played the two notes of the harmony when he was cued in. This later development called for a large number of white players proficient enough to provide the model which Aboriginal players at each level could imitate.

This was the beginning of the introduction, too, of tribal techniques of group teaching, of teaching through imitation, of providing the full and vital musical experience from the outset of exposure by including all ages at the same time. From these fumbling beginnings the Adelaide Aboriginal Orchestra came into existence. It placed the instruments in an important social and cultural framework for the students and enabled further development of the coffee table idea by providing more involved tasks for players who were developing increasing skills. It was similar to the piano class, mentioned earlier, taught by Lundquist.

As teachers developed more skill in teaching in this situation, problems associated with music reading disappeared. Children who could not read music were helped by those who could. The newer students performed alongside better players, each playing a part at a suitable technical level. Playing by ear soon became very important and made possible the arrangement for the whole group of simple parts or of tunes students could play themselves. This stimulated a desire to read music so that everybody could play together those songs which they enjoyed. It also stimulated the players themselves to recognize the need for other technical skills such as good intonation. A few songs in the repertoire of the city people were arranged for the orchestra.

At this level of introducing musical experiences to new Aboriginal students the work of the orchestra was expanded continually. New ideas were frequently tried, some with success; others were discarded as failures, only to be later requested as important; others again were allowed to fall into disuse, until the orchestra itself was gradually discontinued (during 1979/80).

Comments made by Aboriginal students

Comments have been written by urban Aboriginal students

for inclusion in *Tjungaringanyi*. They show how each student felt as a participant in the work of Section A.

I am in the orchestra; I play trombone. It is something to do, something to keep me off the streets. I am employed in the program. I was in the orchestra before but I dropped out because I had trouble with my ears. Finding out what all the other students are doing in the orchestra, what they are doing and what they achieve in playing gradually brought me back. The tutors teach us to get our notes properly ... They come round to our houses and give us lessons or come to the office and give us a lesson or go to the schools and give students their lessons. (Vol. 1, No. 1:7)

The worst thing in my mind is that I have found that a lot of my people are destroying themselves. What I mean is that they cannot do anything on their own, so they go and get drunk because they like to be part of something different for a change. My people don't know themselves, so we are trying to help them understand themselves by showing what is done in the Centre by Aboriginals. Music has helped me to gain confidence in myself as a person. I have learned to type better, read music and mix better with people, and I try to understand people more.

The urban Aboriginal people need more help because they are scared of one another, trying to start fights against each other. They are scared to get jobs because they don't understand what people want them to do. When they go to apply for jobs (filling in forms, etc.) they get scared, then angry because they don't know how to tell people they need help. Then they get angry with other Aboriginals and resent them if they are dressed well and have more money, and because they are refused when they ask for a few bob they pick fights with them ...

But the main reason is that some of our people are scared to face life or to face white people and accept their way of life ... The reason some Aboriginals have problems is that they don't get enough help and encouragement. So, I think we should learn to help each other and share with each other and never to be lonely and scared of your own people. (Vol. 2, No. 1:2)

I feel that we need a lot more Aboriginals, young and old to take up music. You don't have to be a brain to do music. When I was at school, I hated music lessons, where we only studied the theory part of it, but I found it different when I started playing an instrument ... When taking up music, you're not committed or forced to play, or attend lessons; it's up to you, yourself, if you want to progress. It is better to start playing when you're young, but not really necessary. I myself have really enjoyed playing the trumpet and would like to see more Aboriginals playing an instrument. (Vol. 2, Nos. 2 & 3:1)

During 1976 the Adelaide Aboriginal Orchestra was able, with the aid of Community Arts Project workers, to arrange a number of music workshops which gave students an opportunity to observe and hear different types of instruments and music. They saw that an instrument could be used in a number of ways to produce different musical styles. Students were able to see and hear a number of groups perform at the Festival Theatre - jazz musicians, pop groups and artists such as Ray Price, Cleo Laine and others.

It has stimulated a number of students to do better themselves. Through talking to these many performers, they have realized that it is very important to practise regularly. (Leila Rankine, Aboriginal Chairman of CASM and trombone player in the orchestra [Vol. 2, Nos. 2 & 3:5])

Aboriginal students — Section B

Students usually move into Section B after having been involved casually in Section A. This graduation calls for a more serious application to study on the part of the student and much greater effort at individual, unsupervised work.

Techniques Used in Teaching

The work does not differ in nature but constitutes an extension of all that occurs in Section A, and is not in any way separated out in activities from Section A. The difference is therefore one of quality rather than course content. However, students are encouraged to verbalize more about their experiences and to relate more with performers from other cultures. Increasingly they are expected to develop professional kinds of skills and a theoretical knowledge of music. The progress is from casual to more structured involvement in all the activities available, including those belonging within Section C.

Comments made by Aboriginal Students

I think the highlight of the year for me was the opportunity that I and the other staff at the Centre had of meeting and listening to the Japanese quartet who toured Australia last year. The experience was beautiful and moving; it will long be remembered. (*Tjungaringanyi* Vol. 2, Nos. 2 & 3:5)

I got involved in this program about three and a half years ago when I went to a Youth Camp at O'Sullivan Beach. It was a Music Camp and while I was there someone gave me a trumpet and that is how it all began . . .

. . . now in 1975 we are well known because not only have we improved and are really getting good at playing together, but we have played all over the place and are getting better at every concert.

Now there are about twenty-three Aboriginal members in the orchestra and it is really good fun. We have three Aboriginal trainee tutors — one each for the trumpet, clarinet and flute, and these trainee tutors are themselves taught by players from the Adelaide Symphony Orchestra, and instrumental teachers from the Department of Further Education.

Now we are working in the Centre for Aboriginal Studies in Music in the University of Adelaide. When we are at the office we practise or sit in on lectures and learn more about our own culture. We have fully tribal men that come from Indulkana who lecture at our office and they teach us how to talk in Pitjantjatjara and how to sing some of their children's songs. They are really fantastic.

We also have a small ensemble which plays semi-jazz music — things with a bit of spirit. In a few years time we will be playing really hot stuff so you will have to come and hear us some time. (*Tjungaringanyi* Vol. 1, No. 2:1)

Aboriginal students — Section C

Very few Aboriginal students chose to move into the work of Section C. We have one report from an urban Aboriginal adult who worked with a group of university students in the project called Music in the Community, a subject in the music degree course.

The role which music plays in the education of people whether they be physically, mentally or socially handicapped or those who have different cultural backgrounds, was seen to be of utmost importance. The discussion of each participant's paper leaves no doubt in my mind that music can bring about a response where other means of communication have failed . . . I am seeing changes within the group, within the individual students, who are regarded as being almost unteachable or unreachable and who are responding to music. It isn't something which happens overnight, but it is happening.

I have listened to musics from other countries, spoken with people from other countries involved with the singing and making of music and have found a warm response by them towards the group.

The people involved in the studies learned from each other that music from one country is as important as music from another. No one music is more important than the other; music is universal . . . It is very easy to be critical of something one does not understand because one is culturally different, but after the Ethnic experience we must believe in each other's dreams, whether we be Red Indian, Black American, Asian, African, White, Australian Aboriginal or any other nationality, we can still communicate with each other through the use of music even though language may continue to be a barrier. (*Tjungaringanyi* Vol. 1, No. 1:4)

Tertiary students at CASM

To 1977 at least one hundred and fifty university students had studied under tribal teachers at CASM, thirty of these for one entire subject of their degree course. The impact that this training is making on secondary school teaching in South Australia is noticeable. The work has been operating long enough for newly matriculated students to be coming from schools into CASM with previous structured experience of minority group music, and particularly Aboriginal music.

Tertiary students — Section C

The University of Adelaide has long-established, standard courses in music. In these, students examine something of Western cultural history, composition, music in education, electronic music, musicology, ethnomusicology and many different instruments. In the ethnomusicology courses which operate through CASM, students attempt to come to grips with what music means to different peoples, and to understand the effects music can have on a person's behaviour.

The subjects that were available within CASM by the end of 1977 were:

Aboriginal singing: this is a practical course open to students in any section. It is taught by the tribal visiting lecturers, and involves mainly Pitjantjatjara songs. This subject is now named Tribal Singing.

Music in the community: a subject based around a field study of any music functioning within the community (perhaps music from a particular minority group). This subject is now incorporated into Ethnomusicology II and III.

Aboriginal music: the visiting lecturers from Indulkana

present half of this academic/practical subject. The other half covers work such as that presented in chapter 5. It is now called Pitjantjatjara Music.

Cross-cultural instrumental teaching: this subject shows how tribal teaching techniques can be applied to teaching Western music and gives instructions on the nature of the work in the Adelaide Aboriginal Orchestra, rock groups, etc. To stress the absence of white domination, this subject is now called Cross-Cultural Performance.

Ethnomusicology seminar: this seminar for advanced university students covers complex areas of the study of music as communication.

Techniques Used in Teaching

In all cultures, practical music is learned by a student placing himself under the guidance of the master musician. It is possible for a student, or even a master, from the music of one culture to become the student of the master in another. By using this method of teaching about other musics, education through music becomes a real possibility.

There are facets of the work of CASM which place high demands on tertiary students. Those students who rise to meet the challenges before them have an opportunity to experience cross-cultural phenomena not otherwise presented in the normal learning situation. The part-subject Introduction to Ethnomusicology, offered by the Elder Conservatiorium of Music in the first year of the B. Mus. course, is intended to prepare music students for these high demands. Because those who teach at CASM believe in the importance of placing Learning III experiences before students, all teaching belongs within the broad field of performance-oriented ethnomusicology.

Comments made by university students

Although many student comments on work in Aboriginal music have been quoted in chapter 5, several additional comments concerning other aspects of the studies available at CASM are included here. The two students quoted studied under different university lecturers, in different musical cultures, yet each seemed to gain similar insights from the experience.

> This project provided for me, not only an area for gaining knowledge, but also personal growth. The phenomenon of music was considered from all angles. Its elements, uses and functions through time were all discussed individually without losing sight of how one relates to the other . . .
>
> The knowledge and personal experience gained from being involved in this project is immeasurably valuable to me as a trainee Music Educationist. (*Tjungaringanyi* Vol. 2, No. 1:48)

> Another aspect of the work which impressed me was the relevance of it to today . . .
>
> I really felt that I was contributing something new and important to the literature of the Australian Bush Song, something which is not always possible when doing a historical topic. The satisfaction of this work was heightened by a new awareness of other people and their culture . . .
>
> Overall the project helped me to be a more tolerant person. I do not use the word tolerant meaning "to put up with"* something but simply to explain that now I can try and meet someone halfway in a common dilemma whether the problem arises from cultural, musical or other factors resulting from different social training. (*Tjungaringanyi* Vol. 1, No. 1:5f)

Aboriginal Singing classes

Within the context of CASM as a whole Aboriginal singing followed on the work with adult urban Aboriginal people through I.N.M.A.

Urban Aboriginal students in the tribal singing classes

Despite protestations to the contrary, there is ambivalence shown in urban Aboriginal people's attitudes to studying under the strong discipline of the tribal elders. Most are very threatened by this form of tuition and, by 1977 only ten had even attempted the studies available. They often say that the most important experience for them at CASM is the

---

* This was the meaning understood by an Aboriginal student in the group. She claimed this was the commonly understood meaning of "tolerance" in the Aboriginal community.

opportunity to learn from tribal people, yet at the same time request that they be excused from these studies because they find them irrelevant and confusing.

A little of this ambivalence is apparent in one urban Aboriginal student's comments:

> I am amazed at the capacity of the Elders to retain so much knowledge in their minds with such perfection.
>
> It is not easy to understand at times the difference between the two cultures but only by working together can we hope to gain an insight into the depth of training in history and value systems of both cultures. (personal communication)

Secondary school children in tribal singing classes

Ruth Buxton, then Principal Education Officer in Music for the Education Department of South Australia, came into CASM as a student after many years' experience teaching music in secondary schools. She has written about taking Aboriginal and African musicians from CASM to schools:

> The immediacy of personal involvement made an overwhelming impression. We moved from a document-oriented study to a people-oriented study . . .
> . . . A cultural explosion occurred. The kids were totally involved in the performance. The tribal educative process was foolproof. Listening may make us aware, but performance makes the music live. The students were then confronted by the exciting discovery that they had moved behind the facade of initial contact to an examination of deeper cultural values. The special education class took an avid interest in an African social studies project and the musically literate group felt a sense of profound ignorance when presented with the knowledge, wisdom and performance techniques of the elders.
> "I forgot he was black", said one.
> "I thought our music was the only sort", said another.
> Joe summed it up —
> "When he played I could feel his heart beating." (1976:2)

8
The Challenge of the Present —
Living and Learning in a
Multi-cultural Society

In this book I have repeatedly emphasized the different ways people think, and the need to transcend these differences. There are a number of aspects which are frequently overlooked by persons not involved in close cultural interaction and these need now to be spelt out more clearly in order to begin the process of drawing useful conclusions and attempting to integrate what has already been said.

Given the fact that readers themselves come from groups with different value orientations, this is no simple task. The book could, theoretically, be concluded with reference to the impact of exposure to the tribal teaching on non-Aboriginal people, reiterating what this has meant for those involved. This, in turn, could be summarized by saying that it has been possible to re-evaluate what has happened in Western music education and to understand and recognize the importance of education through music, the process which acknowledges music as both experience and message. But this does not go far enough.

The experience of tribal music teaching is valid only for those involved. Education through music has to involve the whole person and requires a high level of commitment, without which the music cannot fulfil its role as both experience and message. No matter how theoretical work on Aboriginal music is written, it does not inspire a feeling of empathy for the musicians. It is thus all too easy for the reader to dismiss what has been said as of no personal relevance, of concern only to ,the specialist. It was for this reason that I gave an autobiographical account early in the book: any information concerning experience of inter-cultural relationships is important for survival today and is therefore of direct concern to every individual.

In chapter 6 I drew attention to Freire's view (1973) that dependent people become alienated not only from their own culture but also from their own thinking. The imagined world is so unlike the world that exists in reality that the alienated person responds with many negative attitudes, particularly apathy and lack of motivation, and often with aggression. Freire points out that the educational way through this dilemma is to seek authenticity of expression. I have attempted to show how this can be done through music.

However, in daily interaction one cannot rely exclusively on music, important though this is. One must develop verbal communication which is not liable to misinterpretation if one is to survive. This communication essentially came to be, for each of us in CASM, the statement of our own personal experiences and how we saw these. The statements may not have been "correct" interpretations of our own lives, but they nevertheless came to be the only points on which we could speak with certainty.

Implicit in the idea of multicultural education (whether through music or through any other medium) is the notion that there is equal validity in the cultural experience of any person (see, for example, Freire, 1973, 1974). This applies to both student and teacher. It may seem self-evident, yet putting the theory into practice is far from easy. Ethno-centricity, that deep-seated belief that the only right way to do, to know, or to perceive is the way one's own culture accepts as right, is an extremely strong force in all education. Indeed, education is often defined as *enculturation,* the process of training in what is right and wrong in a given culture.

In multicultural education, ethnocentricity is dangerous. Both student and teacher must attempt to step beyond ethnocentric limitations. Success in such education lies in learning to see everything from a broader base of reference than that accepted within one's own culture. Yet as soon as this broadening takes place the student and the teacher are at serious psychological risk because their expanded view of the world is seen as an aberration by those enclosed within ethnocentric values and attitudes.

A notable feature of the experience of CASM was that those of us who worked there for some time could be honest enough with one another to discuss our individual experiences. In doing this, we were certainly working within Gooch's System B, dealing with feeling rather than with logic. However, we found that it was rare to meet a person outside CASM who could comprehend this type of personal revelation in the terms it was intended. Always we faced ill-considered criticism of our actions and our statements. In such cases, our personal sharing, which was intended to increase perception, did not contribute at all to another person's understanding of the cross-cultural situation.

For this reason, I have reluctantly decided not to include any direct reference to my personal experiences within CASM. For those who have experienced acculturation – the adoption of patterns from more than one culture – it becomes routine to learn that even the most obvious facts, regardless of who states them, are interpreted by various ethnocentric groups according to their own value orientation, with little or no attempt made to perceive the orientation of the speaker.

One of the features of Western education which is not often discussed is its potential for developing critical thought. Through this means, the majority of the community has acquired some capacity for looking objectively and critically at many things. However, an appropriate use of this faculty presupposes a thorough understanding of the problems being examined, and this is rarely the case in cross-cultural education.

There are a number of reasons why such a high level of uninformed criticism is directed at all people who speak and work from a base of experience in more than one culture and there are several factors which follow from this. The first is that individuals with acculturated experience are forced into silence on the very experiences which are crucial in understanding multicultural education, because their every comment or action is subject to misinterpretation.

Those who are subjected to this constant lack of understanding need therapeutic assistance to retain psychological stability. This must be in a form (preferably non-verbal) which itself is not open to misinterpretation, and music therapy provides an obvious channel. My own experience of tribal therapy, given in the *Proceedings of the Third National Conference of the Australian Music Therapy Association* (Ellis, 1977), is an example of an immensely valuable cross-cultural experience which cannot be recounted without many people grossly misinterpreting its nature.

The relationship between this experience and Western music therapy is similar to the relationship between shamanism and psychoanalysis which Lévi-Strauss (1972: 198ff) discusses. In both cases the therapist seeks to align the patient with memories of events or feelings in the patient's past and one way to achieve this is through myth. It seems, if we accept this information and that on myth presented in chapter 2, that life experiences of an individual are built around his personal and cultural myths, the structure of which can be used to tap the deepest levels of his thinking through either mythic or musical form.

The second implication of this constant criticism centres on the critic himself, representative as he is of the vast majority of the community. If it is not possible for the critic to see the stance of the acculturated person, then it is certainly important that he understand his own position in relation to cross-cultural experiences. Usually, critics are unaware that this is necessary; and there seem to be a number of reasons for this lack of awareness, each of which will now be discussed separately.

Levels of learning and their implications in cross-cultural education

In chapter 2 I outlined Bateson's concept that beyond zero learning there are three different learning experiences available to human beings. It is possible to show these three levels of learning diagrammatically: an informal one acquired from the childhood environment and shaped by the culture of those to whom the child is closely related; a formal one shaped by the education system which, ideally, builds on the informal level of learning; and a spiritual, visionary one concerned with learning about, and discarding, elements of the second level, while developing new insights.

Since that area of learning which Bateson calls Learning III — the transcending and deeply spiritual experience of life — is so important for multicultural education, a little more time spent attempting to define it more rigorously may help in understanding the emerging diagram. Assagioli, in his work, *Psychosynthesis* (1965:16ff), defines the structure of the personality as best understood at the time he wrote.

Speaking about two different selves, the conscious self or "I" and the higher self, he draws attention to the duality within the personality, the opposition between the conscious self and the higher self. He sees this duality as resolved by awareness and expereince of the whole self. This synthesis is probably the same as that spoken about by Bateson as Learning III and the difficult process of achieving this higher level of learning, Assagioli notes, is usually accompanied by personality disturbance.

The nature of perceiving at this higher level can be seen in some of the writing of Le Shan (1975) who speaks about Alternate Realities. In the light of much scientific evidence, Le Shan postulates at least two realities: a Sensory Reality and an Alternate Reality. His description of the Alternate Reality brings points of Western thought, and descriptions consistent with traditional tribal beliefs, together in a common mould. In this experiential frame occur those universals which overcome the polarities of culture-bound sensory realities.

Le Shan arrives at his definition of an alternate reality after close examination of the statements of physicists, mystics and clairvoyants. He found all three groups of people discussing a form of reality which, in everyday terms, could not be "real". In attempting to overcome this apparent paradox he examined the nature of this other reality as discussed by all three groups of people. He found four basic characteristics of this Alternate Reality (1975:64), at least two of which are significant for our present purposes. Firstly, there is a central unity to all things. The most important aspect of a "thing" is its relationships, its part in the whole. Its individuality and separateness are secondary and/or illusory. Secondly, pastness, presentness, and futurity are illusions we project on to the "seamless garment" of time. There is another valid view of time in which these separations do not exist.

This description, which presumably indicates something of the nature of thought occurring within level III, and which has arisen from examination of aspects of Western thought, is remarkably similar to many concepts frequently discussed as essential to tribal thought.

Reimer's statements (1970:126ff) on aesthetic education as the goal in music performance programs are also related to these ideas. Earlier in this book on music education (1970:25) he gives a list of the many words which have been used to describe the aesthetic qualities of a work of art. I have italicized those I believe to be most relevant to Learning III, but include the full list because of its importance to all the material being discussed throughout this book.

Art:
is expressive of
is analogous to
is isomorphic with
corresponds to
is a counterpart of
has the same pattern as
is a semblance of
gives images of
gives insight into
gives experience of
gives understanding of
gives revelation of
brings to consciousness
makes conceivable

subjective reality
the quality of experience
the emotive life
the patterns of feeling
the life of feeling
sentience
the depth of existence
the human personality
the realm of affect
the patterns of consciousness
the significance of experience

These items are critical elements in any performance of music. Reimer summarizes his comments on performance programs with this statement:

> When helped to achieve an integration of musical mastery with musical understanding at least some children will achieve a third value which transcends the benefits of both: they will have gained a sense of becoming *part of the act of aesthetic creation.* That experience is among the most fulfilling a human being can have, as all who have had it know full well. (p. 138)

Figure 8:1 shows how these different theories, which have been elaborated in various forms in earlier chapters, fit within the diagram of levels of learning.

Figure 8:1 Theoretical outlines of levels of Learning I, II and III.	
SPIRITUAL VISIONARY (level III)	Perceiving Alternate Realities (Le Shan) which go beyond formal, self-centred learning and reach toward the higher self (Assagioli) and universals. This may be experienced through the act of aesthetic creation (Reimer)
COGNITIVE TECHNICAL FORMAL (level II)	Formal training; learning to learn (Bateson); centred on the conscious self (Assagioli)
INFORMAL (level I)	Informal learning; extinction of habituation (Bateson)

The critic of acculturated actions is often unaware of these three levels of learning and may base his assumptions of correctness of behaviour entirely within one of these categories. In such a case he certainly will not realise that Shankar (see chapter 2) was speaking about all three when he emphasized the importance to the study of Indian classical music of humility (level I?); practice and discipline (level II); and self-realization (level III). He may also fail to understand the nature of the difficulty any musician faces once he has experienced the heights of level III through music making yet has thus far been unable to transfer these insights to personal growth.

Systems of thought and their implications in cross-cultural education

Even where a critic of cross-cultural work is aware of different levels of learning, he may not take account of the importance of different processes of thought. The denial of the validity of individual experience because of its necessarily subjective expression indicates this. It is, essentially, an example of the attempted domination of Gooch's System A over System B. It is also a denial of the authenticity of expression stressed by Freire. The use of techniques modelled on System B or System C is misinterpreted by those who feel the need to take refuge in rationalism and objectivity. These techniques may be seen, for instance, as a statement of prejudice, or as too embarrassing a display of private information. About this domination of rational processes, Yehudi Menuhin, a great performing artist of our time, says:

> One of the most disturbing symptoms of the superstitition of our day . . ., that blind faith in a monstrous god so antagonistic to man and his art, is our passion for the abstraction. (1972:139)

The importance of different processes of thought has been raised a number of times throughout this work, and the writings of Gooch, Rattray Taylor, Lévi-Strauss and others, as well as the inherent duality in the structure of the personality and of tribal music have been used to explain this paired division.

There are four important aspects which concern us about theories of paired systems of thought: that the majority of people in any one group develop a preference for either A or B; that most Western European people of the educated classes develop a preference for A over B; that most Aboriginal and other people coming from oral traditions tend to develop a preference for B over A; that an additional, integrative system of thought is of vital importance in improving communications between those who have opted for A and those who have opted for B (Figure 8:2).

There are many good examples of writings on race relations which stem from each of these systems. For instance the collection of research writings edited by Watson (1973) provides valuable informative data. This, however, can be interpreted with greater feeling after reading the writings of Eldridge Cleaver (1970), who speaks from the depth of personal experience. An anthropological novel which gives an account of the personal and field experiences of the research-er, E. S. Bowen's *Return to Laughter* (1964), achieves a synthesis of this objective/subjective approach in such a way that the factual information is illuminated by the personal experience. Writers such as Bowen achieve the integrated level of discussion of the problems encountered.

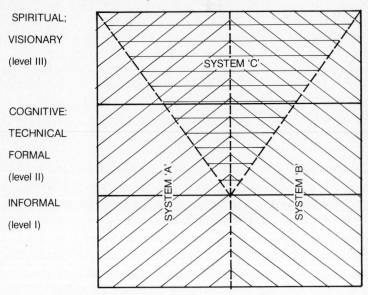

SPIRITUAL;
VISIONARY
(level III)

COGNITIVE:
TECHNICAL
FORMAL
(level II)

INFORMAL
(level I)

SYSTEM 'C'

SYSTEM 'A'

SYSTEM 'B'

Figure 8:2   Systems of thought within any culture.

Common and cultivated music and their implications in cross-cultural education

Another misunderstanding can arise concerning the quality of musical interaction. Here the critic may be a person who looks exclusively for motivation or initiative in music making at the cost of quality, or he may be concerned with assuming the quality of his own music to be superior to that of any form of music. I have already frequently mentioned the danger of the cross-cultural value judgement made without consideration for the values in the unknown culture. Music occurs at various qualitative levels in any culture. Each level has its importance in the community, and the denial of one or the other level leads to imbalance.

Often, however, there is confusion over these levels when cultural interchange is involved. Music intended for everyday use and requiring little or no intellectualization may then replace music of a deeply spiritual nature from another culture. If interchange or acculturation is to occur without loss to either group, the levels of musical activity involved in this interchange must remain qualitatively comparable. These levels (Figure 8:3) seem to be directly related ot the levels of learning appearing in these successive diagrams. Failure to understand this type of division can result, for instance, in criticism which sees racist the placement of children's tribal songs in the category common music.

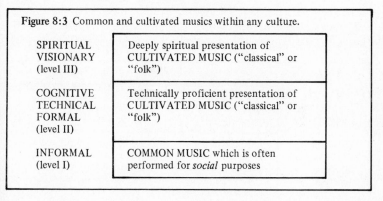

Figure 8:3 Common and cultivated musics within any culture.

SPIRITUAL VISIONARY (level III)	Deeply spiritual presentation of CULTIVATED MUSIC ("classical" or "folk")
COGNITIVE TECHNICAL FORMAL (level II)	Technically proficient presentation of CULTIVATED MUSIC ("classical" or "folk")
INFORMAL (level I)	COMMON MUSIC which is often performed for *social* purposes

Contexts in which learning occurs and their implications in cross-cultural education

Bateson frequently stresses the importance of context. Learning that occurs in any given situation depends on the context in which the learning takes place. Just as the critic may have missed other boundaries which are crucial to understanding statements and actions occurring in different cultures, he may also misinterpret the nature and significance of the context. Culture is that body of learning which is presented to the child initially from the environment, and later developed within the confines of this initial set of perceptions. The success of multicultural education lies in the ability of students to see events from wider perspectives than those which arise from their original culture. Since this represents growth, it is appropriate to consider each move to wider cultural perception as a further stage in development.

However, the acculturated view cannot be one that is seen objectively only, but must be one which is experienced through relinquishing those aspects of our own culture which are detrimental to others, as well as accepting those aspects of other cultures which are a means of growth for us.

The three levels of learning in Figure 8:1 can now be included in a diagram with two markedly different contexts, each representing a further stage in the development and education of the multicultural individual. The first stage comprises that learning which concerns itself solely with the values of the original culture; the second concerns itself with

Figure 8:4 Three levels of learning occurring in two distinct contexts.

SPIRITUAL VISIONARY (level III)	Heights of spiritual experience	Maintaining supreme levels of quality experience in more than one culture
COGNITIVE TECHNICAL FORMAL (level II)	Formal education which enables questioning ("How?" "Why?") and application of techniques to answer the questions	Considering the experiences gained in other cultures and accepting, integrating, discarding and re-experiencing
INFORMAL (level I)	Informal and unreflective learning about one's own culture	Unreflective experience of another culture
	ETHNOCENTRIC (stage I)	ACCULTURATED (stage II)

incorporating or discarding elements of one's own and other cultures as they best facilitate or damage intercultural and interpersonal relations in a multicultural situation.

An example of acculturated thinking is given by Yehudi Menuhin who is knowledgeable in both Western and Indian music, when he talks about this process of give and take across cultural boundaries as it refers to a particular musical problem:

> To the Indian quality of serenity, the Indian musician brings an exalted personal expression of union with the infinite, as in infinite love. Few modern composers in the West have achieved this quality, though we revere it in the works of Bach, Mozart, and Beethoven. Perhaps we should not admonish our contemporary composers for having lost this sense of serene exaltation, for indeed we have little enough of it in our civilization for them to draw upon; yet what quality is music, the organization of pure sounds, better suited to express? If the Indian musicians who are now beginning to bring their genius to us - musicians like Ravi Shankar - can help us to find this quality again, then we shall have much to thank them for. (1972:66)

So far I have spoken about learning within the frames of reference of one's own culture (ethnocentric learning), and within the possible patterns which emerge as acceptable if several cultures interact (acculturated learning). In both cases it is possible to move through the three levels of learning to arrive at a point where the wholeness of the individual makes it possible for him to be accepting of others through his understanding of universals and his greater awareness of his higher, rather than his competitive, conscious, self.

There are situations, for instance in newly emerging urban cultures, where the individual arrives at an awareness of universals without moving through the three levels of learning in the manner outlined above. Moreover it is probable that the occurrence of the third level in any group of people maintaining common heritage and beliefs is directly dependent on the age and stage of development of the traditions they maintain. In newly emerging traditions, therefore, this third level may not occur. The higher awareness that some individuals from these urban centres achieve seems to have been gained by moving across different cultures to universal principles rather than moving intensively through one culture.

Figure 8:5 Progressions of learning within and across cultures.

	ETHNOCENTRIC (stage I)	ACCULTURATIVE (stage II)	TRANSCENDENT (stage III)
SPIRITUAL VISIONARY LEARNING (level III)	Heights of experience and communication of these within one culture through aesthetic or religious processes	Heights of experience in aesthetic or religious forms which derive from sources in different cultures	Being universal
COGNITIVE FORMAL LEARNING (level II)	Intellectual activity within and about one's own culture, and one's own position in it, as well as intellectual activity based in one's own culture, but *about* another culture (e.g., anthropological study)	Intellectualizing and *experiencing* across cultures	Researching and discovering and experiencing universals. *Intellectualizing and feeling* about the nature of culture as a prop for daily behaviour
UNREFLECTIVE INFORMAL LEARNING (level I)	Unreflective informal learning about one's own culture	*Experiential learning* about another culture, or sharing experience of own with another	Awareness of unimportance of cultural difference ("We are all children of the universe.")

Figure 8:5 combines all these possibilities within one diagram. It represents various types of learning which we have found relevant within CASM and explains many paradoxes which previously seemed incomprehensible to us. This diagram helps to clarify the causes of so much misunderstanding. It seems that agreement can be reached if both the perceiver and the perceived are within one particular level and stage of learning. If, however, there is a boundary between them, the likelihood of each understanding the other is reduced. Where there is more than one boundary (for example where perceiver and perceived operate from squares which are diagonally separated in Figure 8:5) understanding is unlikely to occur unless both make special efforts.

The progression from an unreflective view of life to a more intellectual approach can be seriously disrupted if it is necessary for the person to shift from ethnocentric informal learning too soon, or with too little preparation. It may not be possible for such a person to begin progressing through the levels of learning because the move to acculturated forms has meant that formal education is built on patterns that are not directly related to the patterns of his earliest learning.

While such a benefit to another culture can be the consequence of external events (e.g., change of country of residence), it is often the case that people who seek to prove themselves in a culture other than their own are people who feel alienated from their original culture. They are often critical of many aspects of the culture and expect the problems they confront in their own to be absent in the new culture. This is usually a false notion and can lead to serious problems of personal identity. Menuhin makes important comments on this when he speaks about the significance of learning where more is available to the student than that within the ethnocentric sphere. He says:

> Unless modern man can develop a strong and healthy relationship with his *own* family, his *own* people, his *own* background, his *own* language, music, dance, while at the same time cultivating the abstractions and idioms of the new age, he will never be a balanced human being, but will remain forever dazed and confused. (1972:16)

In other words, to be successful in acculturated thinking we must first and continuously be successful in ethnocentric patterns.

It is possible to regard the lines or boundaries which separate the vertical levels of learning and the horizontal stages representing the cultural context within which this learning takes place as milestones in the educational process. The crossing of a boundary by an individual marks an achievement of growth irrespective of whether the movement is horizontal or vertical in Figure 8:5.

It is not intended to suggest that once a person passes over such a boundary the earlier learning is discarded. This is not so: the earlier processes are subsumed in a larger framework. Viewed in this way, both the white university student and the initiated tribal Aboriginal of the same age have achieved a comparable amount of learning, each within his own system, from the informal levels of ethnocentric learning to the formal levels of that learning.

However, an urban Aboriginal, studying at university, has probably had to progress first to the informal level of acculturated learning. Thus, although he is now operating at level II, he has had to cross two boundaries where the others crossed only one, and may therefore have achieved more growth than either the white student or the tribal Aboriginal student, each within his own culture. Conversely, if the movement has been horizontal on Figure 8:5, a person having crossed the same number of boundaries (and therefore, presumably, having the same amount of learning experience) will be operating at a different level of learning from the one who has moved vertically without diffusion of effort through cultural relearning.

Another point emerges from the diagram which relates directly to many accounts referred to in chapter 6. Western and other cultures which do not acknowledge or understand level III learning as part of education cannot provide conceptual models or personal examples of the process of development through to this spiritual, visionary level which is primarily experienced through aesthetic or religious processes. Hence when people from such cultures interact with people from another culture which does recognize this level (such as tribal Aboriginal culture), they may fail to perceive the higher learning even if they are taught about it.

The diagrams help to show why there are so many paradoxes of cultural difference which belong within the informal and formal levels of ethnocentric and acculturated learning. These must be recognized and accepted as differences, but not seen as the ultimate possibility for human growth. However, unless the transcending level III and/or stage III is kept within reach of the students' awareness at earlier levels and stages (through the use of System C media) no recognition of higher forms will ever be available to those grappling with cultural contradictions at lower levels and stages.

Since the boundaries between these levels and stages are difficult to cross, and what lies beyond them is often feared, each change of learning involves a psychological risk which is completely normal and which must be passed through if growth is to occur. However, the difficulties of negotiating boundaries often produce symptoms which appear as personality disorders. If this is not understood, people undergoing these difficulties of cross-cultural education may suffer severe identity problems at points of crisis, irrespective of their culture of origin.

If music is used therapeutically and there is no confusion between common and cultivated forms, these boundaries between various levels and stages all disappear for the duration of a performance. Further, people unable to pass over difficult boundaries can do so temporarily during performance, thus reducing the fear of passing through them at other levels of interaction after the performance. (This temporary tapping of the Learning III experience has not been represented in Figure 8:5. To do so would require a three-dimensional diagram with a central core of Learning III which could temporarily be tapped from any outer position, but which becomes a living force only once informal experience and formal mastery have been achieved.)

These are some of the points that become clear once the position of individuals is more carefully stated and understood. The fact that Learning III can be tapped temporarily also indicates that it is possible to solve some of the outer problems of cultural alienation and blockages resulting from difficulties in crossing various barriers in the matrix by the process of education through music.

Results of the outer problem solving can be seen, for example, when young urban Aboriginal musicians from CASM begin taking their place alongside white student musicians, where the professionally developed skills of each are comparable. But these Aboriginal students still find themselves caught in the dilemma of inner, personality-based alienation which arises from the constant criticism they have had to face in the white community all their lives. To reach this deeper level of the problem, thus enabling a student to grow through a boundary of the matrix in Figure 8:5, requires meticulous self-examination with some guidance. The tribal music teacher provides this guidance for the tribal person through music therapy in the traditional setting and this is carried over to the tribal teaching at CASM.

Where can the non-tribal person, caught in cross-cultural conflict, find assistance that is not culturally biased and preferably leaves untouched the confusing area of verbal interaction?

In order to answer this question it is necessary for me to write about my own experiences. When I returned to work exclusively among Western thinkers I had a strong need to reaffirm my own ethnocentric values without, at the same time, facing denigration of Aboriginal ones. For this reason I began serious study of the performance of Western music again even though I knew my potential for again achieving the professional status I had ignored for so long was limited. Many students twenty years my junior were infinitely better performers. I suffered some sense of guilt at taking my place as a student of one of the fine musicians on the staff of the Elder Conservatorium of Music, knowing that another, younger student, more able to win credit for his or her teacher and present a better image of professionalism in musical performance was thereby denied access to the limited teaching resources.

The basis of proficient music making in any culture is an adequate technique which enables the performer to express the deeper meaning of the music. Until this technique is achieved, little can be expressed. Once a certain level of facility occurs, the perceptive teacher constantly directs the student's attention to technical problems which are in some way preventing the free flow of the music.

These problems are, at one level, entirely concerned with motor skills. However, as my teacher worked patiently, eliminating faulty co-ordinational problems and reshaping my technique after its long disuse, another factor emerged which was apparent to me only as a result of my long training with tribal musicians. Persistent technical problems in my playing which prevent the free flow of the composer's intentions as well as inhibiting my own ability to express myself through music, are without exception due to personality problems, of which I have been unaware. For instance, the failure to move a musical phrase to its point of greatest feeling may be caused by failure to co-ordinate fingers, wrists, and arms appropriately; but it is also caused by my personal tendency to pay too much attention to small detail, thus losing the essence.

The statement of this technical problem, even though presented exclusively in terms of the desirable musical technique within one culture only, is a diagnosis, a statement about personality which is not culture bound. Not only this, but the technical correction (skilfully determined by the teacher) of the purely motor processes can reach back into the personality. Thus, by increasing my capacity to allow the technical expression to flow and thereby reach the essence of the music, my teacher was in a position to reduce my generalized personal problem of inhibiting free flow of thought.

The music teacher may argue that it is his role to be involved in musical, not in personal, development. (This comment is connected with Seeger's differentiation, quoted in chapter 1, between the musician as educator and the educator in music who is interested in the growth of the student.) Despite this, evaluation of personality-based problems as they appear through my playing has provided a means of guidance for me which is not culture bound; it provides access to information at a deep level of my personality, and an indirect remedy.

The process perceived in action is one in which the music making is a reflection of the integration (or disintegration) of the personality. While either may affect the other, the teacher is normally showing only how the reflection may be altered and thus incidentally the substance, the personality.

His aim, however, is not this. It is to teach how the reflection, the playing, may be *separated* from the substance; and how to acquire the technical and musical facility which is available irrespective of the personality basis of the reflection. This separation of reflection from substance can produce large numbers of proficient players, none of whom need have any perception of themselves as people. Often their performances are a brilliant facade.

The Western music teacher is forced to earn his living in a competitive commercial world in which primary emphasis is placed on the second, cognitive and technical level of learning. His rightful place, however, is within the more spiritually-based learning of level III. He does not have time, in this alienating climate of competitive survival at level II, to wait for the slow process of a student discovering a reflection of his personality.

The teacher must necessarily concern himself with the reflection alone, and do the best he can to make it a competitively successful reflection, irrespective of what it is reflecting. The teacher's diagnostic skill and ability to treat the problem diagnosed is therefore being channelled into community activities which are almost exclusively commercial. Yet my own experience leads me to believe that these outstanding teachers have a major contribution to make to education in today's multicultural society. This suggests an entirely new role for some music teachers as educators of integrated people. It also implies the need for special training for these selected music teachers of the future.

While what I speak about is close to music therapy, it is in fact education through music. There are important relationships and differences between this and music therapy. In the first place I am suggesting that music can be used as a tool in the diagnosis of the difficulties of a "normal" person; and the appropriate technical correction, if understood in these terms, is a perception for both musical and personal growth. This occurs in music therapy too, and when describing musically-elicited behaviour in a therapeutic situation Sears says:

> . . . the individual may come to discover what he really is — to find his own ways of living, of valuing and appreciating himself as an individual with potentialities. He may come to discover that these potentialities have sufficient meaning to himself to be used for experience in relating to others. (in Gaston 1968:39)

However, I am not suggesting that the professional roles of

music therapist and music teacher should either be combined or separated, but rather that the music teacher of the future who chooses to operate in cross-cultural situations should become more aware of the therapeutic nature of his work. He must see it within the scope of the extra-musical as well as the musical concepts which may be learned by his students (as the music therapist already does). The difference in the two professions — the music therapist's and the music teacher's — that would then emerge would primarily concern who the students are and where they are placed on the matrix of Figure 8:5.

According to this last point, the music teacher and the music therapist would need to develop techniques suitable to their own and their students' level of operation in order to achieve the goal of greater personality development in their students. Education through music has to move beyond itself. It is the use of music as both message and experience; and the message is not only the one intended by the composer (whether a Dreaming ancestor or Beethoven) but one which comes directly from the personality of the performer.

There appears to be a contradiction between the strong ethnocentric values of any musical performance and the ability of the teacher to determine characteristics of the performer in a way which is not culture bound. It seems that in diagnostic teaching from the music of any culture, the information reached transcends ethnocentricity.

This point needs some further elaboration. In the first place, it is never possible for the teacher from one culture to make an accurate interpretation of the reflection in music of the musician from another culture, within which this teacher is not trained. Only those skilled in the music concerned can do this. The reflection is shaped by different technical demands in each culture and can only be interpreted by an expert from within that technique. (It was this lack of awareness that led my earlier teachers to denigrate my folk music background.)

A related point is the importance of this type of diagnostic teaching as a means of therapy in cross-cultural situations.

The person who faces misinterpretation of his every action may spend much fruitless time and personal effort in an endeavour to correct faults for which, in fact, he is not responsible. It becomes exceedingly difficult under constant negation to know what positive attributes one still possesses. It is here that the diagnostic music teacher can help so much. He has access to an objective evaluation of his student's personality through music making.

Several examples may explain this complex aspect of the teacher's role. In CASM, the teachers of wind instruments all commented on the beautiful tone urban Aboriginal children achieved almost from their first lesson on the instrument. One of the most important technical requirements for producing a good tone is relaxation. This suggests that Aboriginal students may be more relaxed than the white students with whom these teachers were most experienced. However, others watching these students at school, in the community at large, or at CASM, often labelled them "apathetic". The two attitudes can appear similar outwardly, yet in musical performance there was no question of apathy (which in any case would be likely to produce a lifeless tone quality). Thus the music teacher was in a position to reinforce the positive aspect — relaxation — and thereby help the student to understand the negative interpretation — apathy — as part of his critics' stereotyping.

A similar Western example can be given. White musicians working in CASM were often criticized for insensitivity. A Western musician who is by nature sensitive to other people's needs can mould his interpretation to that of other performers in ensemble playing. All these teachers were sensitive musicians and a skilled diagnostic music teacher would have been able to reinforce in them their awareness of their own sensitivity to others, thereby enabling them also to see the negative interpretation of their behaviour as part of their critics' stereotyping.

My renewed experience in the realm of Western professional music making has clarified many problems of interpretation for me concerning the nature of music making and music teaching. I have known, since my earliest exposure to tribal music, that the diagnostic skill of the good tribal teacher is comparable to that of a good Western music teacher; and that for either, nonverbal communication of the nature of a musical problem is often more effective than verbal description. (I have also known that many Western music teachers are quite unable to detect what, precisely, is the technical cause of a particular fault in playing. I do not consider these to be good teachers.)

The differences in action between the good tribal teacher and the good Western teacher seem to lie both in the ultimate goal each perceives and in the medium through which the music teaching takes place. In the case of the tribal performers discussed in this book, attention is always, ultimately, toward the third, spiritual or visionary level of learning and the medium is always that of vocal music. Both these centre the teacher's attention closely on the development of the individual. In the case of Western musicians being discussed here, attention is directed toward tangible reward in the form of commercial success and toward techniques used to manipulate an instrument which is not part of the performer's physiology. Both these factors tend to lead to depersonalization.

The tribal teacher is primarily concerned with the substance of the person performing the music. The Western teacher, on the other hand, works in a society which believes music is a useless channel of communication and is primarily concerned with the reflection. It is the good fortune of the Western student if he discovers that these two things are intimately connected.

For myself, the discovery of the potential for education of the personality through Western music, whether or not my teacher is aware of the process, has been an integrative force. I know now that nonverbal guidance on my own personality development is available to me not only through tribal Aboriginal music, but through my own culture. More importantly, through the agency of the skilled music teacher, it is available to me in a form which transcends cultural bias. Even so, during performance I am involved in an action which is strongly reinforcing my own cultural norms. This is unlike any other help available to a person in a cross-cultural situation.

The music teachers of the future, who choose to develop these skills in order to become master musicians in the process of education through music in a multicultural society, need special training if they are to be able to teach music so that students may use this medium as an authentic reflection of their personality and culture. At the moment, the most skilled teachers available in Australia to train these future music teachers in the areas of personal growth through music are tribally-qualified Aboriginal musicians.

In this book I have endeavoured to move the reader through concepts about music which are not widely accepted in our own culture. I have attempted to show how crucial the well-trained tribal musician has been in the development of my own understanding and that of other Western musicians who have studied with them.

I have also aimed to demonstrate the importance of music for the emergence of urban Aboriginal people in today's world. Through approaching Aboriginal music from the basis of my own multicultural experiences, coupled with analytical research, I have arrived at a different appraisal of both Aboriginal music and the music of my own tradition.

Appendices

Appendix to Chapter 4

Texts of Verses of Inma Langka from 1977 Recording

S—— = starting point

——F = finishing point

The listing of the number of times a text is presented does not include the incomplete sections from S—— to the end of the text, or from the start of the text to ——F.

1a. kurkaran p^{S——}alatja kurkaran palatja

      putipurtjunku mantjinu^{——F} putipurtjunku

      mantjinu   3 times

1b. putipurtjunku m^{S——}antjinu putipurtjunku

      mantjinu^{——F}   3 times

      kurkaran palatja kurkaran palatja

2à. nguntila tj^{S——}atutjunu nguntila tjatutjunu

      nyaratja makulpanyi nyaratja^{——F} makulpanyi   3 times

2b. nyaratja makulp^{S——}anyi nyaratja makulpanyi

      nguntila tjatutjunu ngunt^{——F}ila tjatutjunu   3 times

3a. tjilira tjaranya tjilira tjaranya

      wauralka tj^{S——}aranya wauralka tjar^{——F}anya   4 times

3b. wauralka tj^{S——}aranya wauralka tjaranya

      tjilira tjaranya tjilira tjar^{——F}anya   3 times

4a. yilingkarkaralu tjana wata waralu

ngumi ngumi witinu ngumi ngumi witinu   3 times

4b. yilingkarkaralu tjana wata waralu

ngumi ngumi witinu ngumi ngumi witinu   3 times

5a. yurkatira kulpangu yurkatira kulpangu

tali wanmankar wanmankar tali wanmankar

wanmankar   3 times

5b. tali wanmankar wanmankar tali wanmankar

wanmankar

yurkatira kulpangu yurkatira kulpangu   3 times

6a. yurtjanpana wirarirari

yurtjanpana pulingka pulingka   4 times

6b. yurtjanpana wirarirari

yurtjanpana pulingka pulingka   4 times

7a. ngapalalu walku kanyinu ngapalalu walku

kanyinu

waru kulturiny kulturiny waru kulturiny

kulturiny   3 times

7b. ngapalalu walku kanyinu ngapalalu walku kanyinu

waru kulturiny kulturiny waru kulturiny

kulturiny   3 times

8a. takanpa rakaraka takanpa rakaraka

kantjilpa rakaraka kantjilpa rakaraka   3 times

8b. kantjilpa rakaraka kantjilpa rakaraka

takanpa rakaraka takanpa rakaraka   3 times

9a. papa nyutitjara tjarpara pakanu

tjunpin pirilan pirilan tjunpin pirilan pirilan   3 times

9b. tjunpin pirilan pirilan tjunpin pirilan pirilan

papa nyutitjara tjarpara pakanu   4 times

10a. warpunangi warpunangi

kamilu ngalilinku putalu ngalilinku   4 times

10b. warpunangi warpunangi

kamilu ngalilinku putalu ngalilinku   3 times

11a. miniri miniri miniri miniri

tjuralku kulpangu tjuralku kulpangu   4 times

11b. miniri miniri miniri miniri

tjuralku kulpangu tjuralku kulpangu   3 times

12a. miniri panyanpa miniri panyanpa

walunku ngarangu walunku ngarangu   twice

12b. miniri panyanpa miniri panyanpa

walunku ngarangu walunku ngarangu   3 times

13a. katu kutu minkul ngaringu katu kutu minkul
ngaringu

para wauli waulinu para wauli waulinu   3 times

13b. katu kutu minkul ngaringu katu kutu minkul
ngaringu

para wauli waulinu para wauli waulinu   3 times

14a. maku mingatja maku mingatja

nyatjan talturinganyi nyatjan talturinganyi   3 times

14b. maku mingatja maku mingatja

nyatjan talturinganyi nyatjan talturinganyi   3 times

15a. tjintir tjintir tjintir tjintir

mantjara katilan tjaraya   4 times

15b. tjintir tjintir tjintir tjintir

mantjara katilan tjaraya   4 times

16a. tjintir tjintir tjintir tjintir

kulpi ngalya pututiri   4 times

16b. tjintir tjintir tjintir tjintir

kulpi ngalya pututiri   4 times

17a. tjutururtunan pulyarulyaru

tjunkunan pulyur wantinyan   3 times

17b. tjutururtunan pulyarulyaru

tjunkunan pulyur wantinyan   3 times

Figure A1: Examples of Rhythmic Patterns and Rhythmic Segments of Selected Inma Langka Verses: The rhythm is notated in long and short notes, spacing and beating indicating exact duration. Each verse is presented in the first position listed in the song texts — verse (a) for every number.

▾ = main beat (sticks)   ● = echo beat (sticks)
> = main accent (text)   – = secondary accent (text)

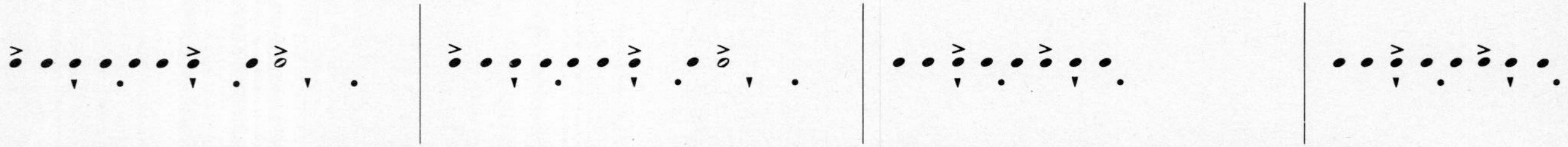

(a) Rhythmic pattern with 4 segments in which segment 2 = segment 1; segment 4 = segment 3. Notation of Verse 7.

(b) Rhythmic pattern with 4 segments in which all four segments have differences. Notation of Verse 14.

(c) Rhythmic pattern with 4 segments in which all four segments are identical. Notation of Verse 11.

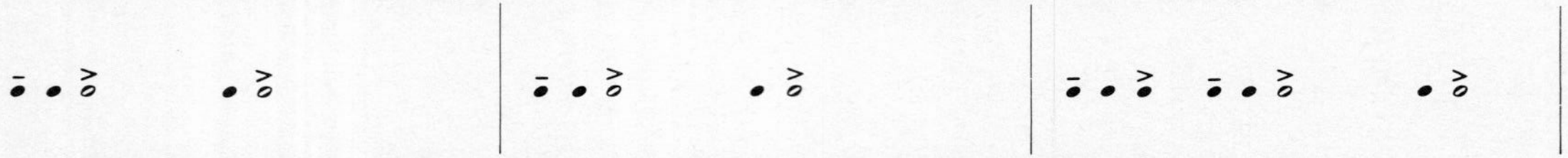

(d) Rhythmic pattern with 3 segments in which segment 2 = segment 1. Notation of Verse 17.

Figure A2: Various aspects of duration (in secs), in particular the stability of time taken to sing the same text in different recordings.

verse no. (1977)	total duration of small song	time between end of one small song and start of next	duration of text — 1977	duration of test — 1970	duration of text — 1969
1a	28.8	5.7	7.6	7.5	7.6
1b	28.1	7.0	7.5	7.5	—
2a	25.6	4.1	6.5	6.9	6.6
2b	25.3	12.0	6.5	6.8	6.6
3a	27.0	9.9	6.0	—	—
3b	24.6	27.5	6.0	—	—
4a	25.6	9.0	5.9	6.2	6.3
4b	22.5	4.2	6.0	6.3	6.3
5a	27.5	7.4	7.3	7.2	7.5
5b	27.3	6.0	7.3	7.3	7.3
6a	27.3	8.0	6.0	—	—
6b	26.0	7.8	6.0	—	—
7a	28.0	8.2	7.5	—	7.8
7b	25.7	13.2	7.4	—	7.8
8a	22.5	5.5	5.5	5.5	5.4
8b	22.9	9.5	5.5	5.4	—
9a	26.9	8.9	7.5	8.0	7.9
9b	32.0	10.4	7.4	7.8	7.9
10a	27.0	7.8	6.0	—	6.4
10b	24.1	9.8	6.1	—	6.3
11a	26.0	13.5	6.2	6.3	6.6
11b	23.8	9.7	6.0	6.3	6.5
12a	29.2	7.2	9.2	9.7	10.3
12b	34.5	5.3	9.1	9.6	10.1
13a	33.0 (25)*	6.8	9.3	9.8	9.8
13b	32.0	9.0	9.2	9.9	—
14a	28.0	7.7	6.9	—	7.0
14b	27.5	10.0	6.9	—	6.9
15a	25.1	9.0	5.3	5.4	5.5
15b	23.5	6.8	5.2	5.5	5.6
16a	20.7	8.4	4.8	5.1	5.2
16b	22.2	1.6	4.9	5.1	5.2
17a	32.4	9.2	8.3	—	—
17b	32.0	—	8.0	—	—

(*This timing, for the 1970 recording, is added to show that there can be substantial change in the total duration of a *small song* while the duration of the *text* and *rhythmic pattern* remains constant.)

Figure A3: Rhythmic segments of Verses 4 and 12, showing similarity of structure.

rhythmic segment

Verse 4

Verse 12

beating accompaniment

1

2

3

4

Figure A4: The same musical information as in Figure A3 is aligned differently here, showing equal duration of the beating and therefore highlighting *differences* in the structure of the segments of the two verses. (Duration of the notes can be seen by allowing that each beat in the accompaniment equals ♩.)

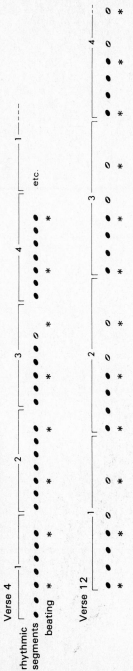

Figure A5: Shows how a pattern, originally assumed to have four segments as shown above the notation (i.e., on a textual basis), provided after careful examination of all features to be a six-segment pattern as shown below the notation. Segments 3 and 4 of the original division have been sub-divided, each smaller sub-division having identical rhythmic structure. The correct definition of rhythmic segments is crucial for understanding how rhythm and melody interlock, and how melodies are identified as the "same" or "different".

Figure A6: (a) The upper stave shows the full melodic movement in Verse 2 of Langka. The lower stave gives it in essence only, using primarily the notes falling at the opening and close of each segment.

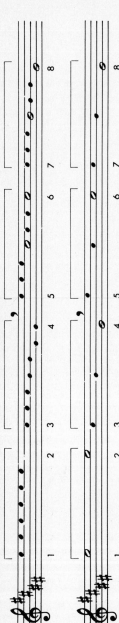

(b) Compares a portion of the essence of the melody as used on the same words in verses 2a and 2b. The two melodies do not appear to be the same.

(c) Shows how the essence of the melody in the two versions of verse 2 appears the same when they are aligned by using the breath at the end of the example as a point of reference. As can be seen by the numbering, the text has been shifted by a whole line in relation to the melody.

Figure A7: Melodic contour of Langka verses 1-17. (See Figure A9 for a diagramatic realization of this).

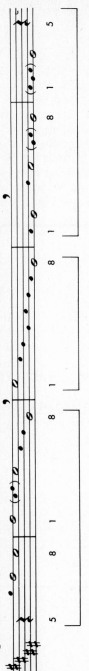

Figure A8: Shows three different versions of the *Urumbula* series. They conform closely to the one melodic shape despite the fact that they cross tribal boundaries, have different performers, different texts and different rhythms. The melodic shape here is, presumably, the sameness of this melody, the "taste" of *Urumbula*. It would not have been possible to identify the "sameness" of this melody without applying the analytical techniques outlined in chapter 4.

Comments on Figure A9

1. Each block of the diagram represents one presentation of the text, the actual duration of which can be found from Figure A2. Verse 13 is the longest, being 9.3 seconds, and Verse 16 is the shortest (in the 1977 version, 4.8 seconds). However, note that the first two segments of any presentation of Verse 16 appear very long. Verse 16 is actually a 3-segment construction (instead of a 4-segment construction) and in order to fit it within the patterning of diagram A9, it was necessary to repeat the duration of segment 1 in segment 2, then double the spacing of the notes within these two segments. These then aligned with changes in other verses.

2. The shading of colours indicates where the notes change in each verse. Points of significance are:

   In every verse the second presentation of the text commences with F sharp and ends with G sharp;

   In every verse the third presentation of the text commences with the upper tonic and ends with the lower tonic;

   In every verse the end of the second segment of the third presentation of the text ends with G sharp; and the commencement of the third segment of that presentation of the text is always A.

   In every verse the commencement of the fourth presentation of the text is lower F sharp.

3. I postulate that it is the consistency of the change of notes in melodic section 2 that is involved when performers identify melodies as the same.

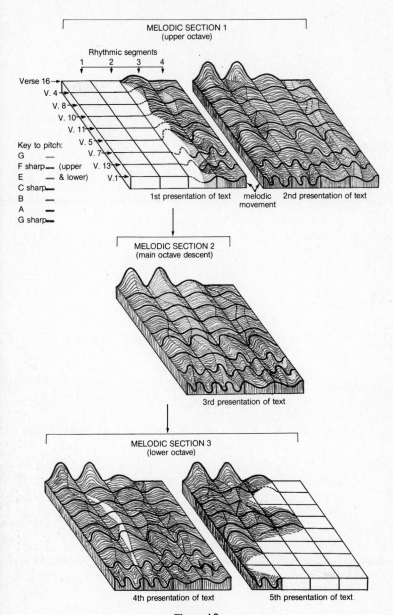

MELODIC SECTION 1
(upper octave)

Rhythmic segments
1 2 3 4

Verse 16
V. 4
V. 8
V. 10
V. 11

Key to pitch:
G
F sharp — (upper
E   — & lower)
C sharp
B
A
G sharp

V. 5
V. 7
V. 13
V. 1

1st presentation of text   melodic   2nd presentation of text
                            movement

MELODIC SECTION 2
(main octave descent)

3rd presentation of text

MELODIC SECTION 3
(lower octave)

4th presentation of text   5th presentation of text

Figure A9

Bibliography

Adorno, T. W. (1941). "On popular music". *Studies in Philosophy and Social Science,* Vol. 9, pp. 17–48.

Alvin, J. (1975). *Music Therapy.* London: Hutchinson.

Assagioli, Roberto (1965). *Psychosynthesis: A Manual of Principles and Techniques.* Harmondsworth, Middlesex: Penguin.

Australian Society for Music Education (1977). *Report of Proceedings of the Third National Conference.* Canberra: Australian Society for Music Education.

Badger, G. M. (1974). *Aboriginal Music.* Paper to the Education Committee, The University of Adelaide, 12 November 1974. Adelaide: University of Adelaide.

Bateson, Gregory (1972). *Steps to an Ecology of Mind.* New York: Ballantine.

Berndt, R. M. and C. H. (1964). *The World of the First Australians.* Sydney: Ure Smith.

Berndt, R. M. and Phillips, E. S. eds. (1973). *The Australian Aboriginal Heritage: An Introduction Through the Arts.* Sydney: Australian Society for Education Through the Arts, with Ure Smith.

Berne, Eric (1972). *What do you say after you say hello?* U.S.A.: Bantam Edition.

Bowen, Elenore Smith (pseud. of Laura Bohannan) (1964). *Return to Laughter.* New York: Anchor Books, Doubleday.

Blacking, John (1976). *How Musical is Man?* London: Faber and Faber.

Brunton, Marylouise (1982). "Western Impact on Aboriginal Music". *Media Development.* Journal of the World Association for Christian Communication, Vol. 29, No. 1, pp. 15–18.

Buxton, Ruth D. (1976). "Ethnomusicology – another man's heartbeat". *Pivot,* Third term 1976, pp. 2–3. The Education Department of South Australia: Adelaide.

Cadar, Usopay H. (1973). "The Role of Kulintang Music in Maranao Society". *Ethnomusicology,* Vol. 17, No. 2, pp. 234–249.

Casals, Pablo (1974). *Joys and Sorrows.* His own story as told to Albert E. Kahn. New York: Simon and Schuster.

Cleaver, Eldridge (1970). *Soul on Ice.* London: Panther.

Covell, Roger (1967). *Australia's Music: Themes of a New Society.* Melbourne: Sun Books.

Crisp, Deborah (1979). "The Influence of Australian Aboriginal Music on the Music of Contemporary Australian Composers". In *Australian Aboriginal Music* edited by Jennifer Isaacs (1979), pp. 49–56. Sydney: Aboriginal Artists Agency.

Davies, E. Harold (1947). "Music in Primitive Society". *Anthropological Society of South Australia Occasional Publication No. 2.* Anthropological Society of South Australia, University of Adelaide: Adelaide.

Dolan, C. M. (1973). "Music Therapy: An Explanation". *Music Therapy Journal,* Vol. 10, No. 4, pp. 172–176.

Ellis, Catherine J. (1964). *Aboriginal Music Making: A Study of Central Australian Music.* Adelaide: Libraries Board of South Australia.

Ellis, Catherine J. (1965). "Pre-instrumental Scales". *Ethnomusicology,* Vol. 9, No. 2, pp. 126–144.

Ellis, Catherine J. (1966). "Aboriginal Songs of South Australia". *Miscellanea Musicologica: Adelaide Studies in Musicology,* Vol. 1, pp. 137–190.

Ellis, Catherine J. (1967). "Folk Song Migration in Aboriginal South Australia". *Journal of the International Folk Music Council,* Vol. 19, pp. 11–16.

Ellis, Catherine J. (1967a). "The Pitjantjara Kangaroo Song from Karlga". *Miscellanea Musicologica: Adelaide Studies in Musicology,* Vol. 2, pp. 170–267.

Ellis, Catherine J. (1970). "The Role of the Ethnomusicologist in the Study of Andagarinja Women's Ceremonies". *Miscellanea Musicologica: Adelaide Studies in Musicology,* Vol. 5, pp. 76–208.

Ellis, Catherine J. (1977). "Experiences in Music Therapy at the Centre for Aboriginal Studies in Music, University of Adelaide". *Proceedings of the Third National Conference of the Australian Music Therapy Association, 13–15 August 1977.* Adelaide: Australian Music Therapy Association.

Ellis, Catherine J. (1979). "Developments in Music Education Among Aboriginals in Central and South Australia". In *Australian Aboriginal Music* edited by Jennifer Isaacs (1979), pp. 27–40. Sydney: Aboriginal Artists Agency.

Ellis, Catherine J. ed. (1971–72). *Report on "Program of Training in Music for South Australian Aboriginal People",* Parts 1–4. Adelaide: University of Adelaide.

Ellis, Catherine J. and Ellis, A. M. (1970). *Andagarinja Children's Bullock Corroboree.* Port Moresby: Papua Pocket Poets.

Ellis, Catherine J. and Ellis, A. M. (1973). "Learning Aboriginal Music". In *The Australian Aboriginal Heritage: An Introduction Through the Arts* edited by Berndt, R. M. and Phillips, E. S. (1973) pp. 227–237. Sydney: Australian Society for Education Through the Arts, with Ure Smith.

Ellis, Catherine J., Ellis, A. M., Tur, Mona, and McCardell, A. (1978). "Classification of Sounds in Pitjantjatjara-speaking Areas". In *Australian Aboriginal Concepts* edited by L. R. Hiatt (1978), pp. 68–79. Canberra: Australian Institute of Aboriginal Studies.

Ellis, Catherine J. and Tur, Mona (1975). "The Song is the Message". *Cultures in Collision,* pp. 30–35. Adelaide: Australian National Association for Mental Health.

Freire, Paulo (1973). *Cultural Action for Freedom.* Harmondsworth, Middlesex: Penguin Education.

Freire, Paulo (1974). *Education for Critical Consciousness.* London: Sheed and Ward.

Gaston, E. T. (1968) ed. *Music in Therapy.* New York: Macmillan.

Gooch, Stan (1972). *Total Man: Notes towards an Evolutionary Theory of Personality*. London: Allen Lane, Penguin Press.

Hamel, Peter Michael (1979). *Through Music to the Self: How to appreciate and experience music anew*. Translated by P. Lemesurier. Boulder: Shambhala Publications.

Hercus, Luise A. (1969). *The Languages of Victoria: A Late Study*. Canberra: Australian Institute of Aboriginal Studies.

Hood, Mantle (1971). *The Ethnomusicologist*. New York: McGraw Hill.

Institute of Papua New Guinea Studies (1978). *The First Four Years 1974–1978*.

Isaacs, Jennifer ed. (1979). *Australian Aboriginal Music*. Sydney: Aboriginal Artists Agency.

Isaacs, Jennifer ed. (1980). *Australian Dreaming: 40,000 Years of Aboriginal History*. Sydney: Lansdowne Press.

Jones, Trevor (1956). "Arnhem Land Music, Part 2, a Musical Survey". *Oceania* Vol. 26, No. 4, pp. 252–339; (1957) Vol. 28, No. 1, pp. 1–30.

Jung, C. G. (1965). *Memories, Dreams, Reflections*. Recorded and edited by Aniela Jaffé, translated from German by Richard and Clara Winston. New York: Vintage.

Kartomi, Margaret (1973). "A Children's Ceremony at Yalata". In *The Australian Aboriginal Heritage: An Introduction Through the Arts* edited by Berndt, R. M. and Phillips, E. S. (1973), pp. 54–58. Sydney: Australian Society for Education Through the Arts, with Ure Smith.

Keddie, Nell ed. (1973). *Tinker, Tailor . . . The Myth of Cultural Deprivation*. Harmondsworth, Middlesex: Penguin Education.

King, Arden Ross (1974). "Review Essay: Claude Lévi-Strauss: Les Mythologiques". *Ethnomusicology*, Vol. 18, No. 1, pp. 101–111.

Kodály, Zoltán (1974). *The Selected Writings of Zoltán Kodály*. Translated by Lili Halápy and Fred Macnicol. London: Boosey and Hawkes.

Le Shan, Lawrence (1975). *The Medium, The Mystic, and The Physicist: Toward a General Theory of the Paranormal.* New York: Ballantine.

Lévi-Strauss, Claude (1969). *The Raw and the Cooked: Introduction to a Science of Mythology: I.* Translated from French by John and Doreen Weightman. London: Jonathan Cape.

Lévi-Strauss, Claude (1972). *Structural Anthropology.* Translated from French by Claire Jacobson and Brooke Grundfest Schoepf. Harmondsworth, Middlesex: Penguin University.

McLaughlin, T. P. (1962). "Music and Communication". *The Music Review,* Vol. 23, No. 4, pp. 285–291.

McLuhan, Marshall and Fiore, Quentin (1967). *The Medium is the Massage.* Harmondsworth, Middlesex: Penguin.

McAllester, David P. (1972). "Teaching the Music Teacher to use the Music of his Own Culture". *Australian Journal of Music Education,* No. 10, pp. 17–20.

Maranda, Pierre ed. (1972). *Mythology: Selected Readings.* Harmondsworth, Middlesex: Penguin.

Menuhin, Yehudi (1972). *Theme and Variations.* London: Heineman.

Merriam, Alan P. (1964). *The Anthropology of Music.* Evanston, Illinois: Northwestern University Press.

Meyer, L. (1967). *Music, The Arts and Ideas: Patterns and Predictions in Twentieth Century Culture.* Chicago: The University of Chicago Press.

Michel, Donald E. and Martin, Dorothea (1970). "Music and Self-esteem Research with Disadvantaged, Problem Boys in an Elementary School". *Journal of Music Therapy,* Vol. 7, No. 4, pp. 124–127.

Mountford, Charles P. (1973). "A Mountain-Devil Myth and Ceremony for Boys". In *The Australian Aboriginal Heritage: An Introduction Through the Arts* edited by Berndt, R.M. and Phillips, E.S. (1973), pp. 59–63. Sydney: Australian Society for Education Through the Arts, with Ure Smith.

Moyle, Alice M. (1967). *Songs from the Northern Territory.* Companion booklet for five 12-inch L. P. discs. Canberra: Australian Institute of Aboriginal Studies.

Moyle, Richard M. (1979). *Songs of the Pintupi: Musical Life in a Central Australian Society.* Canberra: Australian Institute of Aboriginal Studies.

Munn, Nancy (1964). "Totemic Designs and Group Continuity in Walbiri Cosmology". In *Aborigines Now: New Perspectives in the Study of Aboriginal Communities* edited by Marie Reay, pp. 83–100. Sydney: Angus and Robertson.

Munn, Norman L. (1966). *Psychology: The Fundamentals of Human Adjustment* (5th edition). Boston: Houghton Mifflin.

Murdoch, James (1972). *Australia's Contemporary Composers.* Melbourne: Macmillan.

Nettl, Bruno (1964). *Theory and Method in Ethnomusicology.* New York: Free Press of Glencoe.

Nettl, Bruno (1973). *Folk and Traditional Music of the Western Continents* (2nd edition). Prentice Hall: Englewood Cliffs, New Jersey.

Nketia, J. H. Kwabena (1974). *The Music of Africa.* New York: W. W. Norton.

Nketia, J. H. Kwabena (1977). "New Perspectives in Music Education". *Australian Journal of Music Education,* No. 20, pp. 23–28.

Nordoff, P. and Robbins, Clive (1971). *Music Therapy in Special Education.* New York: J. Day.

Nordoff, P. and Robbins, Clive (1971a). *Therapy in Music for Handicapped Children.* London: Gollancz.

Opie, I. and Opie, P. (1967). *The Lore and Language of Schoolchildren.* London: Oxford University Press.

Parry, C. H. H. (1925). *The Evolution of the Art of Music* (9th edition). London: Kegan Paul, Trench, Tubner.

Paynter, John (1982). *Music in the Secondary School Curriculum: Trends and Developments in Class Music Teaching.* Cambridge: Cambridge University Press.

Pearce, Trevor (1979). "Music and the Settled Aboriginal". In *Australian Aboriginal Music* edited by Jennifer Isaacs (1979), pp. 41–48. Sydney: Aboriginal Artists Agency.

Peterson, N. ed. (1976). *Tribes and Boundaries in Australia.* Canberra: Australian Institute of Aboriginal Studies, Social Anthropology Series No. 10.

Pirsig, Robert M. (1976). *Zen and the Art of Motorcycle Maintenance: An Inquiry into Values.* London: Corgi.

Rattray Taylor, Gordon (1972). *Rethink: a Paraprimitive Solution.* London: Secker and Warburg.

Reimer, Bennett (1970). *A Philosophy of Music Education.* New Jersey: Prentice-Hall.

Robertson-DeCarbo, Carol E. (1974). "Music as Therapy: A Bio-Cultural Problem". *Ethnomusicology,* Vol. 18, No. 1, pp. 31–42.

Robinson, Roland (1976). *The Shift of Sands: An Autobiography, 1952–62.* Melbourne: Macmillan.

Rowley, C. D. (1971). *The Remote Aborigines: Aboriginal Policy and Practice – Vol. 3.* Canberra: Australian National University Press.

Rowley, C. D. (1972). *The Destruction of Aboriginal Society.* Harmondsworth, Middlesex: Penguin.

Sadie, S. ed. (1980). *The New Grove Dictionary of Music and Musicians.* London: Macmillan.

Schafer, R. Murray (1965). *The Composer in the Classroom.* Toronto: BMI Canada.

Schafer, R. Murray (1969). *The New Soundscape: A Handbook for the Modern Music Teacher.* Scarborough, Ontario: Berandol Music.

Schafer, R. Murray (1977). *The Tuning of the World.* Toronto: McClelland and Stewart.

Seeger, Charles (1971). "Reflections upon a Given Topic". *Ethnomusicology,* Vol. 15, No. 3, pp. 385–398.

Seeger, Charles (1977). "The Musician: Man Serves Art. The Educator: Art Serves Man". *Australian Journal of Music Education,* No. 20, pp. 15–16.

Shankar, Ravi (1969). *My Music, My Life.* London: Jonathan Cape.

Sharp, Cecil J. (1907). *English Folk-Song: Some Conclusions.* London: Simpkin and Novello.

Sheppard, Trish (1976). *Children of Blindness.* Sydney: Ure Smith.

Strehlow, T. G. H. (1947). *Aranda Traditions.* Melbourne: Melbourne University Press.

Strehlow, T. G. H. (1955). "Australian Aboriginal Songs". *Journal of the International Folk Music Council,* Vol. 7, pp. 37–40.

Strehlow, T. G. H. (1971). *Songs of Central Australia.* Sydney: Angus and Robertson.

Tagore, Rabindranath (1961). *Towards Universal Man.* London: Asia Publishing.

Tagore, Rabindranath and Elmhirst, L. K. (1961). *Rabindranath Tagore, Pioneer in Education: Essays and Exchanges between Rabindranath Tagore and L. K. Elmhirst.* London: John Murray.

Tindale, N. B. (1974). *Aboriginal Tribes of Australia.* Canberra: Australian National University Press. (maps)

Tjungaringanyi (1975–78). Vols. 1–4, Adelaide: Centre for Aboriginal Studies in Music, University of Adelaide.

Tolkien, J. R. R. (1964). *Tree and Leaf.* London: George Allen and Unwin.

Turner, Ian (1969). *Cinderella Dressed in Yella.* Melbourne: Heineman Educational.

Wachsman, Klaus (1971). "Universal Perspectives in Music". *Ethnomusicology,* Vol. 15, No. 3, pp. 381–84.

Waterman, Richard A. (1955). "Music in Australian Aboriginal Culture – Some Sociological and Psychlogical Implications". From *Journal of Music Therapy,* V (1955), pp. 40–49. In McAllester, D.P. ed. *Readings in Ethnomusicology* Johnson Reprint Corporation, New York-London, 1971, pp. 167–174.

Watson, Peter ed. (1973). *Psychology and Race.* Harmondsworth, Middlesex: Penguin.

Wolff, Karen L. (1978). "The Nonmusical Outcomes of Music Education: A Review of the Literature". *Bulletin of the Council for Research in Music Education,* No. 55, pp. 1–27.

Wurm, S.A. (1963). "Aboriginal Languages". In *Australian Aboriginal Studies: a Symposium of Papers Presented at the 1961 Research Conference,* edited by H. Sheils, pp. 127–48. Melbourne: Oxford University Press.

Index